Tempt Me Twice

Royal Bondage
by Samantha Winston, Delilah Devlin, & Marianne LaCroix

Magical Seduction
by Cathryn Fox, Mandy M. Roth, & Anya Bast

Good Girl Seeks Bad Rider
by Vonna Harper, Lena Matthews, & Ruth D. Kerce

Road Trip to Passion
by Sahara Kelly, Lani Aames, & Vonna Harper

Overtime, Under Him
by N.J. Walters, Susie Charles, & Jan Springer

Getting What She Wants
by Diana Hunter, S.L. Carpenter, & Chris Tanglen

Insatiable
by Sherri L. King, Elizabeth Jewell, & S.L. Carpenter

His Fantasies, Her Dreams
by Sherri L. King, S.L. Carpenter, & Trista Ann Michaels

Master of Secret Desires
by S.L. Carpenter, Elizabeth Jewell, & Tawny Taylor

Bedtime, Playtime
by Jaid Black, Sherri L. King, & Ruth D. Kerce

Hurts So Good
by Gail Faulkner, Lisa Renee Jones, & Sahara Kelly

Lover From Another World
by Rachel Carrington, Elizabeth Jewell, & Shiloh Walker

Fever-Hot Dreams
by Sherri L. King, Jaci Burton, & Samantha Winston

Taming Him
by Kimberly Dean, Summer Devon, & Michelle M. Pillow

All She Wants
by Jaid Black, Dominique Adair, & Shiloh Walker

Tempt Me Twice

Jaci Burton

Susie Charles

Beverly Havlir

POCKET BOOKS

New York   London   Toronto   Sydney

Pocket Books
A Division of Simon & Schuster, Inc.
1230 Avenue of the Americas
New York, NY 10020

This Pocket Books trade paperback edition January 2010

POCKET and colophon are registered trademarks of Simon & Schuster, Inc.

For information about special discounts for bulk purchases, please contact Simon & Schuster Special Sales at 1-800-456-6798 or business@simonandschuster.com

The Simon & Schuster Speakers Bureau can bring authors to your live event. For more information or to book an event contact the Simon & Schuster Speakers Bureau at 1-866-248-3049 or visit our website at www.simonspeakers.com.

Designed by Akasha Archer

Manufactured in the United States of America

1 3 5 7 9 10 8 6 4 2

Library of Congress Cataloging-in-Publication Data is available.

ISBN 978-1-4391-5009-2

These stories have previously appeared in Ellora's Cave anthologies published by Pocket Books. "Dream On" appeared in *Fever-Hot Dreams*. "Velvet Strokes" appeared in *Overtime, Under Him*. "Irresistible" appeared in *A Hot Man is the Best Revenge*.

Contents

Tempt Me
Twice

Dream On

Jaci Burton

To Briana St. James, my wonderful editor.
Thank you for helping me realize a lifelong dream.

To Charlie, the man of my dreams. You are my heart and my very soul.
Without you, I would be forever lost. With you, I am whole. Thank you
for making me believe that anything I dream can come true.
I love you.

"We are such stuff
As dreams are made on . . . "
William Shakespeare's *The Tempest* (IV, i, 156–157)

1

Kate stood outside on the porch and wrapped the quilt around her shoulders to ward off the chill of impending night. Dust filtered through the setting sun, coloring the lake a rusty orange. It was spring and the days were beginning to grow warmer, but at night when the sun went down so did the temperature. She shivered, grabbed her cup of tea and sat on the old wooden swing. As she rocked back and forth and watched the orange glow of the horizon, the memories slapped at her like flies at a summer picnic.

Spring used to be Jack's favorite time of year. During the rare occasions he had a weekend to spare, they'd travel out here to the country house and sit on the swing, talking about anything and everything. His job, the kids, what they wanted to do when they retired. They'd made so many plans together, counting the years until the kids were grown and off creating their own lives.

The kids were gone now. Problem was, so was Jack. Only his departure had been more abrupt. One day he was there, sharing his life with her, and the next he was gone. Without any warning, he'd disappeared from her life completely.

Her mellow mood vanished in an instant, replaced instead by the cool chill that had permeated every day for the last five years. And all because of Jack.

The sonofabitch. She'd go to her grave hating him for what he'd done.

He'd made promises. Big promises about their future together, sucking her into his dreams so easily, only to shatter her illusions in one day. Now she was forty-five years old and alone, and all those things Jack had promised her for twenty years had meant nothing. They'd never enjoy making love in the middle of the day because the boys were no longer there to interrupt. They'd never sell their house in the city and retire here in their country house. They'd never grow old together.

Empty words. Betrayal.

"You lied to me, Jack," she whispered to the breeze swirling around her. "You promised me forever and you didn't keep your part of the bargain. How could you do this to me? How could you make promises and not keep them?"

Swiping at the tears rolling down her cheeks, she summoned up the righteous anger that always made her feel better. Screw him! He'd left her after twenty years, destroying her dreams. She'd long ago vowed never to hurt over him again. Better to stay angry. Much more productive that way.

So why did she still dream about him at night? Why did his face, his touch, still haunt her?

Because you can't let go.

She shook her head, refusing to dwell on him any longer. Jack was part of her past now and the house in the city was up for sale. One part of her memories would soon be gone. At least she still had the country house, even though it was way too quiet these days with the boys gone. Both Ron and J.J. were in college, but they came home as often as they could.

They worried about her, and she knew that. They tried to visit as often as possible and she knew it was because they were concerned about the amount of time she spent alone. But she fought them tooth and nail, insisting they make their own lives. The last thing she needed or wanted was her children acting as babysitters.

She was fine alone. She'd even reached the point where she could spend weekends here at the country house like they all used to. Soon she'd live here full-time and could concentrate more on her writing. Being alone would be advantageous then. She could write undisturbed by city noise. Maybe she'd even be able to crank out one extra book a year this way. And occasionally, the boys could visit since the country house was closer to their school. They were supposed to be there this weekend, but she insisted they stay at school for the big game. Besides, the quiet solitude of the country would be good for her muse. Maybe she'd be able to finish that book this weekend.

She stood and headed into the house, locking the door and flipping the light switches off. She undressed and stood in front of the bathroom mirror, shaking her head at how much she'd aged in the past five years. Her face drooped like a basset hound's, her hair hung long and stringy and the once shiny auburn strands looked oily and dirty. She'd gained at least fifteen pounds and felt every single one of them in her belly, thighs and butt.

"What the hell do I have to look good for, anyway?" she mused to her reflection. "I used to take care of myself, worked hard on my body and my appearance. Did it keep Jack in my life?"

Jaci Burton

The reflection shook its head.

"Exactly my point. No one sees me anyway." And her sons loved her no matter how she looked, though they did suggest she get out more and away from her computer.

What they really meant was they thought she should find another man.

The thought of dating anyone made her shudder in revulsion. Never again would she put her trust in a man, only to have her dreams of paradise ripped away when he didn't live up to his promises.

She grabbed her pajamas and slipped them on, remembering the days she and Jack would slide under the cool sheets stark naked, using their bodies to warm each other. With a sigh she shut off the light and climbed into bed, staring out the window at the half moon shining overhead.

They used to make love while looking out this window. The moon always had an erotic pull for her, reminding her of hot and sexy whispered promises in the dark, warm, calloused hands reaching for her breasts or between her legs, eliciting cries in the night that she hadn't experienced in far too long.

Her breasts ached and a tightness formed between her legs. Her clit throbbed, her pussy moistening at the memories of hot sex that went on all night long. She reached down, sliding her hand between her legs and resting the heel of her palm against her clit. Pleasure burst inside her, but she quickly drew her hand away, refusing to give in to the desire that seemed all too insistent these days. Orgasm would only make her wish for something she couldn't have.

Sexual reawakening wasn't what she needed right now. She'd long ago lost the urge to bring herself to orgasm, afraid the memories would wash over her and she'd end up hating Jack, and herself, for what they could have had together. So she fought back the urges, determined that her mind was stronger than her body and she didn't need sex of any kind to feel fulfilled.

Disgusted by her unruly body, she flipped over onto her back and stared up at the ceiling. "Damn you, Jack, will I ever get over what you did?"

Maybe the boys were right and she should get out and start dating again. If she did, thoughts of Jack would dwindle until there was nothing left but vague memories. But could she really do that? Thoughts of having another man's hands on her or another man seeing her naked made her physically ill. Jack was the only one who'd ever touched her, the only one she'd ever wanted to touch her.

Could she actually take that step and start over again? She let the thought permeate her mind for a few minutes, but came up with no answers to her dilemma other than the same old feeling that she belonged to Jack and nobody else. That she'd never let another man touch her.

But was that fair? Why did she have to be punished because of what Jack did?

"Somebody please tell me what to do." She laid there quietly for a few moments, but the darkness provided no answer. Not that she expected one. No one had answers or explanations for why Jack had left her. Only the standard diatribes of *these things happen and no one can explain why,* or *give it time and you'll get over him,* and of course her favorite one of all . . .

. . . *it's not your fault.*

With a disgusted sigh, she squeezed her eyes shut and refused to think anymore tonight.

Sleep, Kate. Turn your mind off. Maybe one day you'll actually be able to get through an entire day and not think about that bastard who left you.

Maybe one night she could sleep without the dreams haunting her.

If only . . .

"KATE? WAKE UP."

Kate pulled the covers over her shoulders and turned away from the offending voice. "Go away. I'm sleeping."

Warm breath caressed her neck and goose bumps broke out on her skin when a hand touched her shoulder.

"Babe, you need to wake up."

So used to him invading her dreams every night, she ignored the realistic sound of his voice. Why wouldn't he just go away? How long would this torment continue? "Get lost, Jack."

"I've *been* lost, Katie. I'm home now."

Something wasn't right. This conversation didn't *feel* dream-like. It felt real.

But that wasn't possible. Jack didn't live here anymore. He wouldn't be here. No way. She was hallucinating, or so deep into the dream that it seemed like the real thing. Yet she'd dreamed of him every single night since he left and this wasn't like all those times before. Her nightly sojourns had been more surreal, more distant. Though she saw him, touched him, made love with him over and over again, there was a definite lack of reality to her dreams. It was if she was observing her own body, watching the way he touched her and kissed her.

This was different. The covers moved down and she felt the chill of cold air on her skin. When the brush of warm fingers trailed down her arm, she knew what she felt was no dream.

Her heart lurched and she sat up, blinking back the sleep from her eyes. The room was dark, but she heard the soft inhalation of breath that wasn't her own. She broke out into a sweat and fought to still the trembling of her body.

Someone was in the room with her!

Too afraid to even swallow, she clutched the sheets and prayed to God one of her kids had come home for the weekend to surprise her.

"Don't be afraid, Kate. It's me."

She blinked, as if the act of doing so would cast a light over whoever was in the room.

"Baby, shhh, it's okay."

That voice. She knew that voice. But it couldn't be. It wasn't possible. When he left she knew he was never coming back. And he hadn't in five long years.

It couldn't be him.

She lifted her arm, ready to search the darkness, but dropped her hand to the sheets and shook her head, realizing that she'd completely lost her mind. "You're not real." This was the weirdest dream she'd ever had.

But when a calloused hand caressed her cheek, she froze. Dammit, she *felt* that! It *was* real! She wasn't asleep now, so it had to be real. Surely she wasn't still dreaming.

"Don't be afraid."

Her eyes adjusted well enough to the darkness to make out a silhouette of a man sitting on the edge of her bed. "Who the hell are you?"

It's not Jack. It couldn't be him. He would never come back. Yet the more she cast it aside, the more real it became.

"You know damn well who I am. Wake up, Kate. This isn't a dream."

It *had* to be a dream. No way in hell would Jack have come back to her. Not after . . .

This was ludicrous. And it wasn't happening. If she reached for him, she'd grasp nothing but air. Lifting her hand, she stretched toward the apparition in the darkness and grabbed a fistful of . . .

. . . shirt. Shirt surrounding hard muscle of a man's upper arm.

Oh, God. This wasn't happening. Jerking her hand away, she scooted toward the other edge of the bed and lunged for the lamp on her nightstand, afraid to turn the light on and too afraid not to. She sucked in a breath of courage and flicked the switch.

Holding her breath, she turned around. Her heart tumbled over as she drank her fill of the man she both loved with all her heart and hated to the deepest recesses of her soul.

"Jack."

2

IT COULDN'T BE. HE wouldn't be here. How would he even know she was here? Why would he even *want* to find her? Not a word in five years. Nothing. No contact.

Why now?

"I can explain," he said, running his hand through his thick black hair. "If you want to hear it."

He hadn't changed at all in five years. She had aged like an old hag and blamed stress and misery as the reasons her appearance had changed so drastically. Apparently he'd not had that problem. His body was still all corded muscle, expansive chest, flat abs and sexy, muscular thighs encased in jeans that hugged his form like a second skin. She pulled the covers up to her chin, suddenly wishing she'd never turned that light on.

How dare he look so goddamned sexy!

Drawing up the anger she lived with every day, she lifted her chin and said, "No explanations necessary. You left. There's nothing else to say. Get out."

He stood and walked around the other side of the bed to sit next to her. She tried to scoot away but he grasped her wrist. Heat surged through her body at his touch. She might hate him, but just the whisper of his skin against hers flamed her long-dead libido to life again.

"I have a lot to say. And I left for a good reason."

She snorted. "Sure you did. There's always a good reason to dump a twenty-year marriage just like that." Okay, she sounded like a shrew. A bitter one at that. But she didn't care. She'd spent five years wishing she could get him alone in a room and tell him exactly what she thought of him. Now was her chance. And no matter what her heart said, no matter the joy that wanted to spring up inside her at the sight of him, she held onto her anger like a comforting weapon to use against him.

"I never stopped loving you, Katie."

Oh, now that wasn't fair. Wasn't fair at all. She'd been prepared for excuses, for apologies and explanations, but not this.

Pull that anger and feeling of betrayal out of their shell, Katherine. Tell him how it felt when you woke up one morning and he was gone.

"You never loved me. Hell, you barely even told me you loved me the last few years before you left." *And if you really loved me, you'd never have left me.*

Furrows creased his brow. She itched to trace every single line on his face, all the way down to the curve of his full lips. His gray eyes darkened like a thick cover of clouds in the night and he dropped his chin, looking at her through hooded eyes. "I'm sorry. You're right. There's a lot I have to atone for, if you'll let me."

She jumped out of bed and paced the room, brushing her hair away from her face, no longer caring that he could see her gray hair and flabby body. "Atone? Atone! How *dare* you show up here claiming 'Gee babe, I'm sorry that I left you five years

ago, but I'm back now so everything's okay, right?'. How stupid
do you think I am? Do you think I've sat around for five years
mourning what we had, missing you so bad I couldn't breathe
and just wishing I had one more day with you?"

He didn't smile, but he nodded. "Actually, I think you did
just that. And that's exactly how I felt, too. That's why I'm
back."

Damn. Fury rocked her body and she trembled. She dropped
into the chair next to the desk and bent her head down, refusing to let her ire completely overtake her. She clasped her hands
tightly together to still the tremors. He wouldn't hurt her again.
She'd never allow it. Once was bad enough. Twice would be
unbearable.

"Why are you here? What do you want from me?"

He didn't answer and she refused to look up at him. But she
heard him move off the bed and toward her. She couldn't help
but watch as he knelt on the floor in front of her. She squeezed
her eyes shut so she didn't have to look at him, afraid if she did
she'd weaken, and all those years spent erecting the protective
shell around her heart would have been wasted.

"Katie, I love you. And I made some serious mistakes with
our marriage. I screwed up our lives and our future together.
But I didn't leave because I didn't love you anymore. I left
because I had to, because I had no control over certain events.
It wasn't until after I'd left that I realized there were things I
needed to fix about myself."

"And did you?"

"Did I what?"

"Did you fix them?"

"I don't know. I hope so. Actually, I thought you could tell
me, if you give me a chance to show you."

His words filtered through her anger like honey into a comb. Her shell weakened at the husky plea in his voice and she remembered all those whispered promises in the dark, when his hard, thick cock had filled her, his hands stroking her to one whimpering orgasm after another. He'd played her body like an artist inspired to greatness, each brush of his hands and mouth on her like a masterpiece of rapture that made her cry out and beg for more of his genius.

The bad times had been all too frequent, but the good times were incredibly memorable.

"Let me prove it to you, Katie. Tell me what you want."

How easy it would be to tell him to stay, to let him know that all she'd ever wanted was forever with the man she loved. But the last five years wouldn't disappear so easily, even if her body was starved for attention and her heart felt empty and cold without him. She looked him in the eye, making sure he read every one of her emotions. "What I want is for the last five years to have never happened. What I want is for the five years before that to have been more than fleeting glimpses of you while you stopped at home to unpack and repack in between business trips. What I want is to start over again and this time have a husband who'd be there for me and the kids instead of focused only on his career."

She refused to feel sympathy for the pain in his eyes. None of this was her fault.

"You're right. About everything. I screwed up. But I can't go back. I can only go forward. Let me show you that I've changed. Let me give you back what I took from you when I left."

"You can never give me back what I've lost, Jack. Never." And she didn't care how much she hurt him by saying it. It was the truth.

Besides, she'd had this conversation with him almost every night for the past five years, when he appeared in her dreams. This time seemed real, but she knew better. She was still dreaming. She had to be.

She jerked when he swept his hand over her hair.

"Let me try."

She pushed at him and stood, crossing over to the sliding glass doors and looking out at the moon. "I don't want anything. I don't want you here." She turned fully away when he stepped behind her, determined not to let him touch her again. "You showing up out of the blue like this after no word for five years is ripping my heart out, Jack. Please leave me alone. I was doing fine without you."

Because despite her anger, her misery, her desperate prayers to bring him back and then giving up when she knew her pleas fell on deaf ears, she'd never once stopped loving him. Standing here with him now opened up wounds that had taken years to close. This wasn't fair!

"I'm not leaving this time, Katie, no matter what you say. I'm here to stay, for as long as it takes to show you I've changed. I'm staying until you realize that I love you, that I've always loved you and I never stopped."

Then why did you leave me?! The words dangled on the tip of her tongue, but she refused to give them voice. What difference would explanations make at this point?

"Just go away, Jack. I don't want or need you anymore." She pushed past him and went into the bathroom and shut the door. She sat on the lid of the toilet and counted, hoping he'd get the hint and leave.

Twenty minutes later her butt was numb. Was he gone or had he stayed? It was quiet and he'd long ago stopped talking to her through the door, so maybe he'd finally given up and left. She unlocked the door and opened it, both relieved and disappointed that she didn't find him waiting for her in her bedroom.

Oh, sure. Just like that, in and out of her life once again. She tasted the bitterness, reveled in it, wrapped it around her like a shield of thick armor. Anger felt so much better than pain. It strengthened rather than weakened her, filling her with its lusty power like a weapon she could use against her enemies.

Or enemy. The man she once loved had become her nemesis. Only this time she wasn't going to come out the loser. She didn't need him in her life again, didn't love him anymore and he wasn't welcome in her home.

Giving up on getting anymore sleep, she glanced at the clock.

Five in the morning. Might as well fix some coffee, clear her head and try to get some writing done. Sleep would come later, after she thoroughly exhausted herself.

She padded into the kitchen, stopping in the hallway as she picked up the scent of coffee. Wary, she peeked around the corner, her shoulders slumping in defeat as she spied Jack leaning against the counter, a cup of steaming coffee in one hand, holding another out to her with the other.

"How about some breakfast, babe? I'll cook."

Oh, God. She wanted to fall into a heap right there in the doorway, pound her head against the wood floor and scream out in rage, letting all the emotions she'd held in pour out of her. She wanted, no, *needed* an epic tantrum.

Why was he doing this to her?

3

KATE REGARDED JACK WITH a dubious expression. Okay, if this is the way he was going to play the game, so be it. She'd let him know that she had changed in the five years he'd been gone. That she was self-sufficient and didn't really need him anymore. That she was impervious to his dark good looks, his steely body, his sexy smile and voice.

Yeah, right. Now she just had to convince herself of it.

True to his word, he fixed her breakfast. Didn't let her do a thing except sit at the table, forcing her to watch the way he moved, the way his ass looked when he bent over to retrieve a pan from the lower cabinet, the way his muscles moved under his tight T-shirt.

Even with bacon sizzling in the pan, the scent of Jack over-powered her. Crisp, clean, smelling like his favorite soap. She'd left his brand of soap in the shower long after he'd left, torturing herself by lifting it off the shelf and inhaling the smell that was so much a part of him it made her heart hurt.

Smelling it again and seeing him standing in their kitchen cooking for her made her hands shake. Fighting off the quiver in her fingers, she lifted the coffee cup to her lips and took a deep draw of the life-infusing caffeine, hoping it would jolt her out of the cloud of bittersweet memories.

Remember the bad stuff, Kate.

Bad stuff. Right. That she could do. Like a life preserver, she held tight to those memories. Jack had been all about work. Owning his own business was time-consuming, he'd told her in the beginning. And it eventually consumed all of him. He never took the time to do the things she wanted. But she was always there for him, and for their kids, standing by Jack when things went badly at work, taking care of shuffling the kids back and forth when he had yet another out of town business meeting. And through it all, she'd loved him, lived for those fleeting moments when he gave her his attention. They were rare, but when they happened, they were unforgettable.

She'd been such a fool. All those years she'd struggled as a writer, putting her own career on the back burner while she nurtured his and took care of the children because he was too busy to do anything but work.

Now she was poised on the verge of success. Her agent told her a sale of her latest book to one of the big publishers looked promising. Very promising.

She allowed her first smile of the day.

"What are you grinning about?"

She jumped when Jack spoke, so immersed in her own thoughts she'd forgotten he stood nearby. He slid a plate in front of her and sat, occupying his usual chair that had stood empty for too many years. Now it was like the past five years had disappeared, as if they'd been some kind of dream and this was her reality now. A sense of comfort overcame her and she knew it was because Jack was here, smiling at her as if he'd never left.

Obviously she was still dreaming. This was no reality. "I was thinking about my latest book."

He scooped up a forkful of eggs, arching a brow as he swallowed. "Tell me how that's going."

"It's going great. I've sold a few books to a smaller publisher, but my agent has my latest and claims there's going to be a bidding war by some of the big names out there."

His beaming smile was like an arrow to her heart. "Always knew you could do it, Katie. You've always had amazing talent."

She sniffed. Yeah, right. As if he'd ever taken the time to even ask her what she was writing or take the slightest interest in her work. How would he know how talented she was? He'd never read a word of what she'd written.

"I've read every book you've written. You have a gift, Kate. An amazing gift that I'm so glad you're utilizing."

Good thing she was sitting down or she'd have fallen to the ground. Shock made her eyes widen and she nearly choked on the orange juice she'd just swallowed. "You've read my books?"

His smile was sheepish and he hunched his shoulders. "Yeah. I'm sorry it took me so long. You're incredible, Kate. I wish I hadn't been so selfish all those years so you'd have had more time to get your writing going. My leaving was actually the best thing for you. It made you write and submit your work."

She sat back and regarded him, unable to believe this was the same Jack who used to sit across the table from her, on the rare occasions he was actually home, of course, so engrossed in his newspaper he'd never know whether she was there or not. And when he wasn't busy with paperwork for his business, he was off on a trip. By the time he'd get home, he'd be exhausted and barely have time to spend with the boys, let alone inquire about her writing.

This Jack seemed relaxed, focusing all his attentions on her. She wasn't used to this version of her husband and didn't quite know how to react. Suspicious, she waited for him to launch into detailed explanations of what he'd been doing for the past five years, but so far, nothing about himself. Only about her.

Bizarre.

"You're looking at me funny."

She arched a brow. "Funny?"

"Yeah. Like you can't believe I'm really here."

Well, duh. What she couldn't believe was the version of Jack that sat across from her. "This is too weird. You know it as well as I do."

His lips curved into a grin. "Well, yeah, you could say that. But I'm here, so let's make the best of it and not question why."

Easy for him to say. He wasn't the one with questions.

And more questions, especially when he got up, cleared the table and did all the dishes. This had to be a dream! Jack never did domestic chores around the house. Ever.

"Let's go shopping."

She stared at him as if he spoke a foreign language. "Huh?"

"Shopping. Go take a shower, get dressed and let's go. Daylight's wasting."

Shock prevented her from objecting, especially when he grabbed her hands and hauled her to her feet. She stood and mutely allowed him to direct her down the hall toward the bathroom. She stepped into the hot shower, convinced she'd just dreamed the past couple hours and when she came out, she'd find Jack was still as gone as he had been the past five years.

But he wasn't. She dried her hair, dressed and opened the bedroom door. There he stood, looking completely edible and way too good-looking for her. She cringed at the thought of being seen with him in public.

Then again, they really didn't know anyone in town. The country house sat on over two acres of land overlooking the lake, and they mainly kept to themselves. The chances of running into anyone they knew in town were slim.

When they stepped outside, a brisk gust of wind caught her jacket and flung it open. She held it tightly closed with one hand and looked around the circular driveway.

"Uhhh, Jack, where's your car?"

"Don't have it anymore. I took a taxi out here."

"A taxi. From town?"

"Yeah. I grabbed your keys off the dresser. We'll take your car."

Stunned speechless, she slid in the car and buckled her seat belt. Jack never went anywhere without his expensive luxury sedan, his pride and joy, his status symbol of success. He'd never sell that car. And why didn't he have another car to drive?

"Jack, I don't under—"

"Why I'm going shopping with you?" he asked, cutting her off mid-question. "It's simple. I'm going to do all the things I never did with you before. All the things I claimed to be too busy to do. Like shopping and buying you things and spending time with you." He glanced at her and said, "I've missed just being with you, Katie. I've missed touching you, holding you and kissing you. I've missed pressing my body up against yours at night, breathing in the smell of your hair and skin. I miss all of that so much it makes me hurt inside."

Tears pooled in her eyes and she willed them away, turning

quickly to look out the window. She would not fall for his charm again. Nothing he said mattered to her. In an hour or two he'd grow tired of this game and be off on a phone call or a trip. He may have had an attack of nostalgia and maybe a little guilt, but that didn't mean he'd come back to her. Not really.

She'd lost Jack forever a long time ago. Nothing he did or said now would bring back the man she once loved.

4

"ARE YOU INSANE?"

An hour into their shopping trip, Jack stood her in front of the town's trendiest hair salon.

"Of course I'm not insane. You're getting your hair and nails done today, and a pedicure. I'll wait."

"I am not getting anything done and you're crazy."

With eyes that sparkled like they had when he was young, he turned her toward the entrance of the salon where two smiling women waited to work on her. Hell, it would take them at least a week to make her look good.

"Go," he whispered, his warm breath caressing her neck and making goose bumps pop out all over her skin. "I'll be waiting for you. I'm not going anywhere, Katie, I promise."

I'm not going anywhere. Those words both chilled and warmed her during the two-hour hair and nail extravaganza. She expected at any moment to look up and find Jack had disappeared, but he hadn't. He sat in a chair at the front of the salon the entire time, reading magazines and occasionally glancing up to smile over at her.

The looks he gave her heated her from the inside out. The way he used to look at her, before he got too busy to notice whether she was even in the room or not. Hot gazes filled with the promise of scorching sex.

The result was a complete biological meltdown. Her breasts ached and her nipples tightened. Her long-ignored pussy flamed to life, her clit quivering with the need to be touched, licked and sucked. She squirmed in her chair and tried to ignore her betraying body's signals to leap from her seat, straddle Jack and fuck his brains out before he left her again.

God, she missed sex with him. Even when they had reached the point where they'd become nearly strangers, when they came together at night it was explosive. They may have had a full list of problems, but sex had never been one of them.

All those old feelings of desire and need and want came crashing down over her with every one of his seductive glances. Damn him. She was supposed to hate him, not crave him.

His gaze caught and held hers, and she read the heat in his eyes. Something passed between them at that moment and she shivered. It had been a long time since he looked at her with barely controlled hunger in his eyes. And she wasn't immune, either. Her body was so in tune to him that it screamed from the inside out, waking with a sexual vengeance she wasn't prepared to handle.

"Okay, honey, you're all finished!"

Finally. She smiled apologetically at Mary, her hairdresser, who no doubt had to struggle with the messy mop on her head. But instead of looking disgusted, Mary beamed, winked and flipped Kate's chair around so she could look in the mirror.

Okay, *wow* was the first word that came to mind. Who was that woman in the mirror? Ten years had just been peeled away as she stared, openmouthed, at her reflection in the glass.

Two hours, a facial, eyebrow wax, haircut, color and makeup could not have made that drastic a change to her appearance. But it sure looked that way.

They'd chopped off at least six inches of lifeless hair, giving her a newer, trendier cut that skimmed just along her chin. The color was a deep, rich auburn, bringing out the amber in her eyes and highlighting her cheekbones.

The makeup they'd applied hadn't hurt, either. As a stay at home writer she usually wore her pajamas and no makeup. Since Jack left she'd had no reason to get dressed, do anything with her hair or go out unless she met the boys or had a meeting.

But this new hairstyle and makeup brightened her face like it hadn't been for . . . years. That had to be the reason she looked so much younger now.

"Get over there and show that hunky man of yours the new look," Mary suggested.

He wasn't *her* hunky man. Not any longer. Nevertheless, she stood and headed toward Jack, who was currently engrossed in a weekly gossip magazine, of all things. He looked up when she stopped in front of him, his eyes widening and his jaw dropping. She suppressed a smile at her purely feminine reaction to his look of shock and pleasure.

"Wow," he said, standing up and walking around her.

She felt more self-conscious than she ever had before, like Pygmalion's creation at the grand unveiling. Had she really looked so bad before? The answer was yes, she realized with a huge rush of embarrassment. How could she have let herself go that way?

Jack stopped in front of her again, took her hands and pulled her against him. The first contact of her nipples against his hard chest was electrifying. She stared into his eyes, knowing she should object, push away. Something to maintain a careful distance between them. But for the life of her she couldn't help but enjoy the way he looked at her right now.

"There's my girl," he whispered, slanting his lips across hers.

It was a simple, gentle brush of mouth to mouth, but in a heartbeat all was lost. She breathed in the scent of him, thrilled to the softness of his lips against hers, the way his body fit against hers as if they'd been made for each other. She was suddenly sixteen years old again, being kissed for the very first time by the boy she'd fantasized about for years. Her relationship with Jack went so far back she couldn't remember a time he wasn't part of her life.

Which had made his abrupt departure so much worse.

Cruel reality intruded into her moment of nostalgic bliss and she placed her palms on his chest, gently pushing away. Her lips tingled, her nipples beading against her bra and her panties moistening. In an instant she'd forgotten everything he'd done to her, the years of feeling betrayed by his broken promises. How easily she'd been seduced by male appreciation for surface appearance.

Jack searched her face and she realized he knew her thoughts.

"I know. I still have a lot to make up for, Katie. You don't trust in my love and I don't blame you for your lack of faith. One step at a time, okay?"

She nodded, wary but willing to keep an open mind.

"Let's go shopping," he said.

He took her hand and led her out of the salon and into the

town's trendiest clothing boutique. It was small and very, very expensive. She'd never been one to spend money on clothes, especially those that came with a price tag she could feed her family a month on.

"Why are you doing this?" she asked as he led her to the evening wear.

"Because I have to. I need to. I want to shower you with gifts and attention and everything you missed out on all those years because I was such a selfish bastard."

She couldn't argue with the selfish bastard part. "I don't need any new clothes."

"You have anything at the house to wear to go dancing at the country club?"

Country club? Who was he kidding? They weren't even members there. "Jack, we don't even belong—"

"We do now. Come on. Let's go see what they have in here."

They were greeted by a very tall, statuesque blonde who couldn't be more than twenty-five. She smiled enthusiastically and led them to the cocktail dress section, no doubt smelling a sale. A big sale.

Hell, one outfit here could feed an entire third-world country for a month! But Jack insisted, grasping her hand and dragging her around while Suzie the salesclerk brought out a stack of dresses.

None of those dresses would either fit or look good on her. They were too short, too tight and would reveal way too much of everything she was desperate to conceal. But Jack chose five dresses and all but pushed her into the dressing room to try them on.

"I've also brought some undergarments and shoes to go with these dresses," Suzie enthused, then shut the door and left Kate alone. She stared at the dresses and then her reflection in the mirror.

Too tight blue jeans and a bulky sweater did nothing for her figure. Then again, they suited her lifestyle. Those . . . things . . . hanging up in the room were not her and it was about time she made her choices clear to Jack and Suzie both. She turned and opened the door, stepping out and running smack into Jack's chest.

"Oh, no, you don't," he said, pushing her backward and shutting the door behind him. "I thought you might try to make an escape. I'm here to see you don't."

"You're not supposed to be in here!" she hissed.

He waved a hand toward the door and shrugged. "Oh, Suzie doesn't care. She knows if she sells at least one of those dresses she's going to make a bundle. Now try them on."

"I will not." Especially with him standing in the room with her. He hadn't seen her naked in five years. Well, longer than that considering they hadn't had much sex at the end and when they had it had typically been in the dark. No way was she going to let him see what her body looked like now.

"If you don't take your clothes off, I'm going to do it for you."

His threat sent her mind careening into visuals she had no business visualizing. Like Jack peeling layer by layer of clothing from her body, touching his hot mouth to every spot he revealed. The room temperature increased by ten degrees and she broke out into a sweat. She could call his bluff, but the determined expression on his face told her he wasn't kidding about undressing her. "Get out, Jack. I'll try the damn outfits on, but not with you standing in here."

He tilted his head to the side, then nodded. "I'll be right

outside the door. Just holler when you have one on and I'll come take a look."

Great. Just what she needed. Why was she even allowing herself to be pulled, prodded, and forced in a direction she didn't want to go, anyway?

She knew the reason. Because deep down . . . really deep down . . . she wanted this. Maybe it was a challenge to see if she could somehow squeeze her body into one, just one of these gorgeous dresses. She hadn't worn anything pretty in years and it was about damn time she made some changes.

If only she had the body to match the dresses, she could really show Jack what he'd given up when he left.

She wanted to hurt him. The realization hit like an icy chill on a wintry day. She wanted him to feel the same pain she'd felt when he left, to realize that maybe what he'd left hadn't been so bad after all, that maybe, just maybe, he should have worked a little harder to stay.

Get over yourself, Kate. He left for a damn good reason and you know it. Quit trying to make it something it isn't.

With a heavy sigh she struggled out of her jeans and sweater, then removed her underwear, refusing to even glance in the direction of the full-length mirror while she slipped into decadent underthings. Lord, it was amazing they fit her. She chose the dress she liked best. A black, slinky, clingy short cocktail dress that hugged every one of her curves. What the hell, it was good for a laugh before she took it off, right? Smoothing the matching black hose against her legs, she slipped into the heels and braced herself for disappointment when she turned around.

"You still in there?" she heard Jack say through the door.

She froze and stared at the door. "Yeah."

"I'm coming in."

"Wait!" But before she could reach out to lock the door, he'd opened it.

"Holy shit, Kate," he whispered, his gaze traveling from her eyes down to her feet.

He was being kind. Okay, he scored points for that. "Thanks. Gimme a minute and I'll slip another of these dresses on."

"What the hell for? You got me hard in a second just looking at you in that thing. Jesus Christ, Katie!"

She rolled her eyes at him. "Give me a break, Jack. I look like a sausage."

"Have you looked in the mirror yet?"

"No." And she planned to slip off this dress and put on another without once turning around to stare at herself in the mirror. Mirrors revealed all flaws, especially dressing room mirrors.

He grasped her shoulders and turned her around. "Then take a peek so you can see what I see."

Ugh. She didn't want to, but she had no choice when he fully spun her around. She looked down at her feet first, not recognizing the slim ankles and shapely calves that led up to slender thighs and . . .

"Oh my God!"

5

WHO WAS THAT WOMAN in the mirror? Not the same one she'd seen last night, that was certain. Was she hallucinating? The lighting in the dressing room couldn't be that good.

But she definitely looked . . . different. The dress clung to her, all right, but she didn't look fat or out of shape. The snug fabric slenderized her shape and showed off all her curves.

Well, okay. Her curves were a bit ample. Hell, she wasn't twenty-five anymore. What did she expect?

"You've always been overly critical of yourself," Jack whispered as if he'd heard her internal thoughts. "You look hot as hell, Katie. Delectable. I'd like to eat you alive, right here."

There went the temp in the room, notched up another ten degrees. Good thing the dress was sleeveless. What kind of game was he playing with her? Before, he'd never noticed whether she'd been dressed in sweatpants or an evening gown with a tiara on her head.

"You've never seen what I see in you," he said, stepping

behind her and resting his hands on the curve of her hips. Her skin burned at his light touch.

"You stopped looking at me a long time ago," she shot back at his reflection in the mirror, irritated that he was giving her the full-court press. He had to be after something. Some ulterior motive for his oddly attentive behavior. But what?

He frowned, his lids half closing. Then he looked up and met her gaze head-on. "I never stopped looking. I was just . . . I don't know what happened to me, Kate. Somewhere along the way I lost sight of what was important. You, the boys, everything that should have mattered. I told you I screwed up. I've spent the past five years thinking of nothing but that, wondering if you realized how much better off you were without me causing you such pain."

"Leaving me caused me more pain that I thought I could bear." But she *had* borne it, had survived it, had learned to live with the sense of betrayal and mistrust ever since the day he left. "Why did you come back, Jack?"

"To appreciate you the way I never did before. To make you appreciate yourself the way you never did. Beyond your surface beauty, there's a kind, gentle heart that always gave and gave and gave without hesitation, while I took and took and took. You were always there for me, Katie. Me and the boys. You were unselfish and loving with a hundred percent of your heart and soul, and that's what makes you beautiful to me."

His words knifed through her middle, making her ache to turn around and throw her arms around him. But she held back, the part of her that still hurt hesitant to allow her to open her heart again.

He bent his head and pressed a soft kiss to the side of her neck. Her nipples tightened against the snug fabric of the dress as, despite her irritation at him, her body responded with a wild flare of desire.

"I don't need you to appreciate me." But the words sounded as hollow as they felt. She *did* need him to appreciate her, more than she could admit to herself.

"Yes, you do. Now look at yourself and let me tell you what I see."

"I don't want to play this game, Jack."

"It's not a game. I'm serious. Look."

She did, meeting his gaze in the mirror, forcing herself to face who she really was now.

"Your face has a glow about it. That always mesmerized me about you. The way your eyes light up when you smile and your cheeks turn pink when you're embarrassed. Do you remember how shy you were when we first met?"

"Yes." She'd almost died when he'd asked her out the first time, sure he was playing some kind of joke on her. He was a senior football player and she was a geeky, gawky sophomore who hadn't a clue how to act around boys. But he'd been kind and gentle, never pressuring her for more than she was ready to give. And she'd fallen hopelessly in love with him. He'd been her first love. Her only love.

"The way you used to smile at me when you thought I wasn't looking drove me crazy. God I loved that yearning in your eyes, Katie. That sweet innocence in those warm eyes that made me want to take care of you and protect you forever. I fell in love with your eyes first, and I still love them best about you. They tell me everything you're feeling."

She studied her reflection as if she could see any telltale signs in her eyes. They had a dark, honeyed look to them right now, as if there was molten fire behind them. Is that what Jack saw when he looked at her? Were her emotions always that transparent?

Memories did that to her. Made her remember all the good times, instead of concentrating on the bad times like she should be doing.

His hand on her hip caught her attention. Squeezing gently, he caressed the curve from waist to thigh, his breath hot against her neck as he bent down to pet her body. "You know, I love your eyes, but there's a lot more. Especially the way you feel under my hands." He pressed his palm against her hip. "I love this part of you. Every curve in your body entices me. I'd like to undress you and lay you out naked in the sunlight so I could study every inch of you."

She cringed at the thought of every bump of cellulite exposed to the glaring sun.

His laugh was husky and dark, his chest rumbling against her back. Her legs trembled. "You always thought I scrutinized every flaw. I don't. I adore the perfection of you. You are an amazing creature, Katherine Mary McKay. From your remarkable intelligence to the fierce way you protected our sons to the unselfish way you gave up everything so I could do my job. It will take an eternity for me to repay you for all you did for me, and even that won't be enough."

This side of Jack was so new, so unexpected, that she was at a loss for words. A snappy comeback to an empty promise was easy. But she heard sincerity in his words, and a depth of his soul he'd never revealed to her before.

He kissed her shoulder, drawing one thin strap down her arm, his fingers blazing a trail of sensual promise that made her shiver despite the heat in the small dressing room. Thoughts of anger and betrayal fled as her body tuned in completely to his touch, his scent, the way his hard body felt pressed against her.

"Let me love you, Kate," he whispered, drawing the other strap down and pulling the dress to her waist. The black bra lifted her breasts and squeezed them together, offering an enticing bit of cleavage.

Jack moved his hands in front of her, caressing the swell of her breasts. "You always had beautiful breasts, babe. So full and soft. And your nipples, now those are a work of art." He drew the straps of her bra down and pulled the fabric away from the mounds. Her breasts fell into his hands and he cupped them, using his thumbs to draw circles around the pink areolas, tantalizing them with unbearably soft strokes until she gasped. He circled the distended nipples, plucking gently at first, then a little harder.

Watching him touch her was embarrassing and yet so erotic her panties flooded with cream. She'd definitely have to buy the underwear now.

"Jack, please," she begged, not sure whether to plead for him to stop touching her in public or urge him to fuck her right here. She had no idea what she wanted, and was tired of thinking. It had been too damn long since she'd been touched, too long without feeling alive and desirable. She deserved this moment and to hell with how she *should* feel!

His hands worked magic on her breasts and nipples, firing her libido to life in a wickedly tortuous way. He licked her neck, scraping his teeth along the side of it to take a bite from her nape. She shuddered and backed against him, instinct driving her ass against the rigid bulge in his jeans.

"You make me so fucking hard, Kate," he ground out. She switched her gaze from the movement of his hands to his face.

His jaw was clenched tight and a bead of sweat formed along his temple.

A sizeable erection was evident in the firm swell pressed against her buttocks. Her throat went dry. But the rest of her was wet. Hot and wet. He rocked against her and more moisture spilled from her pussy lips onto her panties.

"I smell you," he said, licking her neck like he thirsted and she was his drink. "I've missed that sweet smell of sex, that sweet scent of you when you're hot and wet and needy for me."

He trailed his right hand over her rib cage and abdomen, pausing to squeeze her hip before moving down to the hem of her dress. He bunched the fabric in his hand and yanked upward, revealing the decadent stockings she'd slipped on earlier. The black garter belt was hot. Even she thought so, revealing only a smidgeon of the pale skin of her thighs peeking between her panties and the stockings.

"Ah, Christ, Katie." He jerked the dress all the way up, then moved around to face her. His expression was tight, fierce, almost as if he was angry and trying to hold it in. He pulled her against him, his mouth crashing down over hers.

He took, he ravaged, plunging his tongue between her parted lips and fucking her mouth with an intensity that left her breathless. She moaned at the sheer exquisiteness of tasting him again, familiarity as exciting as the newness of his bold domination of her. She clutched his shirt, her nails digging into his chest as he drew her even closer. His erection rasped against her swollen clit, shooting off sparks and flooding her with more of her juices. She'd never wanted like this before, not even in the beginning.

Now she was starving for it, for Jack, desperate to grab onto whatever fleeting moments they could have together, no longer caring that she was supposed to hate him for what he'd done. She palmed his cock and caressed the part of him she was desperate to feel embedded deep inside her.

"No," he said, his voice rough with passion. "Not yet." He dropped to his knees, his gaze locked with hers, and reached for the thin straps of her panties. With agonizingly slow movements, he dragged them down her hips and legs, each brush of the silken fabric against her skin making her grit her teeth in anticipation.

She held onto his shoulder as she stepped out of the panties, shocked when Jack held them to his nose and inhaled, his eyes closing for a second. When he opened them, the gray orbs had darkened like a pitch-black night. "I love the smell of your pussy, Kate. Just the scent of you makes me so fucking hard I could come in my pants right now."

Her knees buckled and she squeezed his shoulder for support. But he withdrew her hand, backing her up against the door and following her on his knees. He spread her legs apart, lifting one over his shoulder. Like this, her pussy was right in line with his face. He studied her, tilting his head from one side to another, then breathing deeply as if he couldn't get enough of her aroused scent.

His words were whispered, his voice a gravelly softness that curled her toes. "Do you want to come, Katie? Right here? You want me to eat that sweet pussy until you have to bite your tongue to keep from screaming, don't you?"

God help her, she couldn't hold the words back. "Yes!"

6

Iт нар веем тоо long since she'd been touched. When Jack's
hands cupped her buttocks and drew her closer to his mouth, his
hot breath teasing the curls covering her sex, she knew she was
going to embarrass herself by coming almost immediately. He
leaned his forehead against her belly and stilled, breathing heavily.

Was he having trouble maintaining control? Cool, calm col-
lected Jack McKay was ruffled? Amazing. But then she heard it,
a low growl coming from his throat, so primitive and arousing
her pussy responded with a quaking shudder, a welcoming call
of the wild.

He dipped down and licked through the curls on her
mound, nipping at her with his teeth. She had nothing to hold
onto and was afraid her legs wouldn't hold her, especially when
she felt the warm wetness of his tongue along her folds. Unbid-
den, a moan escaped her lips. Reaching for his head, she tangled
her fingers in his hair, closed her eyes and held on.

The spark was lit with the first swipe of his tongue against her clit. When he covered the bud with his lips and teased it with his tongue, she burst into an inferno, forcing herself to hold onto sanity and not come yet. Not yet. The pleasure was too great, the sensations too exquisite to let go so quickly.

She opened her eyes and watched him perform his magic. His tongue swirled over the swollen hood to lap at the hard pearl underneath. Before she could shriek from the sheer bliss of such an intimate touch, he'd moved further south, licking along her slit, forcing her pussy lips open so he could slide his tongue inside and lap the cream pouring from her.

It was decadent, wicked, and so damned arousing she sobbed out a whimper. Jack tilted his head back and she saw the half smile on his lips before his tongue blazed a hot, wet trail back to her clit.

"Jack," she whispered, knowing she had nothing to say to him, but still needing him to know that his mouth was magic.

She'd always craved his touch, even when things between them had become distant. Long after he'd left she'd lived in a state of shock that she would never feel the warmth of his hands gliding along her skin, or the magic of his mouth when he kissed her and loved her in this most intimate way.

And now he was back and she didn't care why or for how long. She needed this. No, that wasn't quite right. It went far beyond need. She demanded it, and nothing would stop her from getting what she wanted.

"There," she directed, holding his head in place when his tongue found that magical spot she knew would send her over the edge. But he'd already stilled and focused his attention on that location. She heard his dark laugh of satisfaction, reveled in the intimacy of the man who knew her so well she didn't have to lead him to find her sweet spot.

Release hovered close, teasing and tormenting her. A sweet bliss she craved but wanted to hold back. If she only had this one time she was going to make it last forever.

But he tortured her incessantly, swirling his tongue in circles around her throbbing clit. When he reached up and slid his finger along her folds, then inserted it into her pussy, she felt the contractions in her womb, bit the inside of her cheek to keep from crying out and let the sensations overtake her.

Her orgasm raged through her like a sudden tidal wave, crest after crest battering her body until it shook uncontrollably. She held onto Jack like a life preserver, clutching her fingers in his hair while he continued to fuck her with his finger. Never once did he stop, even when the vibrations became unbearable. She floated briefly before riding the wave to another crashing climax that left her panting and unable to stand.

He rose and covered her mouth with his, letting her taste the sweet release she'd poured onto his tongue. She met his kiss with all the passion she'd held inside, needing to feel one with him, a part of him. Needing him inside her like she'd never needed before.

Jack tore his mouth from hers and laid his forehead against hers, panting heavily.

"We'll finish this later. When I fuck you I want all the time in the world, not just a few minutes."

She felt cold when he stepped away from her. Cold and suddenly feeling exposed way more than physically. What was wrong with her? Five years of gloomy depression simply disappeared with one touch of his tongue to her clit? Was she really that easy, that gullible?

Yes, Jack seemed different in so many ways, but what guarantees did she have that he wouldn't disappear again? The thought of it made her want to curl up in a ball and scream. She doubted she'd survive it a second time, and yet she'd let him back in so easily.

Stupid, stupid, stupid. You're supposed to enjoy the moment and not let your heart get involved. But she'd given it all to him once again, baring her heart and soul for his taking.

And there he stood in front of her, his gaze hot and filled with wild desire, and she wanted to offer herself up to him again.

It's just a dream, Kate. Don't think too much. Go with it, enjoy it, but hold your heart closed.

She could do this. Really, she could. He couldn't possibly hurt her more than he already had, so why not take a little from him this time? God knows she desperately needed what he was offering.

She was nearly naked and he was still fully clothed, standing there staring at her as she fought for control over her limbs. But how could she stop trembling with the way he looked at her? Heat fused her core at the look of raw need in his eyes, the way his jaw clenched tight and his hands balled into fists.

Jack fought for control. He wanted her, the evidence clearly outlined against his jeans. But he held back. Waiting. And she could, too. Dressing quickly, she hurried from the dressing room, hoping the telltale blush on her cheeks and her mussed hair wouldn't give away what they'd been doing in there.

Suzie was thankfully oblivious as Jack placed the outfit she'd worn onto the counter and paid for it, all the while exchanging hot glances with Kate that melted her into a puddle of arousal right there in the middle of the store.

Though she knew him well, had known him her entire life, he looked at her now as if he saw her for the first time, had just tasted her for the first time, and wanted more.

Dammit, she shouldn't, but she liked these feelings he evoked in her. She liked the newness of it all, as if they were just starting a relationship. Deep down she knew that whatever was happening between them wasn't permanent. Despite the allure of rediscovered sex, she had to force herself to remember that.

He's not staying. Don't let your heart get wrapped up in this.

Jack had returned to atone for his abrupt departure, in some way asking for forgiveness. But he didn't fool her one bit. He'd never said he'd come back permanently. So she'd just enjoy the moment and when he left again, she'd get over it. She'd done it before. Surely it couldn't hurt as much the second time as it had the first, right?

Right.

Now if only she could really believe that.

Ah, the hell with it. He owed her. She was going to take it.

They drove back to the house to shower and change for dinner. Kate felt strange putting on the dress and sexy lingerie again, all too aware of what had happened the last time she wore it. But they were going to the country club for dinner. He couldn't very well ravage her in the middle of the dining room in front of hundreds of people, could he?

Though the idea had some appeal.

She giggled as she fastened her earrings and gazed at the finished product in the bathroom mirror. Shaking her head, her hair swept sexily from side to side, little wisps caressing her cheek as she moved.

She looked . . . hot. Giggling again, she slipped on her shoes and went out to look for Jack. He was in the living room staring out the bay windows toward the lake, his back turned to her. Dressed in a long-sleeved shirt and black slacks that framed his well-sculpted ass, she swallowed past the desert in her throat.

Screw dinner. She wanted to have Jack for dinner. His cock in her mouth for an appetizer, a heady sixty-nine for the main course and a nice, long fuck for dessert.

She shuddered at the visual of being spread out on the carpet underneath the big window, the setting sun a backdrop for some glorious, sweaty sex.

But instead, she sighed and asked, "You ready?"

He turned to her and she sucked in a breath. Still so damned handsome her heart stopped whenever she looked at him. The way he smiled at her reminded her of when they were young and first fell in love. That smile held a promise of forever. Funny she should see it grace his face now.

"I'm ready. And you're gorgeous. Shall we go?" He held out his arm and she stepped toward him, sliding her hand into the crook and feeling every bit like Cinderella on her way to the ball.

But Cinderella always knew the stroke of midnight would change things, her fantasy would vanish right before her eyes. Kate would do well to remember that too. Anything magical was fleeting at best. Just like her time with Jack.

"How did you get into the country club?" she asked as they arrived in front of the expansive, one-story Pleasantville Country Club. The golf course was visible from the front porch of their country house and they'd often laughed about how one day they'd be rich enough to afford the ridiculously expensive entry fee.

Another "one day" that had never happened.

"I have connections," he said as he helped her out of the car and tossed the keys to the valet.

Kate went silent as they walked up the marble steps toward the lobby door. Connections. Right. What kind of connections did he have now that he hadn't had five years ago? When he left, he'd given her everything, including his business. She'd sold the business and used the money to live on while she worked on her writing career. Hell, why not? He'd abandoned everything and left it all to her to deal with. At least he'd left her something of value.

There were still so many questions. Why wasn't she grilling him about where he'd been, what he'd been doing and the most important question of all . . . why was he back?

Because you don't really want to know the answers.

The truth of that statement hovered around her like the growing night mist swirling in the air. She cast it aside and preferred oblivious ignorance to knowing the truth.

The country club was everything she'd always imagined it would be. Multiple crystal chandeliers graced the cathedral ceiling of the ballroom-sized dining room, their sparkle like glittering diamonds. Parquet flooring led onto rich, thick carpet colored a soft grey and blue. An expansive dance floor centered hundreds of round tables outfitted with white linen tablecloths and fine china and silver.

They were so far out of their league here she almost laughed, but didn't want to call attention to herself. Though no one looked their way as the hostess led them to their table. They could be invisible for all the attention they gathered. Which suited her just fine. At any moment she expected a tap on the shoulder followed by an announcement that they weren't allowed to stay.

A very attentive waiter brought them wine, took their food order and acted as if they truly belonged in this opulent lifestyle of the rich. Whatever. If Jack paid them a bundle to get them in for the evening, so be it. She was going to enjoy the food, the drink and dance her heart out.

For tomorrow it could all be gone.

And no one knew that better than her.

7

"HAVE I TOLD YOU tonight how beautiful you look?"

No more than about a hundred times, she mused. But she wasn't complaining. "Thank you, Jack."

They'd eaten and had wine, enjoying conversation about the boys and her life since he'd left. Not once had he offered an explanation about the past five years, nor had he given her an inkling to what would happen in their future.

A small part of her wanted, needed to know the answers. A large part of her wanted to stay in the moment and quit worrying about things she had no control over.

Certainly a new and improved version of herself, that was certain. But why not? Jack wasn't going to stay. He was here to wine her, dine her and give her screaming orgasms for as long as he deigned to remain. She was going to sit back and let him.

Hell, for all she knew she could still be dreaming. If she was, then she could do anything, be anything, act any way she wanted to and it wouldn't matter in the light of day what had happened in her dreams.

"Dance with me."

When was the last time they'd danced together? He stood and held out his hand. Smiling, she slipped her palm against his and followed him onto the dance floor.

Their favorite song played, an old fifties song about romance and finding the love of your life. As she stared into the unfathomable eyes of the man she'd loved forever, her heart clenched and tears pooled in her eyes.

"I've missed you, Jack," she finally admitted out loud. "So much."

He allowed her a fleeting glimpse of the pain in his eyes before he shielded them and smiled. "I've missed you too, Katie. I've thought of you every day, every night, wishing I could go back and change everything. I would, you know, if I could."

She believed him. "I know. It's enough that you're here now. Let's not talk about what neither of us can change."

He nodded and pulled her against him, her softness against his rock-hard solid strength. More than anything, she missed this feeling of protectiveness, of knowing nothing bad could happen to her as long as Jack held her in his arms.

They swayed together, oblivious to the other couples dancing around them. Kate laid her head on his shoulder, absorbing his scent, the comforting strength of his hard chest against her breast and the feel of his body under her hands.

Time suspended, memories washing over her so fast she couldn't keep up with the visions coursing through her mind. From the beginning . . . the first time he kissed her, the first time they made love, their wedding, the birth of the boys . . .

everything came rushing back to her. At that moment she knew exactly what she wanted.

"Take me home, Jack. Make love to me."

He drew back and searched her face, his eyes turning dark. He nodded and led her to the car. The drive home was made in silence, but he held her hand the entire time, his thumb rubbing against her fingers.

Kate watched the way his hand moved over hers, memorizing every stroke of his thumb, committing the feel of his touch to memory. Before, she hadn't been prepared for his departure. This time she would be. Like a clock ticking in her head, she knew the countdown had started. Somehow, part of her knew that her time with Jack was fleeting.

Maybe that was part of this dream. Spending nights with him, letting her imagination run wild into scenarios of "what if," trying out how she'd react if he ever really did come back to her. The safe haven of her imagination allowed her to break free of the anger and hurt and truly live again in the arms of the man she loved.

Jack pulled up in front of the house, turned off the ignition and got out, making his way to her side of the car. Everything that happened after that seemed like a slow-motion play on a movie. He opened the door, lifted her out with both hands, then swept her into his arms, taking the steps two at a time. She tilted her head back and laughed when he stood on the porch and twirled her around in circles. She was dizzy, ecstatic and crazy in love with him. Unlocking the chains around her heart made her soar with freedom again. Even if this was a dream, it was a catharsis, a reawakening she'd desperately needed.

Nudging the door open with his shoulder, he kicked it closed with his foot, driving his mouth down hard against hers as soon as she heard the click of the door lock. She tangled her fingers in his hair and pulled him closer, desperate to feel no barriers between them except their own needs and desires.

In an instant she was on her feet, Jack's hands sweeping around her and drawing her hips against his. His cock was erect, hot and thick. He rocked against her and her sex wept with need for him. A whimper escaped her throat when his hand found her breast, kneading her flesh and scraping his thumb against her nipple.

Too many clothes separated his hand from her skin. "Jack, please," she begged, thrusting her breast into his hand.

He laughed, the sound low and husky and driving her arousal to a near fever pitch. He lifted her and carried her into the bedroom, turning on the small table lamp. Soft light filtered the room, not too much to glare harshly, but enough that they could see each other.

Typically she'd want the light off, not wanting him to see the way her body had changed. But after today in the dressing room, it was pointless to try and hide the ravages of time. Besides, she thought with a soft curl of her lips, he thought she was beautiful.

He set her down on the bed and stepped away. The light shined behind him, casting his face in a dusky glow, silhouetting his body. And oh what a body! He yanked the tie from around his neck and began to slip each button from its hold. Shrugging out of his shirt, he stood and stared at her while she nearly drooled over his chest and flat abdomen, amazed that a man his age could still make her juices flow uncontrollably.

Truthfully, he looked about thirty-five. Tanned, well-muscled with a healthy glow that suffused his entire body. Dark hairs without a single gray among them scattered across his chest and lower, leading to a soft down of black fur that teased her by disappearing into the waistband of his pants.

She stood and reached for his belt, keeping her focus on his face. Slipping the belt loose, she popped the button on his pants. When she tugged the zipper down, her knuckles brushed his erection and he swore softly, moving his hips forward.

"Touch me, Katie. It's been too long."

She nodded and drew his pants down his hips, dropping to her knees to gaze at his cock. Thick, pulsing, the head engorged and dark, a pearl-sized drop of fluid lingered at the slit. She leaned forward and swiped her tongue over it, then covered her mouth over the head and sucked him inside.

"Christ!" he cried out, holding her face and slowly thrusting forward until his shaft was buried between her lips. She lapped at his cock head and swirled her tongue around and over the shaft, cupping his balls and massaging them while she loved his cock with her mouth.

His body trembled. The power to pleasure him was an amazing thing. To realize that he needed to be close to her, as much as she needed the same from him, made her love him more than she ever thought possible.

The soft sacs under his shaft tightened, drawing close to his body as she engulfed his cock deep into her mouth. She stroked the base of the shaft, propelling it between her lips, then drawing it out to lick the head, making sure he watched the movements of her tongue and lips. He uttered soft curses and kept his hands on her head, guiding her mouth over his shaft again and again.

She could do this all night long, but Jack pulled her to her feet and kissed her, parting the seam of her lips with his tongue. He swept it inside her mouth, thrusting and withdrawing until she was all but weeping with the need to feel those same motions inside her quaking pussy.

Jack pulled away and yanked at the straps of her dress, drawing them down her arms. The bra soon followed after he impatiently tore it away from her body, baring her breasts to his hungry gaze. He devoured her, first with his eyes, then with his hands, and finally, blissfully, with his mouth, tugging one nipple with his teeth while plucking the other with his fingers.

Her legs trembled and she held onto his shoulders for support. His pursuit of her body was purposeful and relentless. There wasn't a part of her he failed to touch as he slowly unveiled her skin, inch by inch, finally drawing her dress down over her hips and to the floor. She stepped out of her shoes and away from the dress, then stood there and waited for him to remove her garter belt, stockings and panties.

But he pushed her backward and she fell onto the bed. Jack followed, positioning her so her head was propped up on the pillows. He knelt between her spread legs, reached for the dainty panties and graced her with a devilish grin. With one quick jerk of his hands he ripped them off. A flood of cream poured from her slit. She'd never seen him like this before. His face was dark, dangerous, his jaw clenched tight and his lips pressed together. He used to look like that when he was deep into a project. Now he looked at *her* that way, as if she was the only thing that existed in his world.

"You have the most beautiful pussy I've ever seen," he murmured, studying her sex as if seeing it for the first time. He ran his fingers up and down her slit until she whimpered at the exquisite torture. "Pink, with plump, juicy lips that I'm dying to bury my dick between. Do you know how much I want to be inside you, Katie?"

To prove his point, he pushed back and took his shaft in his hand, clasping his fingers around the thick rod and stroking from base to tip. His eyes rolled back and he let out a soft groan. With his free hand he roamed her sex, patting her clit. Hot sparks shot deep inside her womb, melting her from the inside out. He tormented her, stroking himself and her at the same time, showing her his cock but not letting her have it.

"Dammit, Jack, please!" She didn't care that she begged. If he didn't fuck her and soon, she'd push him onto his back, straddle and ride him until the pressure inside her exploded. Then she'd take him along for the ride. She wanted his cum inside her.

He slipped two fingers between her pussy lips and buried them inside her cunt, pulling them out and fucking them in again, deeper and harder this time. Her pussy was soaked, cream running down the crack of her ass. She lifted her hips, driving her sex against his hand, clenching the coverlet in a death grip as she rode his fingers toward her impending orgasm.

"Oh, no," he said, withdrawing his fingers. He lifted her legs and pushed them backward, nestling his hips against her thighs. With one quick thrust he buried his thick wonderful cock all the way inside her. "When you come this time, I'll be in you, feeling your pussy shudder and grip my dick, forcing me to come with you."

Exactly what she wanted. She tugged at his hair and drew his face close to hers, needing the full contact of his body against every inch of hers he could possibly touch. The years apart dissolved, the pain with it, as they became one for the first time in a very long time.

When they'd been young, it had been hurried, both of them

too inexperienced to understand the pleasure of taking their time. As they'd gotten older and had the boys, it had continued to be fast and furious. There had always been something else that needed their attention. Then his work had gotten in the way and sex had been an afterthought, a quick tumble to ease the tension, but somewhere along the way they'd lost the romance of making love.

Now they had time and used it to their advantage. Jack teased her clit, brushing his pelvis up and against her, then withdrew his cock until just the head remained inside her. She ran her fingers over his skin, digging her nails into his flesh when he didn't give her the intensity she needed.

"Fuck me, Jack," she demanded.

"As you wish," he teased.

It seemed to last forever, this giving and taking. His mouth devoured hers, at once hard and passionate and yet achingly tender. His cock did the same, moving slowly and gently at first, then hard and pounding as her need rose higher and higher. Jack seemed to instinctively know just where to take her, finally pushing her knees toward her head and pounding relentlessly, slamming so hard inside her that his balls slapped her ass. She welcomed it eagerly, wanting to hold him there for an eternity and never let him go.

But release loomed ever closer and try as she might, she couldn't hold it back. Like an oncoming train, it came faster and faster, careening toward her until she couldn't run from it anymore.

"Jack, I'm coming!" she cried out, her voice ragged. The answering cry was his as he jettisoned hot cum deep into her pussy, dragging her into a crashing orgasm that tore her in two. She cried, knew she drew blood as she buried her fingernails in his back, but she was helpless to stop. Pleasure like she'd never known before swept her into a frenzy. Tears rolled down her cheeks as she screamed again, a second, more powerful orgasm shooting through her like lightning, melting her from the inside out.

When she could finally feel his weight on top of her, could feel her trembling legs lowering onto the mattress, could feel their bodies entwined in the moist sweat of their own frantic lovemaking, she knew that what had just happened was special.

He held her against him, stroking her hair and her skin, pressing light kisses to the top of her head. Her heart squeezed painfully and she fought back the melancholy that threatened to overwhelm her.

Dreams were a magical link to her desires, and she knew there was a reason she'd dreamed of him every night. But what she experienced now was no dream and hadn't been since Jack had reappeared in her life. It was time to stop living in a fantasy world of her own making and face the reality of what was happening.

She'd been given an amazing gift, and no matter how much it hurt, she wouldn't rail at the injustice of it all.

But not yet. She needed a little while longer to feel him against her, to commit every touch, every look, every kiss to her memory.

Sometime later they still stroked each other, still kissed each other, and Kate could no longer hold her questions in silence.

Despite the tenuous hold they had on each other right now, she had to know.

"Jack?"

"Yeah?"

"Why did you leave me?"

He rolled over onto his back and took her with him, cradling her against his side. Her head rested on the left side of his chest, and she knew as soon as she lay her ear against it what she'd hear.

Nothing.

"I had to leave, Katie. It wasn't my choice. But I didn't want to. You know I didn't. Not with so much left unsettled. I had things left to do. Mistakes I made with you that I didn't have enough time to fix." He sighed and squeezed her hand. "You know, you always think you have all the time in the world to do the things you want to do. I wish I had known what was going to happen in time to fix it. But I didn't. Or maybe I did. Hell, I don't know now. Maybe I saw the signs and ignored them. But I swear I didn't know about my bad heart, about how the years of stress and overwork would take their toll."

She lifted her head and looked deeply into his eyes, seeing the sorrow, the regret, knowing that the past five years had been as miserable for him as they'd been for her.

"I didn't know I was going to die, Kate."

Neither did she. But he had. Without warning. Just like that, he was gone. One day he was fine, the next he was dead. The doctor told her that the heart attack was devastating, that he had to have felt some pain for weeks or months beforehand.

But he hadn't said a word. Instead, he'd died at the office after working late one night. Leaving so much unsaid and unfinished between them.

"Is that why you're back? To make up for all you didn't do before you died?"

"Yes. I wasn't finished, Katie. Not with you, not by a long shot. I wanted that forever with you that we'd talked about. I hated that I'd allowed myself to get so sidetracked. I hated that all we planned for was ripped away because I was too stupid to recognize the signs."

She couldn't believe she was even having this conversation. But she was. And whether she believed in it or not, it had happened.

This was no dream at all. She'd just spent an amazingly glorious day and night with her dead husband.

8

THEY STAYED CURLED TOGETHER for the longest time, neither of them saying a word. Kate held tight, afraid to move or say anything that would cause him to vanish from her life again. Somehow she knew what was coming and wasn't ready to face it yet.

Not yet, not when she'd just gotten him back.

"I can't stay, Katie."

She sat up and looked at him, nodding. She'd known that from the first. How, she had no idea. She'd just known that whatever this was, whatever had happened, was only temporary. If she thought she had to be strong five years ago, she was wrong. Now she needed that inner strength more than ever, because she knew that no matter what she wanted, she'd have to let him go. She'd been given a gift, and she was damn lucky to have gotten this much. "I know."

He reached for her hand and brought it to his lips, kissing every knuckle and every finger. "I wish I could. God, I wish I could. You have to believe me. Funny how we never seem to appreciate what we love the most until we don't have it any-more. Why is that?"

Which was why she'd held onto the feelings of betrayal and anger for so long. They'd protected her from hurt, from her own guilt at not insisting that he slow down, see a doctor more often, anything that could have prevented his death. She laid her palm against his cheek, loving the feel of stubble against her hand. "I should have taken better care of you."

One corner of his lips curled into a half smile. "Like I would have let you. I was stubborn, arrogant, full of bravado and the feeling of immortality. I ignored every single warning sign until it was too late. I never told you how I felt. If I had . . . oh, hell, Kate. I don't know anymore."

She brushed his hair away from his forehead, realizing how much both the boys had grown to resemble their father. "We both screwed up, Jack. We didn't take enough time to love each other. Instead, we spent our lives letting anything and every-thing come between us."

And then one day, he was gone. The tears flowed freely now, but she didn't care.

Jack swiped at a tear across her cheek. "I've been watching you ever since I left. This . . . I don't know what you want to call it . . . heaven, maybe? It's hard to explain, but I've been able to see you. My heart hurt watching you, baby. You had so much to live for, so much left to do with your life, and you've done nothing but wander through the city house and out here, angry at me because I left and angry at yourself because you couldn't stop it. What happened to me wasn't your fault at all. It was mine and mine alone. You need to start living again, Kate. You need to find . . . "

"Don't say it!" She pushed away from him. "Don't you dare tell me to find someone else! There is no one else but you. There never has been and there never will be! When you . . . died, my heart died too. When I married you and promised to love you forever, I goddamn well meant *forever*. 'Til death do us part doesn't mean shit to me, Jack. You are my heart, my soul, not just in this life, but in the next! So if you dare to suggest I fall in love with someone else then you don't know me at all, Jack McKay!"

He sat up and pulled her against him, stroking her hair as she finally let out all that she'd held in since the day he died. Anger fled, replaced by an abject sorrow at all they'd been denied. She sobbed, exorcising the pain that she'd forced deep inside herself for years. And through it all, Jack held her, whispering words of comfort, telling her how much he loved her and holding her tightly against him.

"Why do you think I'm here?" he finally asked. "Yes, I was supposed to encourage you to live out the rest of your years without me, but even now I'm still selfish, Katie. I don't want any man to touch you but me. I don't want you to ever love anyone else but me."

"I never will," she whispered against his chest. "I can't, Jack. I don't know how to love anyone but you." She touched his chest, wishing she could still feel the strong beat of his heart against her palm. "I don't want you to go."

"I'll never leave you, Kate. I'm here, like I've been, by your side, every single day."

He reached under the covers and pulled out a pink rose. She took it and wiped away the tears, staring in awe at the flower. To see something that could materialize out of nowhere made her truly believe in the magic. Then again, wasn't that what brought Jack back to her?

"Put this in a vase. Every day when you wake up, there'll be a fresh one in there for you."

"I'd rather have you here."

"You will. You might not see me during the day, Katie, but I'll come to you in your dreams. I can't be alive in the way you want, but we can still be together, if that's your wish."

"It is." She didn't care how, she just wanted to know that he wasn't going to leave her again.

"I won't. I'll never leave you again."

He tilted her chin up and pressed his lips against hers. She held onto his shoulders and fought the tears, instead letting her love for him well up inside her and burst forth. Passion replaced despair and she straddled his lap, kissing him deeply. Her breasts brushed his chest, her nipples aching as they scraped the fine hairs there. Jack grabbed her buttocks and rocked her against his erection, moistening the shaft with her juices.

The time for feeling sorry for herself was gone. For some unknown reason she'd been given a magical gift and she wasn't going to turn her back on a chance to love her husband for the rest of her life. No matter how it happened, whether in her dreams or some kind of alternate reality, she knew now that they would never be separated again.

It would be an unusual relationship, one that she couldn't explain to anyone, but it would be enough to know that they'd been given a second chance to be together, that the rest of her nights would be spent in the arms of the man she loved.

Lust for life renewed her and she found the strength she'd lacked for the past few years. She suddenly felt like a young girl again, her body infused with passion, eager to explore her own sexual desires and those of her man.

She dragged her pussy across his shaft, smiling when Jack let out a wild curse and dug his fingers into her hips, drawing her back and forth against his heat. She loved these moments with him. This time when they melded together as one, when she knew that all the pain she'd been through had been worth it. Loving Jack had been worth any price.

"You're going to make me crazy, Katie."

"Oh, I hope so."

He leaned back against the pillows and lifted her hips. "Ride me, baby. Fuck my cock with that sweet pussy."

Positioning his cock at her entrance, she slid down over him, leaning forward to rest her palms against his chest. She drew down on him slowly, tugging her lip with her teeth as he stretched her, filled her, his cock head striking deep. Her pussy gripped him tight and spasmed in ecstasy, her fluids pouring out and coating his cock and balls with her juices.

"So fucking hot and wet. I swear if I wasn't already dead you'd be killing me right now, Katie."

She laughed this time, no longer afraid or in pain. Rocking against him, she pleasured herself and him, splinters of fiery delight shooting straight to her core.

Jack reached for her breasts, his fingers finding her nipples and plucking them gently, adding fuel to her already consuming fire. His hands were hot, demanding, tugging, pinching, each agonizing touch against her nipples making her whimper with pleasure.

"Harder," he commanded, and she lifted, slamming down against his cock and balls, loving the way he groaned, the way his jaw tightened. "Yes, like that. Fuck me, baby."

She dragged her nails across his chest. He gasped and grabbed her wrists, pulling her chest against his and grinding his mouth against hers. He lifted his hips, powering his cock deep and hard until she felt the oncoming rush of climax.

When it hit she cried out, her moans captured by his lips as he drank in her orgasm by plunging his tongue inside her mouth. Hot jets of cream shot deep into her core as he groaned against her lips and came with her.

If she had this to look forward to the rest of her life, she'd die one very happy woman.

Drenched in sweat, they clung to each other. Kate was afraid to stop touching him, wondering when he'd disappear from her arms.

"It's not daylight yet," she whispered in his ear.

He responded by moving against her, letting her feel his shaft hardening once again. She smiled in the darkness.

It was quite possible *he* could be the death of *her.*

They made love again, all night long, each time pouring more emotion into their touches, their kisses, their whispered words to each other. The ability to give him everything made their lovemaking so much more powerful. When dawn broke, she couldn't keep her eyes open any longer. As her lids fell closed, Jack kissed her temple. "I'll always love you, Kate. I'll see you tonight."

BRIGHT SUNLIGHT NEARLY BLINDED her. She squinted and pulled the covers over her head, but knew it was well past the time to get up.

She didn't want to get up, knowing exactly what she'd find, or not find, when she opened her eyes.

But there was no sense evading the inevitable. With a groan

of protest, she threw the covers back and slid out of bed, facing the offending sun with an evil glare.

Sunlight used to be her salvation from the dreams that plagued her. Now it was her enemy and she welcomed the thought of tonight and bedtime.

A single ray of light shined on a bud vase centered on the nightstand next to her bed. In it was one pink rose.

The one Jack had given her last night. She looked around, but knew he wouldn't be there. Waiting for the inevitable despair to hit, she was surprised to feel suffused with energy and happiness. She had a million things to do before it got dark tonight.

Inspiration struck and she wrote like a woman possessed for four hours straight. The prose flowed so easily, almost as if she had been inspired.

She laughed at that. Of course she was inspired! She wrote romance! Finally, she could feel the emotions pouring through her like a life-sustaining transfusion. She was in love and she wanted to write about love, about passion, about happily ever afters. Because now she knew it was possible, that dreams really could come true. It wasn't just fairy tales and fiction. In her dreams she'd wished for Jack to come back to her, and he had.

After spending the morning writing, she showered, dressed and drove into town. The boys met her at their favorite restaurant for lunch.

"You look way too happy today," Ron said, looking more like his dad every day, all the way down to brushing that unruly thick hair off his forehead the same way Jack did.

J.J. nodded. "No kidding. You get laid last night or something?"

"J.J.!" Lord, he was just like his father, too, with his devilish grin and bawdy sense of humor. Heat suffused her cheeks. Sometimes children were far too insightful. "Actually, that isn't it at all," she lied. "I've just had a breakthrough in my book and I'm really excited about it."

"We can tell," Ron said. "Look at you. This is the liveliest I've seen you since . . . "

"Since your dad died," she finished. "It's okay. I'm not going to get angry or fall apart anymore. Life is too precious to waste." She reached for their hands. "Boys, I need to tell you something."

She took a deep breath, then expelled it. "I realize that I've spent the past five years angry at your father for dying, feeling betrayed that he hadn't lived long enough to see our dreams come true. And that wasn't right. Your father was an amazing man who made me happy from the time I was sixteen years old until the day he died."

And even after that, but she couldn't tell the boys about Jack's sudden reappearance in her life. First off, they'd never believe her and second, she knew this magical gift had to be kept between her and Jack. "But your father will never really be gone unless we forget him, and that I won't allow to happen. I don't want you to do it either. Remember him, remember his smile, the way he used to play catch and soccer with both of you when you were younger. Remember how much he loved you."

Ron pressed a hand over hers. "We knew that already, Mom. We've never forgotten Dad, or ever stopped believing in how much he loved us. It was just . . . "

She knew what he was going to say, what he didn't want to say. So she said it instead. "It was just that I was so miserably unhappy after he died that you felt guilty talking about him around me."

"Yeah," J.J. said.

"Well, that ends right now. I don't want a day to go by without talking about your Dad. We'll keep him alive by remembering his love for all of us. And I will love him with all my heart until the day I die." Fighting back tears, she smiled at her sons. "Now, you two have to make me a promise. Promise me that you will live your lives to the fullest and never take for granted how tenuous life is. We know better than most how quickly it can all be taken away from us."

They nodded, and she felt their love pouring through her. She and Jack had done a great job raising the boys. Now that the cloud of denial had been lifted, she realized what a wonderful father and husband Jack had really been. It hadn't all been bad. In fact, other than the fact he was a total workaholic, they'd had a fabulous life together.

The time for regrets was over. It was time to live again.

She thought a lot that day and well into the night as she prepared for bed. She showered, fixed her hair, sprayed on perfume and slipped on the scandalously sexy lingerie she'd bought at one of the shops today. Exhausted, she drifted off immediately.

A warm hand caressed her cheek. Something soft brushed her lips. She inhaled and caught the sweet scent of roses.

"You look hot tonight, babe."

"Jack," she sighed, welcoming him with a smile and open arms.

Epilogue

Thirty-Five Years Later

KATE FINISHED DICTATING THE last chapter of her latest book, making a note for her secretary who would transcribe it in the morning. She'd long ago lost the ability to type, but she made enough money to hire a staff of people to assist her.

She smiled and shook her head, unable to believe how successful she'd become. Touted as the number one writer of romance in the world, she still managed to wow her readers even though she'd just celebrated her eightieth birthday. Her children, grandchildren and great-grandchildren had thrown her a party, and she realized while surrounded by everyone she loved what a remarkable life she'd led.

But the best part was yet to come. Dragging her worn-out body into bed, she shut out the light and waited. She was tired now. Way too tired to engage in the mad, passionate sex that she and Jack had enjoyed when he'd first returned to her.

He, of course, had never aged, while she'd grown gray and wrinkly and riddled with arthritis. He'd still come to her every night, his eyes filled with love and desire for her, despite her advanced age. To him, she was still exactly the same woman he'd fallen in love with all those years ago.

And in her dreams, she was still the same woman he'd returned to all those years ago. Still young enough to move with him when he made love to her, to feel the sparks of desire and enjoy the feel of him inside her.

She sighed, her chest aching, her old body unable to support her any longer. Her eyes drifted shut as complete exhaustion overtook her.

It didn't take long. It never did. Though tonight it was different. Instead of coming to her in the darkness, he was surrounded by a soft light that made her feel warm and comfortable.

"Katie."

He stood next to her bed and held out his hand. Surprisingly, this time it was easy to spring up and into his arms. The shackles of old age had been thrown off and she met him eagerly, their mouths meeting with passion and a love that went deeper than any words could describe.

"It's time, baby," he said, producing a pink rose. "It's your time."

She'd known that as soon as he'd come to her. That's what was different about tonight. The light was the eternal light. And she was ready. More than ready. She'd done everything she'd ever wanted to in life and it was time to be reunited with Jack.

"Now we can be together, night and day, for all eternity," he said, squeezing her in a tight hug. "No limits on our time together, no day running into night, no leaving you ever again."

What a thrill to let loose of the bounds of flesh. Joy soared within her and she felt ageless, timeless, freer than ever. The moment she'd waited years for had finally arrived. Now she stood on the same plane as the man she loved. The man she would spend forever with.

"I love you, Jack."

His eyes glistened with tears as he pressed his lips to hers. "Forever, Katie. Just as it always should have been. You and me together."

His arms enveloped hers and bright light fused them together, body, heart and soul.

Forever.

Velvet Strokes

Susie Charles

1

W HAT'LL YOU HAVE TO drink, sunshine?" Though the cavernous room was dark, Tom's head pounded in time with the flashing beat of the multicolored strobe lights. Blue, red, green—the pulsing colors shot like steel skewers through his blinking eyes. What had begun as a minor twinge over his right temple when he left his loft had developed into a full-blown, clenching vise of a headache by the time he reached the center of London.

He spun slowly to face the deep, male voice barking in his ear over the discordant thump of the most God-awful music he'd heard in years.

"Are you addressing me?"

"No, I'm speaking to the leprechaun on your shoulder, mate. What'll it be?"

A quick glance at the top shelf gave him enough information to realize that even purchasing a half-decent scotch was highly unlikely.

"Thanks, but I'll pass."

"Well then, if you're not drinking, or even thinking about drinking, move away from the bar."

"Why?" Moving away from the bar would require him to mingle in the sweating, heaving mass of humanity currently gyrating a few feet from the dubious but relative safety of the bar area. He'd come with one task in mind, and getting his body rubbed by some deviant with enough body piercings to pop rivet the Titanic, or have his butt pinched by a leather-clad Lothario in the mostly gay bar was not on his agenda—anywhere.

"Because you're standing there frowning, with a stick stuck up your cute, aristocratic ass, and you're scaring away the customers. That's why. So drink up, or shift it. *Capisce?*"

He gritted his teeth, struggling to maintain his calm under such direct provocation. "I'm here to see Elizabeth."

"Elizabeth who?"

"Elizabeth Burnett," he yelled, trying to make himself heard over the nonsensical, hyped-up jabbering of the DJ. "The owner?"

"Oh, you mean *Lizzy?*"

His lips firmed as he nodded.

"Yeah, well take a load off, sunshine. *Away* from the bar." He tossed his head in the direction of an outbreak of yahooing and catcalling ten feet away. "Your *Elizabeth* is gonna be a bit busy for a while by the looks of it."

Tom turned in the direction of the bartender's smug grin.

A stunning woman with long sable locks, wearing, from what he could ascertain, little more than a hot-pink satin bikini with a handkerchief masquerading as a skirt wrapped around her hips, was being hoisted, laughing, by four hulking brutes with shaved heads. Among the four of them they had enough tattoos, chains, piercings and leather to keep a fetish shop in business for a few months at least. Particularly disconcerting was the short but swarthy one dressed in little more than a leather jockstrap with suspenders going over his shoulders.

The crowd parted before them then surged back like a wave to fill in the gap created by their passing as they carried their precious, giggling cargo in the direction of the stage.

Music suddenly boomed from the speakers around the room. Some banal dance number had the many speakers—and his eardrums—vibrating and crackling from the intensity of the decibel output. At the risk of permanent damage to his cochlear faculties, he watched in appalled fascination as the woman and her overgrown quartet of captors began a libidinous display of dancing that would do a pole dancer proud. Oblivious to the hooting, lewd encouragement from the crowd, his attention fixed solely on the lady.

Elizabeth.

Two years and she hadn't changed.

Full, heavy breasts scarcely contained in the shimmering, straining triangles of pink satin. Glistening skin highlighting a slender waist that flared into an incredibly feminine set of wide hips. Barely concealed by a silky swathe of fabric that made his mouth water as he recalled running his tongue over every inch of exposed flesh.

His groin tightened.

Arms over her head, a smile creasing her beautiful face, she shimmied between two men touching and stroking her, who looked like they could devour her on the spot.

His anger flared. How could she let them paw her like that? It was indecent.

Shameless.

Wanton.

Absolutely and totally erotic.

And it should have been for his eyes only.

The music, the crowd, the flashing lights faded away as he watched her, spellbound. Another night. Another place. Lit by candles, sultry music floating around them as he lay back on the cushions scattered on the floor in front of his fireplace. Watching as Elizabeth danced, just for him. Her eyes holding his captive as she discarded piece after piece of clothing until she swayed in front of him in time to the haunting beat, naked . . . beautiful, the lush curves and sensuous essence a work of art he could never truly capture . . .

But it wasn't just for him any longer.

The truth of that slammed into him as the present came rushing back in to dispel the memory.

In spite of the disapproving grunt from the bartender, he rested his back against the bar, folded his arms, and prepared to wait for as long as it took.

Five minutes . . .

Ten passed.

Fifteen . . .

God, were they going through the whole damn song list? He couldn't watch anymore. Jealousy sat heavy in his gut, a raw burn of possessiveness that seared his insides.

"Where's the office?" he called out to the now occupied bartender.

"See that exit sign over there?" He jerked his head slightly behind him and to the right. "Down the hallway, past the toilets."

"Thank you," he replied abruptly and turned.

"I'd be careful though, if I were you."

Tom paused mid-stride and turned back to the mocking expression of the barman. "Dare I ask why?"

"We got some none-too-fussy clientele here who would just love to snuggle up to your sweet ass, sunshine." He laughed at his own joke.

Let anyone try . . . Tom was less than amused but bit back the retort that sprang to his lips. "Please inform Elizabeth that I'm waiting to speak with her," he said instead, and moved in the direction of the office.

As he strode down the dimly lit hallway, he savored the small amount of relief brought on by the muting of the raucously blaring music. He averted his eyes from the couple fondling and kissing in the small, darkened alcove just before the toilets, hurrying past in the direction of the "office" sign lit up at the end.

Thrusting his hands in his pockets, he leaned against the locked door and closed his eyes with relief, the pounding in his head abating slightly. In some detached part of his mind, he noted that the music had settled down, the catcalling had eased off. Hopefully that was a good sign . . .

"Now, aren't you a pretty one, sweetheart?"

Tom's eyes snapped open as a finger stroked down the side of his face. A Goliath of a man wearing an open leather vest and a studded leather biker cap, stood in front of him, smiling.

"I'm not your *sweetheart*," he gritted out, "and if you want to leave with all your body parts intact, I suggest you remove your finger, and get f—"

"Harry! You naughty thing."

A laughing feminine voice cut him off. But it was sufficient for "Harry" to step back and turn to her instead. The woman, her diminutive height dwarfed by the hulking hormone in front of her, stepped up to him without any fear and poked him in the chest.

"I've just left poor Nigel. He's been looking all over for you."

"Nigel? Is looking for me?" A huge grin broke over his face before he swooped her off her feet to plant a smacking kiss on her cheek. "That's music to my ears. Thanks, Lizzy luv. You're a darling." And strode off.

Elizabeth, her face sweat-streaked, her breath still a little uneven from her exertions, turned to face him, the smile slipping into a frown as she considered him. "It isn't a good idea to tell any of the guys around here to 'fuck off', Tom. It's a gay club—they tend to get a bit literal." She raised an eyebrow at him but didn't speak further as she unlocked the door and led the way into the office, softly lit by a row of recessed lights above the solid red cedar desk. Half a dozen security monitors showing various views of the dance floor and bar were inset into the wall on the right.

He moved into the middle of the room, taking in the professionally equipped space in contrast to the decadent bacchanal outside. In the sudden, blessed quiet, the sound of the door clicking shut behind him had him turning around.

Leaning back against the door, Elizabeth considered him, her startling cornflower blue eyes running down and then back up his body, a tight smile on her face.

"Since it's highly unlikely you've changed your sexual orientation, I can only assume you're slumming. Why is that? What would bring the great Thomas Danville down to my little den of iniquity?"

He shrugged, as if the sight of her standing there practically naked had no effect on him. It did though. And was the reason he kept his hands in his pockets, fighting the urge to reach out to her. He knew it would be less than well received. "A proposition."

"Oh, well this should be interesting." She didn't move from her spot, leaning against her hands on the door. He could only dream that she fought the same need to touch him. Dream was right . . .

"Is this what you wanted, Elizabeth? This . . . this life?" He glanced at the monitors.

"What do you mean 'this life'? I run a very successful club, Tom. 'This life' as you put it, has been good to me."

"I can see. Surrounded by deviants. Letting them paw at you, putting their hands all over you. You left me for this?" One of his hands left its pocket to wave at the monitors.

After a brief flare, her eyes shuttered, going blank, emotionless. "It's *my* life, Tom. And, therefore, none of *your* business," she snapped and pushed off the door.

Glancing down, he noticed red finger marks on the pale, creamy flesh of her arms, her waist, and became infuriated, knowing where they had come from.

"You don't have to do this. I could have given you better, Elizabeth. I offered—"

A sharp, mocking laugh left her lips. "Offered me what? A position as your mistress? A nice, cozy little apartment where you could visit me when it suited you?"

"That's rubbish! It wasn't like that—"

She spun on her heel, no more than an arm's length away, and held up her hand, cutting him off, anger pouring off her in waves. Her words though, when she spoke, were controlled, so cool as to be almost icy. "What is it you want, Tom? I have a club to run, in case you hadn't noticed."

Great, he was managing to alienate her without even trying. And that was the very last thing he wanted to do. "Fine. Let's get back to business then. I need you, Elizabeth. For a special job."

"Yes, well, I hardly expected it to be for anything else. Sorry, I don't do artist's modeling anymore. For you or anyone else."

She turned to walk away, but he grabbed her arm and turned her to face him, anger beginning to simmer in his head along with the headache that had returned with a vengeance.

"You were never just a model to me, Elizabeth." He eased his grip slightly but didn't release her, awareness of the warmth of the skin under his palms filtering through him. Soft too, the skin smooth and silky. "And you damn well know it."

"So true, I was the little bit of fluff you liked to amuse yourself with. The naughty little secret your family wasn't to know about."

"Elizabeth—"

"Look, Tom, whatever it is, I'm not—"

"No. Hear me out. Please. Just hear me out."

"Fine. You have two minutes. Talk fast."

"You recall the 'Aphrodisia'?" he asked.

THE "APHRODISIA"? AS IF she could ever forget. With one word he managed to shatter her calm. Buried pain from the past crept under her guard, the small stab going straight for her heart.

The series of three highly sensual paintings had been the start of "them"—a catalyst for two years of uncontrollable hunger and passion that fed his artistic genius but nearly consumed them both . . . that nearly destroyed her. The past two years, since it all fell apart that winter's day, had been spent picking up the pieces and trying to rebuild her life.

"As you know, the Blonheim Foundation holds the original series," he said. "They've commissioned another set, a companion to the first three."

In spite of the unaffected air she assumed, in her mind Elizabeth gasped. The Blonheim Foundation rarely, if ever, requested works done specifically for them. And they only took the best—their gallery was full of masters, old and new. Tom had taken her to watch as "Aphrodisia" was mounted there, prior to the public viewing. For a specific request to come from them . . . She could understand what this meant to his career. It was on a par with a scientist being awarded the Nobel Prize. A pinnacle few achieved in their lifetime.

She glanced pointedly down at his hand on her arm until he dropped it. "Why me? Can't you find some other starving model to sit for you?"

"They want the original model. *I* want the original model, Elizabeth. I wouldn't do it without you."

She had to wonder why not, since, judging from reports in the press, he and his career seemed to have managed quite well without her—his *muse*—for the past two years. "How very touching. But as I said, I don't model anymore, Tom. No need. I'm a successful businesswoman now." She waved her arm at the office, the monitors, amazed at how easily the lie fell from her lips.

"Please consider it, Elizabeth. You'll be paid well."

Pain sliced through her and she turned away before he could read it in her eyes. Why did it always come down to this, as if it was the crux of their relationship—he who had plenty and she who had none. "You never did get it, did you, Tom? For me it never was about the money."

God, how could he do this to her so easily? She inhaled deeply, bolstering her resolve. She'd known two years ago, in spite of the hurt, there would never be another man for her. Sometimes she wondered if the loneliness, the hunger for him that ate away at her would ever go away.

"Elizabeth . . . "

Strong hands caressed her shoulders, turning her back to face him. Looking into those dark, intent eyes, so close she could see the golden flecks in the iris, was like falling into the past, to a time when nothing mattered but the heat, the need, sating the unquenchable hunger that burned between them. She struggled against his grip.

"It was never, ever about the money, Elizabeth," he bit out in seeming exasperation, his tone gentling, "for either of us." Her heart stuttered as those hands slid up over the curve of her shoulders, her neck, to cup her face. Transfixed, her pulse skittering wildly, she watched as his head lowered, inch by inch, so close that his warm breath fluttered over her lips. "It was only ever . . . about this . . . "

A flicker of panic flared as she realized he was going to kiss her. Then it was lost, swamped under the feel of his warm lips closing over hers, his hands tilting her head so that the fit of their mouths was perfect. The achingly familiar caress that always left her yearning for more, crazy to touch him, taste him.

Her mouth opened on a gasp as his tongue licked, nudged. Stealing between her parted lips as a groan rumbled up his chest and restraint was tossed aside as he thrust deep. His hands freed her head, slipping lower to wrap around her and pull her against him as he ate at her mouth with a fierceness that sent her senses reeling.

Hard. Everywhere her body touched his felt hot and hard. The noticeable bulge in his groin that made her clit throb with unfulfilled need as it pressed up against her, rubbing the ultra-sensitive button as their hips rocked together in a familiar dance. Liquid heat flowed through her to dampen the flimsy barrier of her panties.

Tasting him. After so long without. With a muffled whimper, she sank into the kiss as though the intervening years had never been. And in a heartbeat, the memories she'd tried so hard to bury surged to the fore, supplanted by a new reality as her tongue curled around his, rubbed up against it in a primal form of mating that set her heart pounding and made her knees weak. The electric sensation that streaked through her from even that simple touch made her arch into him.

In a dizzying rush, her feet left the ground. Hands under her buttocks lifted her, the smooth wood of her desk cooling her flesh as she was perched on the edge. Strong male legs parting hers, stepping into the space formed as hers shifted, wrapping around his hips, his erection rubbing against her burning pussy.

So good. It felt so damned good.

Her hand moved down to grasp a tight buttock, pulling him closer. She needed more. Needed to feel him moving inside her, thrusting into her.

As if he shared her thoughts, the kiss deepened, became wilder. His mouth ate at hers with a hunger she matched. Voracious. Insatiable.

All that mattered was his lips on hers. Her body aching for his, for the pleasure she knew could be found there. A pleasure she hadn't known in such a long time.

Moans filled the air—his, hers—she didn't know. She no longer cared.

Her pussy clenched, her clit tingling, preparing for the climax that built faster and faster. Close. The tremors building, her muscles tightening in anticipation.

Until a warm hand slipped under the scrap of silk covering her breast, rubbing the nipple between thumb and finger before pinching it, sending a small frisson of erotic pain arcing through her body directly to her throbbing clit. She gasped, the shock finally jolting her out of the sensual haze fogging her senses.

Even though her body screamed for release, she tore her mouth from his, slipping her hand from around his neck to push him away.

"No!"

Both of them were breathing roughly, Tom's heaving chest rising and falling as he sucked in deep draughts. He stared at her, his eyes dark, heavy, full of the same desire, the same thirst for more that she knew hers must mirror.

She wrenched her gaze away, down, traveling over his body, unable to stop her eyes from moving lower. His cock bulged and strained against the zipper of his designer slacks, a telltale dampness that could only have been from her staining the light gray front where their bodies had met.

Mortified, she considered what she must look like, seeing herself as he would—perched on the edge of her desk, hair disheveled, lips swollen, her legs splayed shamelessly. Part of her bikini top nudged to the side so that a reddened nipple was bared, the tip peaked in wanton display.

God, she must look like a whore.

And that was a little too close for comfort.

Tears gathered, but were tamped down with a deep

shuddering breath as she tugged at her top to straighten it. The feeble attempt at restoring her modesty didn't help calm the emotions rioting through her body. The last couple of years of steeling herself against her body's response to this man, all destroyed with one kiss.

With as much dignity as she could muster, she closed her legs and slid off the desk. Her footing wasn't sure, her legs were like water, and she stumbled in the four-inch heels. Tom reached for her, but before he could touch her, she held up her hand.

"Don't . . . touch me." If he did, she'd be lost. All it ever took was one touch. "Please leave, Tom."

"Elizabeth. No."

Steeling herself, straightening her back, she looked up at him, unable to miss the raging lust—barely concealed by a look of concern—that still darkened his eyes.

"I can't do this, Tom. Not again."

"And if I promise not to touch you?"

Even now he looked like a tiger about to pounce, the tension on his face, through his body, indication enough that he was only just restraining himself. "You're kidding me, right? We haven't seen each other for two years, and in two minutes—*less*—look what happened."

His jawline firmed and he took a step back, thrusting his hands into his pockets as he dropped his head, breaking the connection of their eyes. "If you agree, we wouldn't be alone."

This time the pain shafted a little deeper, nipping at her soul. Of course. How naïve of her to think she, the muse, wouldn't have been replaced after all this time. "Oh, I see."

But as if he could read her mind, translate the straighter stance, the squaring of her shoulders, into what she was thinking, he reached for her, clutching her hand in a reassuring grip.

"It's not what you're thinking, Elizabeth," he offered, and she caught the small flash of dismay in his eyes. "Do you honestly think I'd be so crass?"

"Well then, what?"

He let her hand go, turning away as if to consider his words. When he turned back to her, his expression was neutral, blank. "They've requested a couple this time—a woman and a man. An evolution of the original series."

Taking the half-dozen steps to her chair, she sank into it gratefully, before looking up at him. "And who did you have in mind?"

"Richard."

Her body softened in the chair, some of the tension draining away as a small, weak laugh broke free.

"Richard? That figures. Funny, he didn't mention it last week . . . "

"Where did you see Richard? And why?"

She looked up at the scowl in his voice, seeing a matching expression on his face.

"Richard and I meet for coffee or a drink every now and then. Unlike some Danvilles," she flashed a brief, pointed look up at Tom, "he doesn't have a problem being seen with me in public. But then he never has much cared about what your family and friends think."

No, Richard was the black sheep of the Danville family, a role he relished. After spending ten years in an "acceptable" career in the SAS, he'd resigned his commission and nowadays spent most of his time freelancing as a fitness trainer. Ninety percent of his clients were female, which, she was sure, had a whole lot to do with him having a body that could tempt a saint to sin and a smile capable of melting half the polar ice cap when he turned on the charm. He was a six-foot-two stick of dynamite who had women falling over themselves for a chance to light his fuse. And though they'd kissed once or twice, succumbing to an attraction they both felt, for some reason they'd each pulled back, never taking it further. As if some invisible barrier stopped them.

She tapped her nail on the large blotter on her desk, her mind turning over. At least with Richard there, there'd be a buffer of sorts. "What would you need?" And why on earth was she even considering it? Curiosity? A perverse sense of masochism?

No, she knew why. In spite of what had happened between them, she had loved modeling for Tom. It allowed a sensual, decadent side of herself free, one that rarely saw the light of day lately, even in spite of her choice of occupation. It was the difference between business and pleasure. Not to mention knowing that she was someone's artistic inspiration had always been a heady thought.

"Two weeks. If you could get away from here. I need you full-time. You know how I work."

"How could I forget?"

When he was working, Tom was like a man possessed. Day or night lost all meaning—when the creative urge hit, he had to paint.

To think she'd lived that crazy life for the two years after she moved in with him. But then, she thought with a wrench, they'd mostly been happy days. Days filled with laughter, love, long nights when he wasn't working lying in each other's arms, gazing up through the skylight after making love. Or fucking on the rug, on kitchen counters, in the hallway . . . anywhere, anytime the urge took them . . .

She shook her head to shake off the memories as Tom spoke.

"I'd start with the preliminary sketches of you—Richard's are just about done—then you two together, working out the poses until I find the right three. Then I can get down to it."

His response was so brusque, so businesslike and unemotional, that she wondered if it would be possible after all. "I'll think about it. When would you need an answer?"

"Soon, Elizabeth. Blonheim's next exhibition is nine months away, and they want them for that."

Could she do it? Could she be around Tom and not want to touch him? Not want him to touch her?

His next words brought her back to earth with a thump.

"Since this is a purely business proposition, I'm offering you a quarter of what I'm being paid, Elizabeth. It will be very generous."

Money again. Well that took care of any delusions she might have had that he was trying to worm his way back into her life. But it was just as well, since with her current situation with the club and her finances, she could hardly afford to take a two-week "holiday".

"Naturally. But you realize I need to not only cover my own income, but also whoever I get in to manage things while I'm gone?"

"I said 'generous', Elizabeth. By that I mean it will be more than enough to pay off the loan you have on this place . . . " he looked around her office with a frown, the frown deepening when his gaze landed on the monitors, "and some left over besides."

A disconcerting thought started to work its way into her head. "And how do you know what I owe on this place?"

As she watched, waiting for his answer, he began to pace, not noticeably, but a random path around the office that allowed him to look anywhere but at her.

"The family has a seat on the board at the bank, currently filled by yours truly. I asked them to pull the details for me."

"You did what?" She stood, pushing her chair back so abruptly that it scraped across the linoleum. Anger boiled up inside her.

He stopped his pacing and stared back, his expression shuttered. "I know you've been struggling to make the payments the past four months. Not to mention the nursing home for your mother must be just about crippling you. You need this, Elizabeth."

Damn him! He knew then, all of it. Knew just how bad things were and she hated him having that leverage. "I don't need your stinking charity—"

He leaned over the desk at her, staring her down.

"It's not bloody charity. I just did my homework. That was a lesson *you* taught me, if you remember."

Oh, she remembered. She plopped back down in her seat. After he'd been shafted a couple of times by less than reputable agents in the early days and his career was faltering due to the industry backlash that washed over him, she'd taken it upon herself to show him how to find out about those he did business with. But he was right. She was having trouble making the loan repayments. Her mother's private nursing home care was just about killing her financially.

"Elizabeth, please. I didn't come here to fight with you. I need you."

And as much as it galled her to admit it to herself, she needed what he was offering, if what he said was true. She considered for a moment longer. Somehow she'd just have to keep it together. Two weeks. Surely she could manage that? And Richard would be there, so it wasn't as if they'd be alone . . .

"Okay. But I want a contract. Everything legal, on paper. I

can be there in a week. That will give me time to get things organized here."

"Sounds perfect," he said and gave her a tentative smile. "Deal?"

He held out his hand. After a short pause where she wondered if she'd really, finally, lost her mind, she took it, shaking it lightly.

"I'll see you in a week." He lifted her hand to his lips and kissed it, squeezing it once before letting go and turning for the door.

"And Tom?" He paused and half turned to face her. "This is probably unnecessary, but I'll state it anyway. I want the guest room. I'm not moving back into your bed."

His half-smile dropped and a cryptic look took its place. He nodded. "Understood."

He left, closing the door softly behind him.

She let out her breath. Hell, what had she just gotten herself into?

2

Y<small>OU'RE DOING WHAT?</small>" E<small>LIZABETH</small> flinched as her sister's response rose a few decibels above comfort level following announcement about the job for Tom.

"The man treats you like dirt, totally disses you so that his poor, precious family won't know he's been mixing it up with a lowly little barmaid, has a fling with some rich tart while he's meant to be with you, and you're going back for more?" Debbie's voice rose higher the angrier she became. "You're nuts! Totally bloody certifiable."

"You make it sound terrible. It wasn't *all* bad," glared Elizabeth, steeling herself against the venting she knew was coming. "And it wasn't a fling—it was only a date."

"A date? A flippin' date? Oh, right. I forgot. And he couldn't take you to hobnob with his rich society friends *why?* No, he had to take Lady Muck so *she* wouldn't embarrass him."

"He never said that, Deb! It was expected that he go with

her. It was a family obligation he couldn't get out of. She was a second cousin, or something."

"And one his witch of a mother felt would be eminently suitable for the title of Lady Danville once *she's* pushing up daisies, I'll bet." Debbie shook her head. "I can't believe it. You're defending him. So you've forgotten the bit where he would only ever mention you to his family as his *model,* even though you'd been living together for two blasted years? God forbid they might think he was sullying his pecker with some little nobody. Hell, you loved him, Beth. He supposedly loved you."

"He did love me, Deb. In his way . . . " *Just not enough,* thought Elizabeth, looking away as she felt the tears welling.

"So why didn't he fight for you? You walked out and he just let you go. What kind of love—"

"He called, you know." She shot a quick look at Debbie, catching the surprise on her face. It was a fact Elizabeth hadn't shared with anybody, even her sister. But then she'd withdrawn at that time, using the setting up of the club as an excuse not to have to answer questions or face what had gone wrong. "Many times . . . just after . . . " Her words petered out as she recalled the desolation in his voice, slowly replaced by the brief, curt, almost resigned tone, the calls coming further apart before they finally stopped altogether.

"And?"

"I wouldn't return his calls. What was the point?"

"Well, it still doesn't make it right. Dammit, he hurt you!"

"I appreciate your concern, Deb. But I'm older now. Wiser. Stronger. And this time it's purely business."

"Oh, really?" Her sister's tone was laced with disbelief.

"He knows about Mom. He knows I've been having trouble making the loan repayments on the club."

"How? Is he having you investigated?"

"He's on the board at the bank, Deb. Plus, he's a Danville. Anything is possible. But darn it, I'm so close. Only six more payments and the last two years of struggling and scrimping will be behind me. As it is now, I stand to lose the lot. I'm on a limited extension already—three weeks left to catch up on the three payments I owe, plus the next one, or they foreclose. And if that happens, then what? Go back to being a barmaid? Long hours, on my feet all night, six nights a week for barely a subsistence income?" She hung her head in her hands. "Can't you see what this job would mean? I'd own the club. Mom's care would be taken care of."

"Oh, sweetie, I'm sorry." Debbie looked contrite. "I had no idea things were so bad. And I'm so sorry Jase and I can't help you out financially with Mom. But we're barely breaking even ourselves. Some months not even that. If we couldn't live here, rent-free . . . God, what a mess."

She held her sister's hand and squeezed it reassuringly. "I know, Deb. It's just the way things are. But at least you visit Mom regularly, make sure she's okay. Hell, I feel so bad that I never see her, but I'm either sleeping or working."

"Come on, Beth, don't be so hard on yourself. Visiting Mom is the least I can do to help. If you weren't paying for her care, she'd be stuck in a public home . . . "

They shared a glance. They'd both heard horror stories of patients relegated to the public nursing homes. It just wasn't an alternative either of them could contemplate.

Elizabeth stood, walking over to the wide bay window, pulling aside the lacy curtain to catch the struggling winter rays barely melting the frost off the ground. She let the curtain drop and turned back to her sister. "But you understand why I can't pass up this opportunity, don't you? I received the contracts from his solicitor today. Tom's being more than generous. Much more. It's like he said—the amount will pay out the rest of the loan, go a long way to covering the nursing home expenses, and still give me a small nest egg. And it's only two weeks."

"And once you've paid off the club, then what? Honey, you're not getting any younger. Don't you want to find someone nice to settle down with? You're hardly likely to find anyone at your place. I mean, let's face it, they're lovely guys, most of them, but you aren't exactly equipped to ring their chimes, if you know what I mean."

Elizabeth shrugged. "It's a living."

The phone rang in the kitchen and Debbie excused herself to answer it.

Flopping back in the thickly cushioned old sofa chair—one that Jase had saved from being tossed out at an estate sale he'd attended for his and Debbie's fledgling business, and then lovingly restored—Elizabeth took a long sip of her coffee as she looked around. Their old home. In spite of the differences her sister's deft decorating touch had made, it was still home. The one place on earth she felt like her old self. It was cozy, comfortable. Certainly a lot more homey than her Spartan apartment above the club. That was somewhere to put her head down at night and little more. But it brought Debbie's comment back to her.

Her sister was more right than she knew, and certainly more so than Elizabeth would let on. After two years, she was tired of the endless round of working afternoons and long nights. Crawling into a lonely bed in the wee hours of the morning. Sleeping until lunchtime. Then the same routine again. Day after day. Night after night. How the heck was she supposed to meet anyone?

Apart from her immediate financial concerns, it was a big part of why she'd accepted Tom's offer. A way off the crazy merry-go-round that never seemed to stop. Maybe when she'd paid off the loan, she could sell the club and make a reasonable profit. It was one of London's most popular clubs for the gay community, after all. And even after putting enough money aside to pay for her mother's nursing home for twelve months, there might be enough to just take off for a while. Move. Live somewhere else where nobody knew her. Perhaps even start over. *Doing what?* she wondered.

She closed her eyes and leaned back, savoring the brief respite before she had to leave for the club.

"That was Jase. The delivery from that last estate auction has been held up in traffic, so he'll be late home." Debbie sat down opposite her again, perched on the edge of the sofa. "So when do you leave to do your Lady Godiva thing?"

"In three days. Just enough time to finish showing Graham the ropes so that he can hold the fort while I'm gone. He should be okay, though—he's worked at the club since before I bought it, so there isn't much that happens there he doesn't know."

"Well, don't worry about Mom while you're gone. I'll tell her you love her—even if she can't even remember me most of the time. But promise to call me, Beth. Any time—day or night—if you need to talk. Okay?"

"Thanks, Debbie. I will."

Debbie slipped her glasses down her nose and smirked as she peered over the top of them. "And keep your hands off hottie Richard. The sight of that boy's naked tush would give a Carmelite nun an orgasm."

"Deb!" laughed Elizabeth, relieved the mood had lightened.

"You told me you didn't sleep with him." It had been three years since Debbie and Richard had dated a few times, before he'd had to leave for active service in Iraq. By the time he returned, Jase had moved in. Strange how things worked . . . it was actually through that association she and Tom had met the first time.

"I didn't. More's the pity. We did get naked, though." Her expression became distant, a goofy smile tilting up her lips.

With a mischievous grin, Elizabeth grabbed a tissue and reached over to her sister.

"What are you doing?" At the feel of the tissue, Debbie batted Elizabeth's hand away from her face.

Motioning with the tissue-wrapped finger, Elizabeth pointed in the direction of her sister's chin. "Sorry, sis. It's just . . . the drool. I thought I'd catch it before it ran off your chin."

Debbie scowled and brushed absently at her mouth. "Oh, har, har. Don't be ridiculous. Anyway, that was years ago. Richard's probably all saggy now."

Elizabeth shook her head. "Ah, nope. Not saggy. Far from it, actually. About as far as it's possible to get . . . " Elizabeth sighed and covered her smug grin with her coffee mug.

"And how would you know, missy?"

"We see each other now and then." Elizabeth smiled at Debbie's drop-jaw look. "And boy, oh boy, what that man can do to a pair of jeans . . . or for that matter, leather . . . " She sighed dramatically, earning her a thwack on the knee with a folded newspaper from her sister.

"Bitch!"

She batted her eyelashes innocently at her sister. "But you have Jase, Deb. He looks pretty good in denim too . . . "

"True." Debbie nodded, and sat back, a wicked smile

creeping across her face, her eyes twinkling. "Actually he looks *much* better out of it."

Elizabeth rolled her eyes and held up her hand. "Okay. Enough. TMI." Elizabeth put her cup down and stood. "I would like to be able to look my brother-in-law in the face in the future without blushing, thank you very much. Anyway, I need to get going. I'll call you before I leave town." She leaned down to kiss her sister's cheek.

"And during," reminded Debbie. "I want to know you're all right. Or I'll just have to come up there and make certain for myself."

"Sure, sure. You're just looking for an excuse to catch another look at Richard in the buff."

"Not true!" cried Debbie indignantly. At Elizabeth's raised eyebrow, she blushed and grinned. "Well, maybe just a little look . . . "

"SIT STILL, RICHARD! CHRIST, you're worse than a two-year-old." Tom sighed in resignation and put down his sketchpad and pencil. "Ah, what the hell, let's take a break."

"About bloody time." Forsaking his reclining pose on the velvet-covered antique chaise lounge, Richard swung his legs over the side and stood, stretching, feeling the knots in his spine from maintaining the pose for so long pop and release. He moaned his relief. "Nice couch, by the way. Where the heck did you find it?"

"Would you believe Aunt Hermione's attic? I asked her if I could borrow it for a bit."

Richard's eyes widened and he choked down a laugh. "And

you didn't tell her to what purpose it would be put, naturally."

Tom snorted. "No. Definitely not."

"I daresay this will be the first time in its illustrious history it's cradled naked bodies."

"It's been in Hermione's family for generations." Tom turned a wry look on Richard. "You need ask?"

"And now it will be the scene of my greatest moment." Richard gave a hearty sigh, hand clutched at his heart. "Elizabeth and me. Naked and frolicking on the crushed velvet, oblivious to the pained exclamations of the 'Creative One' as he implores us to 'hold that pose'. Oh, be still my beating heart!"

Tom laughed. "Give it up, you wanker." He picked up his sketchpad and pencil, preparing to put them on his desk, when he paused and turned. "By the way . . . how long have you been seeing Elizabeth?" He swiped Richard's jeans off the floor and tossed them to him.

"Since you two split up." Richard hopped on one leg then the other as he stepped into his jeans and pulled them up. "Why? Jealous?" He snapped the stud closed, watching Tom closely under his lashes.

"Don't be ridiculous."

"Of course. How silly of me." Still observing Tom discreetly while he pulled his T-shirt over his head, he noticed the pensive look on his cousin's face. But rather than ask, he waited, knowing his naturally reticent cousin would spit out whatever was on his mind—eventually.

Tom straightened the pencils, lining them up in a row, so that all the ends were level, fussing until they were perfectly even—a nervous trait of his cousin's Richard was very familiar with. "So what do you two talk about?" asked Tom.

"Oh, just . . . stuff. You know, her work, my work, my

family, my love life . . . her love life . . . " Behind Tom's back he grinned at the rigidity that entered his cousin's tall frame at that. "You know. Stuff."

No way was he letting Tom off easily this time. The damn fool had lost the best thing in his life when he let Elizabeth go. It was about time he realized it.

"Does she ever . . . mention me?"

Bingo!

"In what way?" he asked innocently.

Tom headed toward the kitchen. Richard snagged his boots and socks and followed him.

"Never mind. It doesn't matter, anyway. It's better left as is."

Good God, the man was a bloody moron.

"You're a smart man, Tom. Smarter than I'll ever be. But when it comes to women, and Elizabeth in particular, you suck."

Tom put down the beer he was pouring and glared at Richard, anger flaring in his eyes. "What the hell do you mean by that?"

Richard grabbed the glass of beer, took a long gulp and sighed, feeling the chill all the way down. "If you need to ask, then my man, you do need help. Seriously."

"Might I remind you that *she* left *me*?"

"Oh, I remember. That and a whole lot more, and you fucked up. And like everything you do, you did a damn good job of it. I'll bet you haven't even figured out the reason she left you, have you?"

"She told me she didn't want to model anymore. She wanted a 'normal' life." He scowled as he resumed filling the second glass and took a long drink. "Right. So she buys a rundown club in Earl's Court and becomes the unofficial queen—no pun intended—of the gay club scene. How blasted 'normal' is that?"

Richard shook his head in exasperation, and made a noise like a buzzer on a game show. "Wrrrrrroong. As I said, you suck." He could hardly miss his cousin's perplexed frown. "Look. Think about those days, Tom. From Elizabeth's side, this time. Because you're missing the most important part." He rolled his eyes at the look of confusion on his cousin's face. "Here's a clue. Think back to what directly preceded Elizabeth leaving that day. Remember, you had a couple of visitors. Family, to be precise." Richard curled his lip in distaste. He'd been unfortunate enough to call in himself and caught the tail end of his aunt's visit. The interfering old biddy. "By the way, how is Aunt Caroline? Still trying to fix you up with half the eligible socialites in London?" When Tom continued to look at him blankly, he shook his head and reached down for his leather jacket, slipping his arms inside before braving the early winter chill outside. "Just think about it, Tom. All the answers you seek are right there—you just have to look hard enough." He glanced at his watch and cursed softly, tossing back the rest of his beer. "Look, I have to go. Got a date with a little lady I really don't want to keep waiting. She's hot for my gorgeous bod, you know?" He winked at Tom.

Tom turned a dry glance on him. "I've always felt your modesty was your best feature, actually."

Richard chuckled. "I'll be back in a week. Try not to piss off Elizabeth in the meantime. Be good and play nice."

THAT NIGHT, GLASS OF MERLOT in hand, Tom sat back on the sofa in front of the fire, staring into the flames as he mentally flicked back through the memories to those last days with Elizabeth. It wasn't a place he visited very often, mainly because of the pain that went with it. Never in his life had he felt as desolate, as devastated, as he did watching Elizabeth walk out that door. It was as if all the brightness, all the life was sucked out the door with her, and he was left with a dark, empty space.

The weeks that followed had been some of the bleakest of his life.

It was not a time he particularly wanted to revisit, but perhaps it was time. And if it held the key to losing Elizabeth . . .

Slouching down into a comfortable position, he straightened his legs out in front of him, cursing softly as his big toe kicked the leg of the coffee table. He looked down, his eyes resting not on his throbbing toe, but on the drawer underneath the coffee table that had been nudged open a crack. His lips firmed. Placing his wineglass on the table, he reached for the drawer, opening it to extract the heavy album that lay inside.

His fingers wandered over the hand-tooled leather cover of the photo album on his lap, tracing the indentations of the lettering. It had been one of Elizabeth's hobbies. Documenting their lives. His showings. His "great career." It had sat in the drawer under the glass-topped coffee table since the day she left. Not once had he looked at it.

The leather creaked, a slightly musty smell tickling his nose as he flipped open the cover.

Early days.

Shots of him in his studio—looking up with a paintbrush in his mouth, palette in hand, a startled look in his eye as Elizabeth caught him unawares. Or totally focused on whatever painting he'd been working on, oblivious even to her snapping him, a frown of concentration creasing his brow.

Family shots—Richard and him at Christmas at his parents',
deep in conversation, glasses of wine in hand . . .

At his sister's wedding. His arm around his cousin Ann's
shoulder. He chuckled as he recalled Richard taking the shot.
The damn fool had backed up to get a better angle and had
nearly fallen into the lake behind him . . .

The gallery opening for his "Insatiable" series. The shot with
his mother and father he particularly recalled. Both of them
standing stiffly beside him. While they supported his artistic en-
deavors, it was no secret, on his mother's part at least, that they
wished he'd pursue something a little more "acceptable" than
nudes, however artistically rendered. Landscapes, for instance.

He was halfway through the album before he found one
of Elizabeth. He smiled fondly as the memory came back.
Elizabeth had been posing for hours. He'd lost track of time, so
absorbed as usual. Long after midnight, he realized she'd fallen
asleep. Curled up on the floor like a kitten, the sheet she'd been
draped in tucked up under her chin, she'd looked so beautiful,
so innocent, he couldn't resist snapping her before he carried
her to bed.

He flipped the page and found, it occurred to him with some
consternation, one of the few photos of them together—her
sister's wedding, this time. Elizabeth smiling as she looked up at
him, his arms wrapped around her, the summer sunlight filtering through the weeping willow in the garden of the reception
grounds kissing them with a mottled golden glow. He traced
his finger over the photo, following the line of her hair as it
tumbled down her back . . . When she'd looked at him like that,
her eyes brimming with love, he would have done just about
anything she asked of him.

Happy days.

The smile faded as a disconcerting realization began to filter in, casting a shadow over the happiness from those memories.

Page after page. Flipping further through the album, a sickening understanding settled over him.

It was the final photo of Elizabeth, though, less than a month before she left, he recalled, that hit him the hardest. He even remembered taking the damn photo. He'd spent an hour shooting her in preparation for a private commission. She'd been tired, he'd been frazzled because he couldn't get the pose and angle he wanted with the light just so, and had stomped away to get them both a coffee. When he returned, she'd been standing at the window, sheet wrapped around her, light angled onto her face, the expression exactly what he'd been trying to achieve all afternoon. In his excitement, he'd almost dropped the coffees in his rush to grab up the camera and capture it. What he hadn't realized, hadn't seen at the time, was that the sad look in her eyes hadn't been a pose. It was the look of someone who was truly hurting. But it was the unspoken plea in her blue eyes, the hurt and sadness he could only now read there, now that he opened his eyes fully and truly *saw,* that brought him undone.

His throat tightened. His eyes burned as the honest pain she'd been feeling back then hit him in the heart. Why hadn't he *seen* it? He was trained to pick up things others didn't. Could he really have been so blind to what was in her head . . . her heart?

He snapped the album shut and closed his eyes, willing away the dampness that had built behind his clenched lids as he breathed deeply, fighting the tightness in his chest.

The feeling passed, slowly, and he opened his eyes again, glancing down at the album before tucking it back into the drawer and pushing it closed with his foot. He tipped the last of the Merlot into his glass and held the ruby liquid up to the flame before upending the glass and swallowing the wine in one large gulp, feeling the quick burn as it raced down over the lump in his throat.

He let his mind wander. Fragments of memories, not just from that last day, but weeks and months before filtered in. Memories, seemingly unrelated at the time, but what amounted to a screw-up of truly monumental proportions.

As a documentary of their life together, the album was a damning indictment against him as the world's biggest, most insensitive fool. Photos of him, of Elizabeth, even a few of them together, taken by other people—Richard, her sister, friends of Elizabeth's they'd visited. But never any of her with *his* family. At all the Danville family gatherings, not a single one. As if that was a part of his life—for two years—she hadn't been privy to. To his great shame, he couldn't even remember if he'd invited her to any of them. Where she'd gotten the photos from, he didn't know. Richard seemed most likely, since he was the only one of his family who knew of and understood his *real* relationship with Elizabeth. Mortification hit him hard at just how badly he'd treated her, to what extent he had taken her for granted.

In every way that mattered to a woman, he'd denied her. He'd never doubted that she loved him. She'd shown it every day, in what she said, what she did. How she looked after him so that he could concentrate on his art.

His fucking *art.* His lip curled with disgust.

Why had that been more important than giving back to the woman he loved half of what she gave him? He'd been driven back then. Obsessed. A budding, enthusiastic painter intent on rendering his visions of life as he saw it—his great, blasted masterpieces. Translating the beauty around him, the joy and love, the passion, but somehow missing the one thing, the one person who gave him that gift. Encouraged. Fostered it. The ability to see what others often missed, whose selfless gift of herself, her love . . . support, enabled him to unlock what he felt, saw, and bring a fraction of that passion to life under his brush.

But that final day . . .

His mother had arrived, unannounced as usual for one of her thankfully rare visits. Five minutes earlier and she would have found Elizabeth and him making love on the rug. As it was, he'd wandered out of the bathroom with a towel wrapped around his hips to find his mother interrogating a naked and very embarrassed Elizabeth.

That was bad enough, but he could hardly blame his mother for what had occurred after she left. He flinched at the memory, Elizabeth's words from the club making perfect sense . . .

"Offered me what? A position as your mistress? A nice, cozy little apartment where you could visit me when it suited you?"

Stupid. He placed his now-empty glass on the table and held his head in his hands.

At the time it had seemed like the perfect solution—to him. Since he couldn't really move his studio, he'd had the brilliant idea to put Elizabeth up in an apartment nearby, close enough that he could spend the nights he wasn't working with her. Plus take her out of the line of fire of his mother's viperous tongue, and the rest of his family who disapproved of the "barmaid-model" who seemed to occupy so much of his time.

Instead of putting his damn obsession with his career, his paintings aside for however long it took, facing the whole bleeding lot of them and telling them he loved her and they could take the "good Danville name" and all go to hell, he had taken what he saw now was the easier path, thinking Elizabeth would understand. But he knew now she hadn't. And could he blame her? To make matters worse, if that was at all possible, he'd thought to sidestep the storm of disapproval, so they'd just leave him alone and let him get back to his precious painting, by introducing her—more than once—as his "model."

His fucking model!

But she'd never said a word. Giving him that line about wanting a "normal life." And after leaving a few messages on her answering machine, instead of chasing after her, he'd let her go, because *he* was hurt that *she'd* leave him.

Christ, he was a bastard. A stupid fucking bastard. How could he have done that to the woman he loved? No wonder she'd left. It was a miracle she'd even spoken to him the other night. He would have kicked his ass out the door before he got his mouth open.

But maybe, just maybe, he had one more chance with her. That kiss had been better than a memory. She still felt something for him. And this time, please God, this time, he'd make sure he did it right.

3

Hitching her backpack a little higher to take the strain off her shoulders, Elizabeth slammed the boot shut on her old Beetle, glancing around the deserted parking lot next to the nondescript old brick warehouse with the fading paint.

"Sweet Lizzy Burnett. Well, I'd just about given up hope of seein' you here again, lass."

At the familiar voice, Elizabeth smiled broadly and turned toward the huge double doors, currently splayed wide open.

"Hello, Sara." She held her arms open for a hug from the tiny, gray-haired woman, inhaling the wonderful fragrance of Sara's signature lavender blend.

For years, Sara had rented a portion of the bottom floor of Tom's converted warehouse for her small aromatherapy business. She paid a pittance for the space, but Tom had always maintained he kept the rent minimal just because he loved the way she made the place smell, and she was a cheap guard for his private lift during the daylight hours. As far as Elizabeth knew, the only person who had a key to the building, apart from Tom and Sara, was Richard. Anyone else had to run the gauntlet of the formidable lady in front or her.

Tom wasn't fooling anyone though—he really loved the old lady who treated him like a grandson. For Sara's seventieth birthday he'd presented her with a beautiful portrait of herself. Elizabeth remembered him working for weeks to get it just right. A lot of love had gone into that painting and it showed. And while it usually took a fair bit to render old Sara speechless, he'd managed it—she'd sputtered and stuttered until he picked her up and gave her a big hug.

So many wonderful memories, Elizabeth mused. "So, you haven't retired yet?" she teased Sara.

"And do what? Sit at home and watch the TV with our George? The man sleeps through more shows than he watches. Besides, the old dear is deaf as a post. The volume damn near blasts me out of me chair."

The air was richly laced with a surprisingly harmonious mix of spicy and floral scents. Elizabeth sniffed as she looked around. "I've missed this, Sara, walking in here and feeling as if I just tumbled into a wild country garden."

Sara stood back with her arms crossed and gave Elizabeth a considering look. "Well, you've been missed too, lass. And by more than me." Sara raised her eyes to the upper floor. "Hasn't been the same since you left. Damn near become a hermit." Then she brightened. "But now that you're back—"

"Oh no, Sara," Elizabeth interrupted. "You misunderstand. I'm only here for two weeks."

Sara's mouth firmed, her fists planted on her hips. "You're kiddin' me! Why, I've never seen two people more—"

Elizabeth kissed her cheek to stop the emotional outpouring

of words, patting Sara's hand as she pulled back. "We two just weren't meant to be."

"Poppycock. And you know it. And so does his lordship up there." She jerked a thumb in the direction of Tom's loft. "Stupid man. But then they're all a bit daft. God didn't put women here to keep men company—it was so there'd be someone around with a brain and a bit of bleedin' common sense to run things."

Sara looked at her closely, gripping Elizabeth's hand firmly with both of hers. "Listen to an old woman, luv." Sara's voice gentled, the scratchiness of age apparent when she wasn't doing her usual shouting. "What you two shared isn't gifted to many—don't throw it away."

"It's too late—"

"Bah! It's never too late, lass. Not even when you're as old as me." Sara turned away and walked to her workbench. "Go on upstairs, lass. He's probably been pacing all morning waiting for you to get here."

"I'll see you later, Sara."

"Oh, you can count on it." Sara chuckled to herself, her shoulders shaking. "Just don't forget to invite me to the wedding," she tossed over her shoulder.

Elizabeth shook her head and couldn't resist a grin at the irrepressible old romantic. She pressed the button on the old lift. It slowly shuddered and groaned its way down to her, and she stepped inside, dragging the outer wrought-iron door closed, then turning the lever for the loft.

Memories hit her thick and fast as the lift rose. The familiar smell of turpentine and oil paints. The annoying creaking of the old service lift. Tom bringing her home from dinner at the small pub on the corner and taking her against the wall, ripping clothes open—his, hers—just enough to get skin to skin and his cock inside her, neither of them able to hold off the hunger and wait until they got upstairs . . .

Leaning her forehead against the wall, she closed her eyes and took a deep, shuddering breath. God, she had to stop. *It's just a job. It's just a job.* She repeated the mantra she'd been telling herself for the past week, whenever the memories started to creep in and overwhelm her.

As the lift slowed, she forced a smile on her face, mentally steeling herself for the impact of seeing him again.

Still, nothing could quite prepare her for the sight that greeted her when the lift stopped and the door opened into Tom's living room.

Tom. Paint-flecked jeans. Bare, muscled chest. A faint smile on his face and a palette in one hand as he held his other out to her. Damn.

"Hello, sweetheart. Welcome home."

FROM THE FLEETING FLICKER of sadness in Elizabeth's eyes as the words fell from his lips, Tom could have kicked himself. Shit! Richard was right—he truly sucked. But seeing her standing there, smiling at him, the sense of déjà vu had hit him right between the eyeballs, and the last two years had evaporated as if they'd never been.

"Sorry. I shouldn't . . . what I meant . . . I mean, what I was going to say . . . "

She stepped into the expansive room, brushing past him to wriggle her backpack off. He plonked his palette down on the console table and rushed to help her. The darn thing was nearly as big as she was, and she sighed and rotated her shoulders with relief when the weight was gone.

She turned to face him with a nervous smile. "Tom, it's all right." She looked around the foyer, the smile fading. "It does seem just like yesterday, doesn't it? And I know you didn't mean anything by it." Still, her gaze jumped around nervously while managing to avoid his face altogether, then her arms crossed over her chest so that she was almost hugging herself. She looked up at him. "The guest room's still the guest room?"

"Sure. Has its own bathroom now, too. So you can freshen up or . . . or whatever."

A cheeky but still nervous smile, a hint of the old Elizabeth, peeked out. "Oh, pooh! And there I had visions of stretching out in the Jacuzzi . . . "

So he wasn't the only one. Except he'd been indulging in memories of her in there with him every time he'd used it for the last two years. Naked. While he fucked her slowly, repeatedly, making her come again and again until she screamed his name and begged him to stop.

His cock stiffened in his jeans, pinching against the cold metal teeth of the zipper so that he flinched. His reassuring smile probably came out looking more like a grimace. "Well, if you want to. I mean . . . I meant . . . " He coughed in embarrassment. "God, I need to stop saying that. Look, if you want to use the tub, Elizabeth, feel free. Lock the door if it makes you feel better." He gritted his teeth and turned to walk away before he looked like a bigger idiot. A hand on his arm stopped him.

"Tom?"

He turned and looked at Elizabeth, surprised to see, not disgust or anger, but instead understanding. The hand on his arm gave a reassuring squeeze.

"This isn't going to be easy for either of us, Tom, I can see that. But this won't work if you keep worrying about what to say or what to do. So for the next two weeks, let's just try and be old friends. Sound okay to you?"

Old friends. Sure. Maybe. *Not.*

Still, it was better than nothing. Hell, he appreciated the fact that Elizabeth was being so generous, especially considering the way he'd treated her before. He covered her hand with his, feeling a slight tremble under his palm. "Sure, Elizabeth. And thanks."

"That's okay, I just want that tub later," she laughed, the sound still a little nervous. "Let me go unpack and take a shower for now. Then you can tell me what you want me to do."

She picked up her backpack and spun away before he could say a word. Just as well. He doubted she'd like to hear what he *really* wanted her to do.

Naked.

On the couch.

No, on his lap on the couch.

On his cock on his lap on the couch.

He closed his eyes and groaned, gripping the edge of the table.

Her sliding up and down, eyes locked with his as he cupped her breasts and made love to her slowly, relishing every second of being inside her. Her juices running down his straining cock, dampening his balls when he began to move faster. Elizabeth moaning, her pussy clenching around him as he fucked her, gripping him, milking him . . .

Ah hell!

He looked down and noticed he'd been rubbing his cock through his jeans. God, next thing he'd have it in his hand, pumping it.

Before Elizabeth could return, he ducked into his own bathroom, almost ripping the zipper off his jeans to free the aching, rigid flesh, shucking the jeans in quick movements.

Yanking open the glass door of his shower, he flicked the lever, cold water blasting out, and stood underneath it, eyes closed, shivering while he willed his erection to just die, for God's sake.

THE MAIN LIVING AREA was empty when Elizabeth walked out of the guest room. The shower had done wonders and she felt ready to tackle Tom again. Subtle spices teased her nose, the mix a tantalizing blend of something Asian. Her mouth watered to thoughts of Tom's special Thai stir-fry . . . But before she could head in the direction of the kitchen to find out, she was distracted by the setting Tom had prepared for the painting.

A decadent, plush, red velvet couch, wide, with scrolled, padded arms and finely carved feet, set off by the lustrous sheen of a creamy satin backdrop threaded with gold. A six-foot butterfly palm stood sentinel over the tableau, the rich green and yellow fronds offering a striking contrast to the richness of the deep ruby red and gold-shot cream.

How the hell she'd missed it earlier . . . She'd passed Tom's studio part of the loft to get to the guest room, but the sight of a shirtless Tom had always had the ability to make certain parts of her brain short-circuit. Some things never changed.

Catching movement out of the corner of her eye, she turned to see Tom leaning against the wall watching her, arms crossed over a now-covered chest, the thin white T-shirt stretched taut, showing the toned pecs and hint of dark chest hair, jeans-clad legs lazily crossed at the ankles. God, he was gorgeous. Tall, dark and handsome just didn't do him justice. Her pulse sped up just looking at him.

His hair was damp too, the rich dark brown waves slicked back off his forehead. From the looks of it, she wasn't the only one who'd taken a quick shower. An image of him naked, water sluicing down that hard, muscled body, the hair-covered chest leading down to tight abs, the dark trail of hair arrowing down to the nest of dark curls that surrounded the thickest, most delicious—

Realizing where her eyes had landed, she blinked and looked away, embarrassed at the direction of her eyes and her thoughts, and nodded at the setting. "That's beautiful, Tom. What an amazing couch. Plenty of room for two." Her eyes widened. "I mean, Richard and me. He and I . . . Posing. Later." She rolled her eyes. "You know what I mean. It's nice, anyway. Wonderful ambience." She tugged on the end of the knotted tie of her robe. "I hope this is what you wanted—the robe. I thought you'd rather get started straightaway since we don't have much time."

His expression hardened, his jawline tense. "Actually, I thought you might like to eat first. It's nearly dinnertime. Aren't you hungry?"

"I guess. Normally I don't eat until about nine, when I remember. Just before the rush hits at the club. Some nights I don't . . . " She looked down at her robe, suddenly feeling a little too casual. "Give me a sec and I'll go get changed."

"No need." He turned and walked away. "Come on through. It's ready. We can eat in front of the fire."

Grasping the lapels of her robe together, she swallowed down her misgivings and followed him through the gothic wooden hallway doors to the open-plan living room. Nothing had changed, she realized as she looked around. The large antique stone fireplace was blazing merrily, surrounded by the same comfortable leather lounge suite offset by the richly colored Persian rug.

"Here. Take this and go get comfy."

She turned at the hand on her elbow and took the glass of red wine he offered her. She closed her eyes and sniffed, a smile spreading across her face as the fruity bouquet teased her senses.

Nestling into a corner of the large lounge, she took a sip of her wine before placing it on the coffee table, looking up in time to see Tom standing to the side of her with two large noodle bowls in his hands, fragrant steam wafting up to make her tummy rumble in anticipation.

"Hmmm," she said, inhaling as she took the bowl. "Your cooking skills haven't diminished, I see."

"Limited cooking skills." His mouth kicked up at the corner in a self-conscious grin. "My repertoire is still limited to one dish."

"Yes, but it's a very, very good dish," she encouraged, inhaling briefly before she began to twist the noodles around her fork, her mouth watering in anticipation.

He sat on the floor in front of the fire, leaning up against the lounge beside her with his legs stretched out in front of him, bare feet pointing toward the fire.

It didn't matter that he'd put on a T-shirt. Even his broad, long feet were sexy as hell. She looked down at her bowl instead, trying to concentrate on the food.

As she ate, and they talked, she tried to remember the last time she'd spent a night like this—just relaxing in front of a fire, glass of wine, wonderful food . . . She couldn't remember a single one. Not since she'd bought the club. And until now, she hadn't stopped long enough to remember what she'd been missing.

Debbie was right—she needed to get back to a more normal life. The emptiness of her current one was glaringly obvious.

"Let me take that."

She was pulled out of her thoughts, not even aware she'd wandered off mentally until she realized Tom was standing in front of her reaching for her bowl.

"Thanks. It was delicious."

"My pleasure," he said, and walked to the kitchen. She picked up her glass and finished off the last mouthful of wine, then lay back and sighed. Food. Wine. A flickering fire. It was heaven. She closed her eyes and enjoyed the feeling of total re- laxation.

The couch dipped a little as Tom sat beside her on the edge of the sofa and she hummed when his fingers pushed the hair back off her forehead and then began to slowly stroke. She exhaled with the pleasure the sensation brought. Nobody had cared for her like this for a long time, not since . . . She men- tally shook off the thought. Tonight she just wanted to enjoy. "I always loved it when you did that."

"I know."

She wanted to open her eyes, but she was just too comfort- able, the sensation too relaxing. "Hmmm, that feels so good."

"You look beautiful lying there like that, Elizabeth. Would you mind if I sketch you?"

"Does it involve me moving? Do you need me naked?"

He chuckled, the sound warm and rich. "Talk about loaded questions. Would I be munching on my testicles for a week if I answered yes and yes?"

She laughed softly, opening one eyelid to peer up at him

before turning on the sofa and pushing the cushion under her head. "Bad man. Tonight you're safe—only because you wined and dined me. Am I all right like this?" she asked, yawning.

"Stay just as you are, sweetheart. You're perfect."

A pair of warm lips pressed a kiss to her forehead, and she smiled, her eyes still closed. "Good, I don't think I could move right now if you paid me to."

The seat dipped again as he stood, and she listened as his footsteps padded away.

It wasn't easy, finding his "zone" with an almost naked Elizabeth stretched out in front of him and a painfully hard erection to contend with, but eventually he did. He'd been sketching for an hour before it penetrated that Elizabeth had fallen asleep. The soft snores brought an affectionate smile to his face. She must have been tired. But then with the crazy hours she worked, it wasn't surprising.

The only problem was, he now needed the robe off, but didn't want to wake her. And he didn't want to wait. Knowing Elizabeth, she could sleep for hours.

Bending over her, he loosened the tie, although the knot gave him some trouble at first. As it released, he breathed a sigh of relief. Slowly, so as not to disturb her, he eased the two halves of the gown apart.

His heart started to pound, his fingers tightening on the silky fabric as her body was revealed. Christ, she was beautiful. How the hell had he let her get away from him?

Because he was a stupid fuckwit.

Turning on his heel, he continued remonstrating with

himself while he picked up his pad again and tried to get comfortable in his favorite chair.

With quick, deft strokes, he began to draw. But following the gentle curve of her neck, the way her jaw led to a slightly pointy chin—her "stubborn" chin she used to call it—reminded him of the days and nights he'd spent drawing her before. The pert nose, the soft curve of her mouth, even when she was asleep.

All so achingly familiar.

When his gaze tracked lower, over the feminine little bump of her collarbone, before the first gentle swell of her breasts, he had to grit his teeth to stop his hand from shaking.

Her large nipples were flat, the dark pink circles begging for his tongue to tease them to hardness. His jaw clenched.

A series of sure strokes filled in the shape.

He quickly shifted his eyes to the noticeable ridges of her rib cage, a slight frown forming a crease between his brows. She'd lost weight. Elizabeth had always been curvy, nicely covered so that bones didn't stick out. As an artist, it was one of the things he'd found so attractive about her.

But then his personal preference was for curves. Lush, shapely, like Elizabeth. He loved running his hands over her body and feeling the flesh give underneath, molding around him, cushioning his hardness, softening as she relaxed against him.

Tracing the flare of her hips, he noticed her tummy was still more rounded than flat. He loved the soft swell. To him it was one of the feminine things about her—a hard, flat abdomen on a woman was about as sexy as an ingrown toenail. How many nights after they'd made love had he curled around her, legs entwined, as he caressed and stroked it? Maybe he was weird, but to his mind, if he wanted to fuck a hard muscled body with a six-pack of abs, he might as well fuck a guy. For just a moment, the thought came to mind of her tummy swelling in another way—fuller, the skin stretched over the tiny babe she carried. Thoughts of taking her, making love to her as he ran his hands over the proof of their love . . . their child. The surge of possessiveness, of almost primal protectiveness that powered through him took him by surprise. He blinked his eyes and the image shattered.

Gripping the pencil a little harder, he tracked lower, aware for the first time that the crinkly black hairs previously gracing her plump mound were almost gone. In their place a thin strip that led between her closed legs. Led to paradise.

Christ! The pencil snapped in his hand. When had that happened? And for whom? Jealousy surged through him. He should have questioned Richard more closely about her "love life" when he had the chance. But then it was ridiculous for him to think that a woman like Elizabeth wouldn't be pursued by men. She'd probably been beating them off with a stick, while he'd been sitting around sulking like an adolescent with a chip on his shoulder.

She moved, tilting her upper body a little so that she lay partly on her back. He groaned softly as the puffed lips of her mostly bare pussy became more visible. His mouth watered to taste her, to run his tongue up the pink slit and lick until she came.

He dropped lower in his seat. Damn, his cock was so hard the constriction of his jeans was killing him. Two years of celibacy were now having disastrous effects on his body. He definitely had another appointment with his shower gel. Just as soon as he finished . . .

Dropping the now useless remnants of his pencil, he picked

up another, sketching quickly to finish the drawing. He really needed to cover her up again.

Then another cold shower.

Placing his pad on the floor, he stood to lean over her, intending to pull the robe closed, when she moved. And stretched.

He froze, his hands suspended over her. Breath stopped as he waited for her to open her eyes.

Part of him wanted her to. Wanted her to watch as he leaned down to tongue her nipples into hard peaks.

But she didn't. Instead he looked down at her arms now lying back over her head, her breasts pulled up, the firm curves tempting him so much that he had to swallow before he drooled all over her.

Kneeling on the floor beside her, he lowered his head, his eyes fastened on the tempting flesh of the dusky areola. His tongue flicked out, tracing a damp line around the edge, the circles growing smaller and smaller until he rimmed the tip. He paused, exhaling warm breaths over the dampened flesh, inhaling the sweet scent of Elizabeth—a muted hint of jasmine, so definably her that his cock pounded in response.

Eyes fastened on her sweet face, he opened his lips over the beaded tip of her nipple, sucking gently. He bit back a groan when the nub hardened, lengthening under his lips. She moaned in her sleep, her body moving, her back arching slightly as if searching for more.

"Tom . . . " Her whispered plea nearly made his heart stop. He searched her face, still rubbing the hard nipple over his tongue, expecting her to open her eyes. At this point he didn't care. He wanted her so much. Could she possibly be dreaming about him? Not some other guy, but him?

"More, Tom. More . . . " Her voice petered away on a soft

little moan as he surrendered and flicked the tip with his tongue then took a little more, tugging a little harder as she began to writhe beneath him. Switching sides, he tended to the other nipple, lapping at the sweetness of her skin, drinking in the music of her breathy sighs and pleas. Her nipples had always been her most sensitive spot—she could orgasm from him sucking on them alone—and he loved them.

When he heard her breathing accelerate, quick little puffs of air passing her lips, he pulled back, looking down at her, feeling the hunger for her that had never been far away, gnawing at him. All it took was a thought of her . . . The robe was now fully parted, showing every inch of silky skin.

A glance at the bared flesh of her labia showed the faint glisten of her juices on the dark pink lips. The musky scent of her arousal wafted up to him, pulling him closer until his mouth was over her delicious pussy and his tongue was swiping a slow line through the silky skin of her folds.

Fuck! He closed his eyes, the taste of her spilling over his tongue. Her legs parted as he looked at her delicious cunt, and he breathed deeply. God, this was heaven.

Moving to the end of the couch, he positioned himself between her legs, taking care not to disturb her.

Letting his arms bear the weight, he positioned himself above her, leaning down to lick her again, running his tongue over the velvety smoothness of her smooth labia. So soft, so sweet. Nectar. Ambrosia.

Plump, swollen, the flushed lips made him ache to work his cock inside her. But not now. From the sounds leaving her mouth, the excited shivers over her skin, she needed this. And he couldn't deny her. Would never deny her again.

His tongue slid inside the sweet slit, and he couldn't stop the hum that rumbled out of his chest. Keeping his eyes on Elizabeth's face, he licked, sucked, lapped and nibbled until her hips arched off the sofa, closer to his mouth, nudging against his lips, telling him of her need for more.

He lifted his face, slowly easing a single finger between the slick folds, moving it back and forward, gritting his teeth at the way her muscles gripped him. But he knew when he'd found her sweet spot. Her body began to move, just small undulations, in time with the rubbing of his finger, continuous little pants leaving her lips.

She was close. It struck him just how well he knew her body—the signs, the sounds, the way she started to clench and release on him when she was about to come. As he inserted another finger, the lips of her pussy parted, revealing the swollen nub of her clit.

His face positioned over her again, he flicked and licked the sensitive little button, feeling her body begin to shudder under his mouth and fingers, the wetness building, making his fingers slick with her juices.

Wrapping his lips around her clit, he sucked, not hard, but enough to push her over the edge, and her body stiffened before twitching in time with her contractions as he continued to thrust gently. Gradually the spasming around his fingers eased and she lay still, her breathing slowly returning to normal.

His body ached with the need to move over her and slide his aching cock inside her sweet hole, feel her sheath swallow him up until he was buried up to her womb.

But if he didn't move away now, he'd be inside her and pounding away before he could stop himself.

With trembling hands, he pulled the edges of her robe together, gritting his teeth as a hand brushed against her breast, his palm curving around the silky mound for one brief, exquisite moment before tying the belt loosely, his hands fumbling over the knot. Her body shifted, the movement slight, almost imperceptible, and he stroked her forehead, smoothing over the skin with butterfly-light touches, knowing how it calmed her.

"Shhh, sleep, Elizabeth," he whispered at her ear, his tone soothing, gentle.

Grabbing the afghan off the back of the lounge, he draped it over her, tucking it in at the sides before leaning down to place a kiss on her forehead.

"Love you, sweetheart."

He straightened and stepped back. After one final lingering glance, he turned and left the room.

As HIS BEDROOM DOOR clicked closed behind him, Elizabeth's eyes blinked open and she drew in a deep shuddering breath, exhaling a single word, filled with pain and longing. "Tom . . . " Her arms lowered, her fingers clutching the blanket, as a single tear, followed by another and then another, tracked down the side of her cheek, slipping off her face to dampen the lock of hair beneath.

With the back of her hand, she brushed the trail of wetness from her cheeks. Her mind was confused, her jumbled emotions taking much longer to settle than her body. She knew better than anyone what a tender, giving lover Tom could be, but what had just occurred . . . There had been no artifice, no power, no advantage to be gained from it. Behind the gentle caring, she had sensed his need for her, and even without his final whispered words, the love communicated in the gentleness of his caresses.

It was that same need for him, for his touch, that had made her continue to feign sleep. With the first stroke of his fingers, she had awoken from the light sleep she'd drifted into. But with her eyes closed, she could pretend nothing had changed, and the dreamlike moment wouldn't be shattered.

She loved him—still. It was something she had never denied—not to herself, anyway. But could things be different between them? Could their two worlds ever meet, or would the same conflicts drive them apart again? And would she be able to survive the heartbreak again if it did?

THE WARM SUNLIGHT ON her face roused Elizabeth and she sat up, rubbing her eyes as she tossed off the afghan blanket Tom had covered her with the night before. As she swung her legs off the lounge, her sleepy gaze landed on the folded note on the coffee table. She fingered the note, thinking about the previous night. Wondering what the day would hold. With a shake of her head, she pushed the thought away. Time would tell. She opened the note to discover Tom had gone for a jog, and for her to help herself to whatever she wanted.

Well, what she wanted was a nice, long, hot shower. Feeling the chill in the air, she dressed comfortably in a pair of sweatpants and a thick, wooly jumper, pulling on a thick pair of socks to keep her feet warm on the polished wood floors.

Hunger wasn't an issue, since she rarely ate breakfast at the club, so instead she grabbed a cup of black coffee from the coffeepot keeping warm on the kitchen counter. The rich scent of Tom's personal blend teased her senses, and that first sip made her hum with delight. There was nothing in the world quite like a good cup of coffee.

Not knowing how long Tom would be gone, since she had no idea when he'd actually left, she wandered around the loft, noticing how little had changed since she'd been away. She was on her way up to the garden seat on the roof when she paused before the staircase, noticing the open door to the smaller room that had originally been intended as a spare bedroom, but had long been Tom's storeroom for his completed or semi-completed paintings.

Curiosity ate at her. Refusing to consider it snooping, an innate inquisitiveness to see what he had worked on during her absence had her feet moving into the dark, shuttered room. A quick tug on the cord, and the wooden slat blinds opened to flood the room with daylight.

Knowing Tom's preference for grouping his paintings in chronological order, she started with the rack furthest from the door, recognizing, as she flicked through the first few, paintings he had completed prior to their original introduction.

The next two racks held those he had undertaken while she lived with him. It was like plunging into the past, to a happier time, his choice of colors rich, vibrant—happy colors. Particular favorites of hers were the ones with children—he loved to capture their *joie de vivre,* that playful curiosity or impish mischievousness. In complete contrast were the ones he'd done of her—richly colored, highly sensual, whether whimsical poses or those charged with erotic nuance. Even though she recalled posing for every single one, it was, as always, disconcerting seeing herself through his eyes. The woman in the paintings was so different from the one she faced in the mirror—more earthy, seductive—he even made her look beautiful.

However, it was the final two racks that held the most interest for her. She paused a moment with her hand on the first painting, almost reticent, now that she was here, to pull it back and see what it held. What had inspired him? Or more importantly, who? That thought had trepidation skittering through her, her heart rate pounding, her breathing picking up as an uncomfortable rush of adrenaline flooded her system. Who had replaced her? Which woman had been responsible for firing his passion for his art? Elizabeth felt a stab of unreasonable jealousy at whoever had taken her place—she had left Tom, after all, not the other way around.

But from her own experience with Tom, she knew better than anyone how he unleashed the passion he poured into his erotic paintings. She couldn't count the days or nights he had made love to her, bringing her to orgasm, over and over, only to carry her sated body through to his studio, placing her on his soft old couch to slumber or watch as he attacked his canvas with single-minded focus, waking her hours later as he carried her into bed and wrapped himself around her before total exhaustion took him and he slept soundly.

Did she really want to see? Whatever or whoever had been his "inspiration" once she left? She knew it would be like gazing into a part of his soul—a part she hadn't been a part of.

Her hand tightened on the wooden mount. Taking a deep breath, she made her decision.

Pulling it toward her, she looked down at a painting of a woman. The background was muted in shades of gray, the mood one of sadness, despair. Rather than a full figure, it was a portrait, the woman partially turned away, looking back over her shoulder. But it was the expression on her face—the pain, the hurt almost tangible so that she reached without thinking to touch her, wanting to soothe the pain she knew she was feeling. She knew that pain, that despair. It mirrored her own the day she had walked away from Tom.

It was, in fact, her.

The thought that he had painted her rocked her. But to have captured so accurately what she'd been feeling . . . So much of that day was now a blur, details muffled by the emotional devastation of leaving him. But consumed by her own pain, she'd been unable to contemplate the aftermath for Tom. Now she knew. He'd dealt with it the only way he knew how.

With a distracted movement, she brushed at the tear that had wound its way down her cheek, breathing deeply to stem the imminent flood of more.

Steeling herself, she flicked through the others, painting after painting. A dozen or more.

Her. With one or two exceptions, they were all of her.

As with the first one, he had chosen key moments in their lives together. And she recognized every single one—the happy ones, the quiet ones, those moments where they were so deeply in love that nothing and no one else mattered.

They had each dealt with the separation in different ways. And while she had never been able to let go of her feelings for him, quite possibly it had been the same for Tom. Maybe he did still love her after all.

So where did that leave them now?

She turned and left the room, snapping the blind shut and plunging the room once more into darkness. As she walked up the staircase and stood up on the roof, looking over the sooty London skyline, feeling the wind buffet her, the brisk chill of the breeze clearing the emotional miasma of the past from her head and thrusting her back into the present, she pondered what to do.

She could wait for Tom to make a move. If he loved her as he'd said, and wanted her back, then he had to be prepared to face what had forced them apart. It would require him putting her first, even before his art, to resolve the issues with his family. Could he do it? Was it, as before, asking more of him than he could give?

Or . . . A thought occurred to her and a small smile tipped her lips as she raised the mug and took a long sip of coffee. Perhaps Tom's motivation for action lay with another member of his family.

Richard. In a few days he'd be back. And knowing Richard as she did, it was highly unlikely he'd behave once they were both naked—especially with Tom watching. The only other time she and Richard had posed together had nearly driven Tom over the edge watching Richard's hands wandering all over her body, ostensibly trying to "get comfortable." Until "getting comfortable" had involved a hand cupping one of her breasts. That would have been more than enough for Tom, until Richard had begun to "innocently" fondle her nipple. In less than an hour, the sitting had been over, Richard was bundled into the lift, and Tom had been fucking her with a frenzy on the rug in the living room, where he'd tackled her as she ran away from him after teasing him about the erection he'd developed watching them.

Maybe she wouldn't have to do a thing . . .

4

GOOD LORD! THOUGHT RICHARD. The two of them were worse than a couple of teenagers. Sneaking longing glances at each other when they thought the other one wasn't looking. And the sexual tension . . . Hell, it had been so thick since he arrived, it was nearly choking him. Whatever had happened before he got there, it sure as hell wasn't what he'd hoped would happen once they had a bit of time alone together. Elizabeth wasn't saying, even when he managed to get her alone, for the short spells when Tom finally left her for ten minutes while he showered. And Tom . . . He was strung tighter than a drum.

Still, something had happened. Something they obviously hadn't talked about, judging from the little pantomime being played out in front of him. Although, from the way Tom hovered over her constantly, finding any excuse to touch her, however innocently, he was at least moving in the right direction.

But time was running out for them. In a few days, as per her contract, Elizabeth would be back at her club and Tom would be alone once more, head stuck in a canvas while the love of his life walked out that door—for the second time.

For a guy who wasn't backward in coming forward about taking what he wanted from life, Tom had royally screwed up with Elizabeth from the word "go."

But not this time. On that point Richard was determined. Not if he had anything to say—or do—about it.

He flicked a glance between the two of them. Tom's butt was perched on his stool, long legs stretched out in front, as he fiddled with his pencils again on the round table beside him. Tension, anger, stress, whatever—he always fiddled with those damned pencils. Sharpening them, lining them up, sorting them . . .

Normally it drove him nuts, but this time he at least knew the reason.

Elizabeth was another matter. He couldn't quite work out what was going on in that mischievous mind of hers. She was nervous about something—he just couldn't figure out what. And as if the drink of water she'd just grabbed from the kitchen was going to help quiet those jumpy little nerves he could see written all over her face. Richard smiled to himself.

It was time for Elizabeth to get naked.

For Elizabeth *and him* to get naked.

Together.

Where good old Tom could watch. Jealous as hell that it wasn't him on the lounge with Elizabeth.

And Richard intended for him to get an eyeful.

He planned to ratchet up that jealousy until it jerked Tom

out of that damn stasis he was in regarding Elizabeth and into some positive action.

Reclining back on the armrest, fingers linked behind his head, he looked at the two of them and rolled his eyes. It was pretty damn obvious, to him at least, that they both wanted nothing more than to fuck like bunnies until they blew each other's brains out. However neither one seemed prepared to make the first move.

So, that left him—good old Richard. If he didn't love them both so much, he'd walk out now and leave them to it. But no, if two people were meant to be together, it was these two. And he would do his darnedest to help. Besides, he was really going to enjoy this.

Standing up, he flicked the studs on his jeans, turning away as he bent over and shucked them down his legs, off his feet, tossing them onto the floor out of the way.

As he straightened he caught a glimpse of Elizabeth's wide eyes at his choice of underwear, quietly amused by the nervous little glances she threw from his butt to Tom.

And Tom. Hell, he could give that moody geezer from *Pride and Prejudice* lessons in brooding. Well, not for much longer . . .

Slowly, dragging it out for maximum effect, he slid his underpants down his legs, watching Elizabeth closely as he gave a little wiggle for effect. A smirk tipped his lips when she rolled her eyes at him. Gee, and that was the thanks he got for putting on his silky black G-string just for her. With a flick and a grin, he kicked it to land on his jeans.

"Ready, sweet pea?" Richard said to Elizabeth and winked, earning him a muttered, exasperated "Rich-*ard!*" Grasping her shoulders, he steered her backward until she reached the velvet lounge, pushing her down until her bottom touched the seat. "Now you just lie back and let me do all the work, okay?" He sat down beside her.

"Richard, I don't think—"

"Good," he said, cutting her off as he eased her head back onto the tasseled pillow. "That's your biggest problem right there—thinking."

He caught her widened eyes looking down between their bodies at his growing erection. Even he was surprised—and delighted—by the display. Talk about running up the flagpole. "Now, don't worry about ol' Willy there. He's got a mind of his own, and besides, no man with a pulse could be in the position I'm in and not get a hard-on, love. Anyway, I'm sure Tom will draw me to be a pencil-dick or something in retaliation for putting my hands on you."

Richard grinned as she chuckled, and brushed the vagrant strands of hair back from her face. "It's only good old Richard. So just relax and trust me, okay?" She nodded. "That's the way."

He turned to Tom, seeing the warning darkness in his eyes, the rigid set of his jaw, his fingers gripping the pencil until the knuckles whitened. From the looks of that thunderous expression, a few molars were going to be sacrificed before Richard was done. Tom really needed to let go of some of that pressure. Learn how to vent. All that "stiff upper lip" crap would just give him an ulcer.

"We'll try a few poses, Tom. You just sketch away and let us know when we hit one that does it for you. Okay?" Richard knew damn well none of this was "okay" with Tom, since it involved any man but Tom being naked with his woman, but that was his tough luck.

Without waiting for an answer, Richard turned back to

Elizabeth. *Poses. Right.* He doubted Tom would be drawing too much very shortly anyway . . . "Now, Elizabeth my lovely, what say you and I get nice and cozy?"

Positioning Elizabeth so that she was comfortable—arms draped loosely over her head, legs extended but slightly spread, one knee bent—Richard waited until she had settled against the tasseled cushions, lying back in sybaritic splendor. God, what a delicious sight!

Then, locking her gaze with his, he reached for the tie of her silky robe, slowly working the knot free. For a brief moment, she tensed, her eyes startled.

"Come now, love," Richard whispered, seeking to settle her, "this isn't the first time we've done this. Though I daresay after today's little effort it will be the last." He winked at her, her eyes going wide until she got his meaning. Or *thought* she got his meaning. If she had any idea what he had planned, she'd likely knee him in the balls. Regardless, he felt his cock harden further with the sensual, slumberous look that came over her eyes.

He had modeled with Elizabeth once before for Tom. Two years ago. A couple of hours of having her luscious bod reclining back against his chest, bare as the day she was born. Even though it had been Tom's suggestion, he had been so pissed off at seeing her wrapped up in Richard's arms, he'd finished the sketches in just over an hour.

But Richard had always had a soft spot for her. She had a fresh, open way of looking at life that just made a person feel good about themselves. In fact, the only thing that had kept him from stepping in when his fool cousin let Elizabeth go was the knowledge that some day it would come to this. Or he would have snapped her up the second she walked out on Tom.

"Don't move." Keeping his touch gentle, his movements slow, he reached for the robe. The fabric could easily have slipped open on its own, but instead he parted it, ensuring the slippery fabric teased her nipples on the way before he released it.

He was rewarded by a soft indrawn breath. Moving to his hands and knees, he leaned over her, watching her eyes almost cross as he drew closer.

He placed a soft kiss on her lips, noting how warm, how soft they felt under his before he nibbled along her jawline to her ear. Down lower, his cock hardened further and he could only imagine the view Tom must be getting.

"Watch Tom, love, and don't take your eyes off him," he whispered in her ear. He pulled back a little, noticing she watched him still. "You know I love you, sweet pea, and I won't hurt you. But trust me and keep your eyes on Tom. No matter what I do," he whispered for her ears only.

Her eyes swung back to Tom. He couldn't see him, but he could guess what he looked like, judging from the slight elevation of Elizabeth's breathing.

Lapping his tongue along the velvety skin of her neck, down over the gentle swell of a full breast, he licked up the underside, closing his eyes briefly at the sweet smell of her skin. A soft, ultrafeminine scent . . . Whatever it was, it was Elizabeth all over—warm, sexy, delicious.

Giving himself over to the enjoyment that awaited him for as long as he had, he ran the fingers of a hand up her side, noting how soft, how sensually rich her skin felt, before finally cupping the relaxed swell of a breast, massaging it in his palm. Closing his lips over the other nub, now tight and puckered, he sucked, light tugs, closing his eyes and moaning softly as he enjoyed the taste, the texture as it rolled over his tongue.

★　★　★

WHAT HAD HAPPENED?

As instructed, Elizabeth watched Tom. Trying unsuccessfully to block the sensations that shot through her body like lightning with every tug, every nip of the sensitive tip under Richard's lips.

But Tom . . . The second Richard moved over her, a change had come over him. Jaw clenched. Body tense. Eyes, the blue so dark as to be almost black, swirling with hunger. A wild, possessive hunger.

But more than that, need. The same tale of insatiable need she imagined her own told.

Richard shifted. Moving. Rimming the other nipple before nipping it sharply. And on her indrawn gasp, the jerk of her body, Tom jerked too. Her eyes floated lower, unable to miss the strain caused by the swelling in his jeans.

Good, he was turned on. Annoyed as hell. Furious, judging from his expression. But turned on to see what Richard was doing. To her.

Her breath caught as Richard sucked harder and she began to pant, trying to draw more oxygen into her lungs.

Tom's sketchpad dropped to the floor, her body jumping in response to the sharpness of the noise as it hit the parquetry floor.

Richard shifted again. Lower, his wicked tongue flicking a damp trail down her ribs, tracing each line until she arched against his mouth, trails of goose bumps following in the wake of his lips.

God, how much more could she take—could Tom take? His breathing was deeper, harsher, his eyes blazing fire at her. And still, no words came from his lips.

When Richard left the dip of her belly button, the rasp of his chin leading the way over delicate flesh, gentle hands parting her thighs further, she tensed, knowing what would come.

And that first breath, that initial brush of his tongue, so hot, down the damp folds of her sex, had her arching up, a shuddering groan releasing as she let free the breath she'd been holding.

The pencil in Tom's fingers snapped, a piece of it flying across the room.

And as Richard's tongue took a long, slow swipe, her eyelids fluttered shut, unable to stand the torment, the undeniable, torturous pleasure of feeling one man pleasure her while the man she loved watched.

It was an escape, shutting them out to submit to the sensations.

Her surrender.

"Eyes open, Elizabeth! Dammit!"

Startled out of her sensuous torpor, she blinked. Tom now stood, staring at them intently, ferociously. Lust and desire etched into every line of his body. He had always been the sexually dominant one in their relationship. It was one of the things that made her so hot. And now it looked like her hungry tiger was back.

"Watch me, baby." Tom's eyes darkened, his nostrils flaring as he stepped closer and caught her scent. Her clit tingled, sending the juices flowing at the commanding tone of his voice, confirmed by the moan as Richard lapped faster, pushed deeper at her sex. "He told you that, didn't he? Knew how fucking crazy it would make me, seeing another man touch you, lick you, kiss that sweet cunt that's mine. So you watch me, Elizabeth, and see what it's fucking doing to me."

In spite of the darting thrusts of Richard's tongue inside her, she watched, her eyes wide, as Tom slid open the zipper on his jeans, and his cock, hard, thick, already weeping from the small slit, fell out into his palm.

A small, hungry whimper left her lips as he began to stroke. From root to tip, the movement slow, the grip firm. As he watched her.

CHRIST! TOM HAD NEVER seen anything as beautiful as Elizabeth. Right then. Her face flushed, the rosy color traveling down her neck, over the delicious mounds of her breasts. The rich brown strands of hair flowing around her head like ripples of silk. He could spend a lifetime trying and never capture the many facets that made up Elizabeth's beauty.

Full breasts wobbling as her chest rose and fell as she panted, short, sharp little breaths puffing through the teeth biting into her bottom lip as her excitement escalated.

A few times when they were younger, he and Richard had shared a woman. But that was different. He hadn't been in love with any of them. And though one side of him wanted to kill Richard for doing this, for touching her like he was, some twisted part of him wanted to see Elizabeth's pleasure as another man took her. But with her eyes only on him.

That was the key. That acknowledgment that her pleasure came from and through him. He needed that. And more. He needed all of her. Needed everything she had to give.

Stripping quickly, he felt satisfaction flare inside him as her eyes grew heavy-lidded, the long lashes fluttering once or twice as her gaze landed on his cock. Licking her lips and leaving a glistening, tantalizing swipe across the reddened, swollen flesh.

Moving closer, a step, two. Until the scent of her arousal filtered up to him, torturing him, the familiar fragrance weakening him so that he had to lock his knees.

Her skin glistened now with a light sheen, continuous little panting moans coming from deep inside her chest that shredded his control.

Richard raised his head, his lips shiny from Elizabeth's pussy, his eyes dark and impatient, his eyebrow raised in an unspoken dare.

Jaw clenched, Tom nodded. Watched a moment longer as Richard slipped a finger inside the tight sheath. Then withdrew, working two fingers back inside before lowering his head again to flick at Elizabeth's clit.

Her hips lifted, pushing up against Richard's mouth and fingers.

Tom began to stroke his cock again. "You thinking of me, baby? Wishing it was me?"

"Please," she panted. "Please, Tom."

He grasped his cock hard at the base, waiting until the warning throb eased off. "Shhh, baby. We'll take care of you." He reached a hand down to caress and cup the side of her face. "You want this, sweetheart?" Still stroking the hot cock in his hands, he inclined his head at it, waiting for her answer.

Biting her lip, she nodded.

"Not good enough, sweetheart. I need to hear the words. Give me the words, baby."

Before she could speak, a ragged moan was torn from her as Richard reached deep inside her, his fingers thrusting faster. "I want . . . I want . . . Tom, please. Give it to me."

Christ, he couldn't wait any longer himself. Straddling the arm of the lounge, he cupped her face in his hands. "Open up those sweet lips, baby. That's it." He gritted his teeth against the shocking intensity of that first heated touch. "Take me. Take all of me." Sinking with slow thrusts into the delicious warmth. Her lips tightening around the aching flesh as her tongue flicked the underneath.

His knees swayed. Hell, she had the most magic mouth. Always had.

"Now, suck it. Come on, hard, sweetheart. I need it so fucking hard." As he began to fuck her, those lips stretched around the thickness of his shaft, her moans of pleasure vibrated along the length of his dick. More than sexual hunger ate at him, and words he'd sworn he'd never say to another woman after she left him, leaving his life empty, his heart devastated, escaped from his traitorous lips. "I need *you*, baby," he whispered. "Oh fuck, I need you so much."

Fiery lances of sensation shot up his legs, down his spine, the overload of stimulation centering in the tight sac between his legs. Panting, he shut his eyes, shaking his head to flick off the sweat that threatened to blind him. He opened them with a snap when he felt her hands on his butt, kneading the taut flesh, fingers trailing down the crevice teasingly to push against the tightness of his asshole.

"Enough!" he grunted.

Freeing his grip on her face, Tom grasped her hands and pulled them away, backing up so that his cock slipped free of her mouth, the bobbing, pulsing length shiny and wet.

"Richard," he gritted out. "I take it you're prepared?"

A devilish grin creased his cousin's lips. "Like a Boy Scout."

"Move. Come around behind me."

Alone on the lounge, Elizabeth half sat, her body trembling, the arms that supported her shaking noticeably. She hadn't come. Richard wouldn't have let her, but damn if she didn't look ready to explode. Tom knew his Elizabeth, intimately familiar with every signal her body put out. He reached down to stroke her cheek, his thumb wiping over her bottom lip so that it pouted at him. "This is what you want, sweetheart? Because if you do, I really want to give it to you."

She nodded. "Yes. Yes, both of you."

He bent and kissed her, hard. Thrusting his tongue inside her mouth as she arched up to him, her arms looping around his neck, holding him tight.

Lips still joined, he lay down on the lounge, pulling Elizabeth with him so that she lay over him. The wetness flowed from her pussy, the heat scorching his cock. And he had yet to get inside her. She was going to set his cock on fire.

With a final lick over her lip, he eased back from the kiss, pure satisfaction surging through him at her sexy, disheveled appearance above him.

"Hands on my shoulders, sweetheart," Tom said softly. "Brace yourself."

Her eyes were so deep, the blue so clear he could drown in them. His heart beat harder as he looked at her, seeing her eyes go glassy, one single tear welling up to topple over the lid and slide down her cheek.

"I need you too, Tom. Fuck me. Please, God, fuck me."

"Oh sweetheart, I'll give you whatever you need. Always." He moved her hips, lifting and positioning her until the head of his cock was kissing the lips of her vagina. The second she felt the tip at her opening, she rocked her hips, a grunt leaving his chest as half his length was swallowed up in the searing heat.

"Oh sweetheart, God, you feel like heaven." She was tight around him, the muscles inside flushed with blood, making the channel narrow. He gripped her hips harder to stop her from hurting herself as she tried to push down on him. "Slowly . . . that's it . . . yes, there's no rush, baby . . ." Her inner muscles tightened around him, nearly cutting off the circulation in his cock. "Ease up, sweetheart. Loosen those muscles so I can move, okay?" He sighed when she relaxed slightly, allowing him to work deeper until he was fully seated. He heard the crinkle of foil, caught Richard's eye over Elizabeth's shoulder. Sweat broke out on his brow as she rubbed her pelvis against his, seeking stimulation for her clit.

Her movements stilled, her eyes going wide as she felt Richard move in behind her and touch her.

"JUST RELAX, LOVE," RICHARD said as he nuzzled her ear, his lubricated finger easing inside the tight hole. Sliding in and out, relaxing the muscles, accustoming them to his touch, to the feel of being penetrated anally.

"Do you have any idea how beautiful you look to us, that gorgeous body just waiting for the pleasure we can give it?" He turned her head to kiss her, her lips swollen, her tongue searching for his hungrily.

A second finger joined the first, sliding easily now as she surrendered to the sensation, rocking slowly on Tom's cock, pushing back onto Richard's fingers. He broke the kiss, panting against her neck. "And it will be pleasure, love. So much pleasure . . . for all of us."

"You talk . . . too much . . . Richard," she gasped as Richard withdrew his fingers and lined up his cock at the pouting little hole. "Been telling you that for *years!*" Her voice rose on the final syllable as he nudged and pushed past the tight ring of muscles until just the head was crowned. Her ass clenched on him so that he couldn't move and Richard gritted his teeth against the exquisite shafts of pleasure that raced up his cock.

"Oh my God!" she panted.

Richard's grip tightened on her hips in direct relation to the gripping around his cock. "Fuck, Tom, she's choking me." And she was, but along with the tightness was the most indescribable warmth and tantalizing friction that shot straight to his balls.

"Come here, sweetheart." Tom eased Elizabeth closer to him, holding her face while he bussed his lips over hers. Whatever Tom was doing worked, because Richard felt the relaxation spread through her body, the clenching grip on his cock easing so he could slide more freely. A sigh of relief left his lips.

Three more slow and easy thrusts and he was buried inside her, his groin rubbing against the warm cheeks of her ass. He leaned back and skimmed his hands over the rounded globes. "Tom . . . hell, Elizabeth has the most fucking beautiful ass." He glanced over Elizabeth's shoulder, catching Tom's eye, seeing the strain his cousin was feeling to not move before she was ready for them.

A nod passed between them. In tandem they began to move, timing their thrusts so that as one pulled out, the other plunged in. Over and over, the sounds of their bodies joining, the hungry sucking noises as Elizabeth's cunt swallowed Tom's cock each time, feeling the vibration and rub of Tom's cock against the ultrathin wall separating them.

And Elizabeth . . . Her moans, her broken, stuttered pleas as she lay between them, unable to move, only able to feel, to enjoy, her cries to them, begging, pleading to let her come.

Hell, he hoped it happened soon. He wasn't sure how much longer he could last.

Reaching up, running his hands up over the soft skin of her back and around to her breasts, Richard palmed them briefly, before rolling the nipples in his fingers, pinching them hard, feeling the jerk shoot through her body in response to the small bite of pain.

He tensed, gritting his teeth, his body rigid as she tried to take control and pushed back against him on the down stroke, an impatient "More!" forced from her lips as she gasped underneath him, her body shaking as the first tremors of her orgasm began to tear through her, building, her body jerking between them.

And then she was there, a keening wail of pleasure piercing the air as her channel and her ass muscles clamped around them. The pinching, clenching of her ass ripped Richard's control away. Going deep once more and tensing, holding it, he reared back, holding himself flush against her buttocks, his fingers tightening on her hips as his cock exploded inside her, pumping and pulsing in an endless stream until he was drained, shaking from the power of his release. The tip of Tom's cock rubbed against his through the thin barrier as he, too, thrust deep and tensed, roaring as he blasted deep inside her cunt.

Exhausted, Elizabeth had already collapsed onto Tom's chest, draped over him, gasping for breath. *Christ al-bloody-mighty!* Richard knew how she felt. Panting, he held himself above her, his rigid arms shaking as they kept him suspended until he felt able to withdraw, holding the condom tight to the base of his cock as his rapidly softening erection slipped free.

A shaky step back from the lounge, and Richard looked down at the two of them. Elizabeth was still collapsed over

Tom's chest. Tom's arms now wrapped tight around her, holding her close as he murmured to her.

A look passed between Richard and his cousin as they both glanced at the woman they had shared, but, Richard knew, never would again.

With a wry smile, he picked up his clothes and stumbled into Tom's bathroom for a shower.

When he returned fifteen minutes later, hair still dripping, he noticed that Elizabeth had moved, now lying beside Tom on the lounge, eyes closed, her breathing returned to normal as she snuggled in close. Tom stroking her hair as his chin rested on her head.

With a parting glance at the two of them, he opened the door to the lift and left, a tired but satisfied smile creasing his face.

5

Elizabeth came awake to the feel of cool sheets beneath her and a warm body surrounding her like a blanket. They were in Tom's room, on his huge king-sized futon. Richard was gone. Through the skylight, she could see that night had fallen.

Behind her, an erection prodded at her backside.

"Feel like a bath?"

"Hmmm," she murmured, her body feeling deliciously satiated, "but I'd have to move."

"I could carry you . . . "

"Or . . . " She lifted her leg over his so that his cock slipped along the crease of her buttocks, nudging at the lips of her pussy. She shifted slightly to get a better position. "We could just stay here, and you could—"

She bit down on a moan as she felt him fill her from behind. "Definitely just stay here," she gasped as he began to rock inside her.

One hand began to caress her nipple, the other one moving

between her legs to rub soft circles around her clit, the arc of tingling fire shooting along every nerve ending between her nipple and the ultrasensitive bud at the top of her slit.

His lips nuzzled at her neck, nipping a path to her ear.

"I love you. I've never stopped loving you, sweetheart," he moaned against the shell of her ear.

As the slow orgasm built between them, she leaned back against him, resting her head in the crook of his shoulder and closed her eyes as a single tear leaked between her lashes and skidded down her cheek. "And I love you, Tom," she whispered, her breath catching as the gentle tremors peaked and passed between them, his arms tightening around her as they rode out the gentle release.

A few minutes later he still hadn't eased his hold on her— she could feel the tension in his body, and turned in his arms. The look on his face was serious—his "thinking" face.

She ran her fingers over his brow, smoothing the lines away. "Hey, what's up?"

He grasped her fingers and kissed the tips, then held her hand against his chest so that she could feel the beat of his heart.

"I'm just wondering if you can ever forgive me . . . enough to give me—us—another chance."

Could she? In spite of what had gone before, she could tell this was a different Tom. He'd changed, matured. For that matter, she admitted, they both had. And while putting her heart on the line again was a risk, was the alternative—life without him— any better? It had been a bleak, lonely couple of years. There had been no other men—how could there be when she'd never stopped loving him? And now, lying in the shelter of his arms, knowing he still loved her, going back to being alone seemed even darker than before. For the first time in two years she felt warm again, happy. Content in a way that went soul deep. "It won't be easy, Tom. We need to talk about things this time—as equals. But we could try."

He buried his head in her shoulder, a long shuddering breath warming her neck. "God, I've missed you, sweetheart. So much. Trust me, it will be different this time. I promise you that."

As he hugged her tight against him, she felt hope. For the first time in two years, the future seemed brighter.

SINGING IN TIME WITH the music blaring from the radio, Elizabeth turned the gas flame off, and lifted the last two slices of French toast out of the pan, sliding them onto a plate to keep warm in the oven.

God, she felt great. As though she were surrounded by a big bubble of happiness. And if Tom didn't hurry up and get out of the shower, she'd say to hell with the French toast and go join him.

As she closed the oven door, the intercom phone rang on the wall beside the refrigerator, and Elizabeth stepped over to answer it, knowing it could only be one person. "Sara?"

"Yes, lass. It's me."

"What's wrong?"

"Just a warning," Sara said in a rush. "You have compan—"

The rest of Sara's words were drowned out.

"What is the meaning of this? And who the dickens are you?"

Surprised at the snappish female voice behind her, Elizabeth spun around. A tall, elegant woman, dressed in clothes that Elizabeth estimated at a glance represented at least a month's wages to most people, stood glowering at her, her eyes widening briefly before narrowing as recognition followed. "You! What are *you* doing here?"

Wonderful. Tom's mother Caroline. Just what she needed. Elizabeth quickly said her thanks to Sara and hung up the phone.

"Hello, Lady Danville. It's been such a long time." *Not quite long enough though . . .*

"Elizabeth." The way Caroline said her name, that affected upper-class drawl with a barely hidden sneer, always managed to make her feel like a peasant. Obviously Caroline's disposition toward her and the "risk" she potentially posed to her darling son hooking up with one of the bevy of debutantes she kept pushing his way, hadn't improved any. Even if Caroline had only believed she was Tom's model, her opinion that her darling son could do better was one she'd had little compunction in voicing, even in front of Elizabeth.

But she was not going to let it get her down. Not today.

"Take a seat. I'll let Tom know you're here."

She escaped to Tom's bedroom, glad to see him coming out of the bathroom, showered. Entertaining Caroline was the last thing on earth she wanted to do. Tom's mother she may be, but the woman was a dragon. A dragon with pearls and a twinset. She'd only met Caroline half a dozen times, and that was six times too many.

"Your mother is here. I better go shower and get dressed. I'm sure she was less than impressed to see me waltzing around your kitchen in my robe."

"I don't care what she thinks, Elizabeth." He reached for her, wrapping his arms around her waist. "And you're not getting away from me without a good morning kiss." His eyes held hers a moment, an odd look in them before he lowered his head until their mouths met, taking his time to kiss her thoroughly before he released her.

She reached up for another quick one before she let him go. "Hmmm, I like your good morning kisses."

His eyes turned devilish. "Stand there much longer looking at me like that and you'll get a lot more than just a kiss, sweetheart."

She laughed softly and turned away, warmth filling her. "You can't. Mom's waiting, remember?" she said, rolling her eyes at him before she scampered away, giggling as a hand swatted at her bottom.

"Don't remind me. Now scoot. Before I forget about my mother and fuck that saucy little ass you keep teasing me with."

She peeked out the door to make sure Caroline wasn't around before she ducked around the corner into the guest room.

TAKING AS LONG AS she dared, Elizabeth turned off the shower, toweling the excess water from her hair before running a comb through it and leaving the steamy bathroom.

Opting for a pair of jeans and a sweatshirt, not wishing to aggravate Caroline any more than necessary by swanning around in her robe, she took one final look at herself in the mirror before she planted a smile on her face and walked out of her room.

She refused to let Caroline spoil her happy mood. Tom loved her. He hadn't stopped loving her, and she loved him.

They were both older now. Wiser. They could work out their problems.

They could work out any—

She stopped as she rounded the corner to the kitchen. Tom's words halting her in her tracks.

". . . and I don't care what you think it looks like, Mother. Elizabeth is my model . . . "

Pain hit Elizabeth like a sledgehammer. Memories of that day two years ago. The words the same. The situation a mirror of the day he'd denied her, denied them, and broken her heart.

Her fragile little bubble of happiness popped as she saw Tom looking at her, a pained expression on his face.

No, not again. No! She couldn't stand it. Her breath locked in her throat and she tried to tell her feet to move. To get out of there. He was going to do it again, and she didn't think her heart could take it twice.

Tears filled her eyes, the pounding in her ears blocking out whatever Caroline was saying. She could see Tom's mouth moving as he watched her, but no sound was getting through.

And she didn't want to hear. She didn't want to know.

All she wanted was to leave. Run.

But Tom was walking toward her. His dark eyes holding hers, his expression angry.

Finally getting her feet to move, she took a step back as he reached for her. But his hold on her wrist was firm, halting her escape.

"Elizabeth. Don't." Though his expression was dark and she could feel the anger pouring out of him, his words were surprisingly gentle. "Come here, sweetheart."

She shook her head frantically. *Why?* she wanted to ask. *So you can destroy me again?*

As he pulled her against him, his head lowered until his lips brushed against hers, and she closed her eyes as a couple of tears breached the lids, followed by another and another.

And then he straightened, still holding her, and faced his mother.

"The family, the great Danville line," he said mockingly, "can all go get stuffed, Mother."

Elizabeth flinched at Caroline's shuddering indrawn gasp, the look of pure venom on his mother's face as she locked onto her.

"Along with all those vapid, dimwitted, supposedly 'suitable' young ladies you keep throwing at me," Tom continued.

A finger under Elizabeth's chin turned her face until she could look at him, see the smile in his eyes as he looked down at her.

"I'm marrying Elizabeth, if she'll have me after the total bastard I've been to her."

"But you can't!" insisted Caroline in the background. "When your father goes, you'll inherit the title. You'll be Lord Danville." Her tone turned cajoling. "You need someone who will be an asset to you, darling, who can help you, who knows how to act, how to dress . . . " She looked down her nose at Elizabeth and her tone sharpened. "Not some . . . some cheap—"

"Enough!" Tom's roar was so loud it made Elizabeth jerk in his arms. "Don't you ever, *ever,* dare speak to or about Elizabeth that way," he growled.

"But—"

"What I need," he bit out, cutting his mother off as he continued to glare at her, "is someone who loves me. *Me,* plain old Tom. Not the heir to the fucking Danville fortune."

"Thomas!" Caroline gasped in shock.

"I *need,*" he gritted out, trying to bring his anger under control, "the woman I love, Mother. The woman I've always loved. And if you and the family don't like it, you can go and get f—"

Elizabeth reached up quickly to cover his mouth with her fingertips, stopping him from committing a bigger sin than he already had. He looked down at her and she smiled up at him. "I've told you before about saying that, Tom. Besides, I think that's enough bad language out of you for one day," she said and winked. "And yes," she said softly, "I'll marry you."

"Thank heavens for that."

"You'll be sorry, Thomas. Mark my words, this girl will bring you nothing but grief."

Without taking his eyes from Elizabeth, he answered Caroline. "No, Mother, that's where you're dead wrong." He smiled at Elizabeth, the unmistakable sight of his love for her shining in his eyes, making her heart flutter. "She'll bring me nothing but happiness."

He kept holding her until they heard the lift door slam shut as Caroline stormed out, then kissed her. A slow, heady kiss. Lingering. Gentle. Dancing over her lips, his touch so tender, so full of love, it made her heart clench.

"You're sure, Tom?" she asked moments later when the need for air forced them apart. "I don't want you to be sorry later."

"The only thing I'm sorry about, sweetheart, is that I didn't tell her—and you—two years ago." He kissed her again. "And I don't ever want to see that hurt look in your eyes again, knowing that I put it there. I love you, Elizabeth. And I will always love you."

So . . . ABOUT THESE PAINTINGS . . . " Elizabeth asked later as she lay back in the Jacuzzi while Tom sat opposite her, massaging her feet.

"Hmmm? What about them?" With a devilish look, he lifted one foot to nibble on a toe, the tickling causing Elizabeth to giggle and squirm.

"They're not finished, Tom."

"No. Are you suggesting we do that now?" He ran his hand from her foot up her inner leg, teasing the lips of her pussy so that she was soon squirming for an entirely different reason. "I was really hoping we could find something just as . . . *creative,* to amuse ourselves. I'm feeling particularly inspired right now . . . "

"Do you think we should get Richard back to pose some more?" she asked innocently.

Tom's fingers stopped and looked over at Elizabeth.

"No. I don't," he replied, his words slow and distinct.

"But I'm sure there are a few poses we haven't tr—"

Elizabeth's words were cut off as a sharp tug on her feet pulled her under the bubbling water.

As Tom grasped her around the waist, she came up spluttering and laughing, water dripping from her lashes, her waist-length hair streaming behind her to float in the water. He pulled her flush up against him.

"Minx."

"But darling . . . " she teased.

"Trust me, I've seen enough of Richard's bare butt to last me a lifetime. I'll do the rest from memory."

"And what about me?" She leaned toward him to kiss him, draping her arms around his neck as she floated fully onto his lap, straddling his thighs. She gasped as he thrust up and slid his now erect cock inside her waiting channel. Small grunts of pleasure left her lips as he began to stroke. "Do I . . . get drawn from . . . memory too?"

"Sweetheart, I've been drawing you from memory every day for two years. Never, ever again. Besides . . . " He nibbled a line along her neck, making her wriggle with the pleasure streaking through her. "I have a special idea for a portrait of the future Lady Danville to hang in the family gallery. I was thinking a lovely nude . . . "

"Tom!"

"Hmmm?"

"You wouldn't!"

"Um-hmmm."

Irresistible

Beverly Havlir

Prologue

BUTTERFLIES DANCED IN MADISON Cahill's stomach as she waited for the hotel elevator. She couldn't stop smiling, excitement bringing her nerve endings alive. The man next to her gave her a curious glance. She lowered her face, hiding the blush spreading on her cheeks. As she did, she glimpsed her wedding ring. *Mrs. Cahill.* She still couldn't believe that it had been two months since she and Gavin had been married in a quiet, intimate ceremony. But shortly afterward Gavin had to leave on a national book tour, and it'd been close to two weeks since she'd last seen him. Unable to wait any longer, she'd decided to surprise him. He had no idea she was coming. She glanced at her watch. From the time her flight got in to the ride here to the hotel from the airport, she'd timed everything perfectly. It was just a little bit before seven o'clock in the morning.

Gavin was going to have the surprise of his life.

Madison grinned as she stepped into the elevator, her pulse

racing. As the doors closed, she looked at her reflection in the mirrored wall panels. Her dress was perfectly decent, a deep blue creation with simple lines and a hem that fell to her knees. But it was the body-hugging lacy lingerie she'd donned underneath that was the real treat for her husband. It was red and barely there, revealing the naughty smoothness between her thighs. Her hair hung loose, the curls trailing to the middle of her back, just the way he liked it. She'd even worn the sexy "fuck me" shoes that her friends assured her were foolproof. Hot anticipation slid down her spine. Gavin wouldn't know what hit him.

A giggle bubbled up in her throat, earning her another curious look from the man who rode in the elevator with her. Biting her lip, she clutched her purse and the small case that held a change of clothes, resisting the urge to tap her toes in impatience. When Gavin had called last night, he'd confessed that he missed her and couldn't wait to get back home. Madison had decided to fly out on the spur of the moment and visit him. She'd booked a flight, packed a bag and taken a cab to the airport with plenty of time to catch the red-eye to Chicago. Even a few hours spent with Gavin were worth it.

The elevator pinged and stopped on Gavin's floor. Madison got off and walked down the deserted hallway. She quickened her pace, and she'd given up suppressing her silly grin. She couldn't wait to see her husband.

Her smile froze as she turned the corner.

Gavin stood by the door, his hair tousled, naked except for a pair of boxer shorts. He was kissing a sexily dressed blonde woman in the hallway, in plain view of anyone who happened to walk by. Madison gasped, reeling from shock. It was Kimberly, his publicist.

Gavin looked up. "Maddie!" he exclaimed, the stunned astonishment on his face quickly followed by guilt. Kimberly wore a smug expression, her heavily made-up eyes glinting with triumph.

A horrible silence ensued. Madison couldn't move, and stood there clutching her purse like it was an anchor. *Oh God, oh God, oh God.* Gavin was *kissing* another woman. She trembled in disbelief and tried to speak, but no words came out. All she could feel was the searing pain of betrayal. She was instantly catapulted back to the worst nightmare of her childhood, the rainy afternoon when she'd come home with her mother and they'd caught her father in bed with somebody else. Madison choked on a sob. She was her mother all over again, married to an unfaithful man.

Somehow she got her legs to move and she fled back the way she came.

"Maddie, wait. *Goddammit!*"

She ignored Gavin's call to stop, bypassing the elevator, shooting instead for the stairwell. Scalding tears streamed down her face, blurring her vision. Madison stumbled on the steps, her anguished cry echoing in the silence when her case flew from her hand. Hastily retrieving it, she gripped the banister tightly as she navigated the stairs once more. The tightness in her chest didn't diminish, even when she finally emerged into the lobby and ran out the ornate doors of the hotel where she hailed a taxi and quickly got in.

"The airport, please." As soon as she wiped away her tears, more fell down her cheeks. She gazed blindly at the passing scenery. Her mind was filled with the heart-wrenching image of a barely dressed Gavin kissing another woman, looking like he'd just gotten out of bed. It was akin to a knife sinking into her heart over and over, stabbing into the same spot, wounding her again and again.

"Everything all right, miss?" the driver asked, looking at her through the rearview mirror.

"No," she whispered.

The elderly man shook his head, his dark eyes filled with compassion. "Sometimes things are not as bad as we think they are."

Yes, they are. Madison felt sick, hollow and empty inside, desperate to get as far away from Gavin as possible. The taxi had barely pulled to a stop at the busy departure area of the airport before she scrambled out of the car, pausing briefly to toss some bills on the front seat before running inside the terminal with her case.

"Miss, this is too much—" The automatic doors closed, cutting off the rest of the cab driver's words.

Madison wiped away more tears while she booked a seat on the next flight back to L.A., which was scheduled to leave shortly. Ignoring the speculative light in the airline employee's gaze, she paid for the ticket and sought a deserted corner against the plateglass window. As she waited to board, she called her friend Amanda. "It's me." Madison smothered a soft sob. *Damn it. Why couldn't she stop crying?* "I-I'm on my way back. Can you pick me up from the airport?" She rattled off her flight number and arrival time.

"You're coming back already? What's wrong, Maddie?" Amanda asked, concern in her voice.

She gulped hard. "I-I can't talk right now. Just be there, okay? And . . . if Gavin calls you, tell him you don't know where I am." She hung up, clutching the cell phone tightly. It rang immediately. A glance at the screen revealed the caller. *Gavin.* She ignored it, letting it go to voice mail. A few moments later, it rang again. Unable to stand the incessant ringing, she turned it off and pushed it to the bottom of her purse.

When Madison arrived back in Los Angeles, her two best friends, Amanda and Kylie, were waiting for her at the airport. They took one look at her tear-streaked face and bundled her in the car and drove her to Amanda's apartment.

"What happened, Maddie?" Kylie asked.

The question triggered more of the tears she'd thought were finally under control. Pain hit her anew when she told them what happened. "I was so stupid. I trusted him." Madison gave a choked, self-deprecating laugh. "Before we were married, the only thing I asked of Gavin was fidelity. I trusted him not to hurt me that way." She wrung her hands tightly. "He said he would never hurt me. He lied."

Amanda rubbed her back soothingly. "Have you talked to him?"

Madison shook her head. "What I saw was clear enough."

"He's your husband, Maddie," Kylie countered quietly. "Don't you think he deserves the chance to explain?"

"Explain what? Explain how he came to be standing half naked at his hotel door kissing another woman?"

"Maybe things aren't what they seem." Amanda sighed. "Talk to him. He called us both several times looking for you."

"Did you tell him I was coming here?" Madison asked sharply.

Amanda shook her head. "Of course not. You expressly forbade me from letting him know you were here."

"I still think you should talk to Gavin, Maddie," Kylie urged in gentle tones. "You need to clear things up."

Madison stood by the window, blind to the beauty of the clear Southern California day or the white-capped waves that hit the shore. "I can't," she whispered brokenly. "You both know my father cheated on my mom time and time again. And each time was more painful than the last. I don't want to live that life again."

"What if you're wrong?" Kylie went over to Madison and put an arm around her shoulder. "I think you should give him a chance to explain."

An incredible sense of loss weighed her down. "It's over."

"Just like that?" Amanda asked gently. "Is it that easy to let Gavin go?"

God no. It was tearing her apart. "I have to." Madison wrapped her arms around her middle, feeling cold and empty. The fear that she'd carried with her all her life rose up to her throat, threatening to suffocate her. "I don't want to end up like my mother. I just can't."

"Gavin sounds miserable. He's going crazy looking for you all over the place. Would you please just talk to him?" Kylie entreated.

Unlike her mother, Madison knew when to cut her losses and wipe the slate clean. She wouldn't cling to a marriage hoping that things would turn around. As a young girl, she'd once overheard her grandmother tearing into her mom, her contemptuous words echoing in the silent house. *"You're a fool, Janice, to stick around waiting for Peter to change his philandering ways. Once a cheater, always a cheater. You're a damn fool!"*

Those harsh, unforgiving words had stuck with Madison. They carved a place in her young heart, planting the fear that she'd someday end up like her mother, clinging to a husband who broke her trust over and over again. The determination to avoid the same bitter fate had been rooted in her mind from that day on. Leaving Gavin was the right thing to do.

"Maddie?" Amanda prompted softly.

Sadness overwhelmed her. "My marriage is over." She absorbed the pain that sliced into her with those words. "It's over."

1

A WEEK LATER, AFTER MAKING sure Gavin was nowhere around, Madison went back to the house they'd shared and gathered her few belongings. She left her rings—left *everything* he'd ever given her—and only took what was hers to begin with. Gavin had been searching for her, calling her friends, hanging out at the coffee shop. She'd moved in with Amanda, needing the time away. She couldn't hide from Gavin forever, but she wasn't ready to face him yet.

Later on that day, with some help from her friends, Madison converted the empty apartment space above her coffee shop into her new home. "It's a little small, but it'll do."

Amanda dropped down on the love seat by the window, putting her feet up on the dark cherry coffee table in front of her. "You need to get a *real* apartment, not this dinky one above the shop. You'll never get away from work."

Madison popped open a soda. "This will do just fine. I don't even have to drive to work. All I need to do is go down a flight of stairs and, voilà, I'm there." She looked at Amanda and Kylie. "Thanks for helping me fix the place up."

Amanda grinned. "Thank Kylie's flirting, you mean. The delivery guys brought up not only your new bed but also all the other furniture that we'd have had to carry up the stairs."

Kylie laughed, tossing her hair over her shoulder. "It was nothing. A little wink, a little swing of my ass, and they were putty in my hands."

Madison chuckled. With her strawberry blonde hair and sparkling blue eyes, Kylie had always drawn attention. "You're incorrigible."

Her friend shrugged. "It was no big deal. The dark-haired guy was kinda cute too."

"Not again." Amanda groaned. "What happened to last week's eye candy?"

"Derek is *so* five minutes ago. Time to move on, ladies. Speaking of moving on," Kylie said, raising an eyebrow in Madison's direction. "Are you one hundred percent sure about what you're doing?"

She pasted a smile on her face. "Absolutely."

"He'll show up here. You know that, right?" Amanda pointed out.

"I can't put it off any longer. I'm ready to face him." Madison mentally crossed her fingers, hoping that when that time came, she'd be able to handle it.

"He won't give up," Kylie added.

"Our marriage is over."

"If it was somebody else, I'd believe it," Kylie countered dryly. "But you, Maddie? You're not the type to bounce back easily from this."

"I'm not one of your patients, Kylie." Madison winced as her voice cracked midsentence. She covered it up with a brief laugh. "Please don't analyze me."

"I'm just concerned about you. I know how much you loved Gavin." Kylie put an arm around Madison's shoulders. "If you ever need anybody to talk to, just let me know. The first session's on me." Despite the teasing tone, Madison knew the offer was genuine.

"Are you *sure* you'll be fine, Maddie?" Amanda asked quietly.

Their concern was touching and it nearly drove Madison to tears. *Again.* It seemed these days she cried at the smallest things. "I'll be fine. Don't worry about me. I have the coffee shop to keep me busy, and now I have my own place, instead of having to crash at Amanda's apartment." She infused her tone with a lightness she was far from feeling. "It's a brand-new start, girls. The start of a new life."

Madison uttered those words again later that evening when she was finally alone. Her clothes now hung in the closet and she'd put her computer and desk in one corner, along with all her files and accounting books for the coffee shop. She was doing fine until she plugged in a new answering machine and recorded a message.

"You've reached Madison. I'm not here to take your call, but please leave a—" And just like that, she couldn't go on. Her finger shook on the record button. The realization that she was alone hit her with the force of a hurricane. Gavin was gone from her life.

Madison sobbed as she dropped into her chair. Pain once again cut through her, inflicting new wounds, opening old ones. Tears fell on some papers spread out on her desk. Her gaze landed on the change of address form she'd planned to take to the post office tomorrow. Inexplicably, it made her cry more.

Everywhere she looked, there were stark reminders that Gavin was no longer a part of her life. He wouldn't be there to cuddle her at night, would no longer wake her up with kisses and fresh-brewed coffee.

Gavin had broken her heart and for that, she could never forgive him.

A knock sounded on the door. Wiping away her tears, she looked through the peephole. Her stomach sank as she pulled open the door. "Mom."

Janice Price swept into the room without waiting for an invitation. "I won't say I told you so. I'm sure you've said that to yourself over and over."

Madison closed the door, trying to hold back her sniffles. "I'm really not in the mood for this right now, Mom. I'm tired and—"

"Were you even going to tell me you'd left him?" Janice demanded. "I found out from Stacy, your waitress downstairs, when I stopped by for coffee tonight!"

"You had no right to do that. My personal life is nobody's business but mine."

"That's the only way I find out anything about you, Madison." Her mother's tone was accusatory. "Ever since you married Gavin, you've kept me out of your life."

Maddie closed her eyes and rubbed her forehead, wishing she hadn't answered the door. "Can you blame me? You never liked him. You couldn't even wait until after the wedding before you predicted that my marriage wouldn't last."

Janice lifted her chin, not the least bit apologetic. "Was I wrong?"

"Does it make you happy that you were right, Mom?" Madison asked, resigned to her mother's venomous bitterness.

Janice had the grace to flush. "Of course not. I just wished you'd listened to me. I mean, you hardly knew Gavin before you up and married him. Marry in haste, repent at leisure and all that."

Madison winced, tempted to give in to the urge to cover her ears and drown out her mother's words.

"Besides, I knew right away what kind of man Gavin was. He's not the type to be satisfied with just one woman."

The words shot straight to Madison's heart. Her mother just couldn't resist pointing that out. It was like rubbing salt into an already festering wound. "I'm tired, Mom."

"I just want you to know that I think you're doing the right thing. Cut your ties with him now while you can. Don't be like me, Madison. Don't wait until it's too late," she said firmly.

Madison lowered her eyes, not bothering to respond. Her mother was a disillusioned, unhappy woman who harbored a deep distrust of men because of what she'd endured in her marriage.

"Is there anything I can do?" Janice asked. "Do you need anything?"

Yeah, a new heart. "I just need time to be alone."

"I care about you, Madison." Her mother's voice softened. "You may not agree with everything I say or do, but you're my daughter and I love you." She marched to the door. "Trust me, honey. It's better to suffer now and get it over with, rather than prolong the pain and suffer for the rest of your life. Don't be like me." With that final comment, she left.

With her mother's words still ringing in her ears, Madison lay down on her new bed. She pulled a pillow close to her and buried her face in the soft folds, once again letting her tears flow, hoping it would ease the pain in her heart. Somehow, she doubted it.

★ ★ ★

GAVIN SHOWED UP THE next day.

Madison's knees nearly buckled and she gripped the door for support. "W-what are you doing here?"

"I'm here to take you home."

"I'm not coming back."

Gavin raked a hand through his thick, dark hair. "Maddie, don't do this. I can't lose you."

She flinched at the deep voice she'd once loved to hear. How many times had she lain on his chest, simply listening to him talk? "It's too late. You should've thought of that before you cheated on me."

His nostrils flared. "I didn't cheat on you."

"You were kissing her right outside your hotel room, Gavin." The memory brought forth more anguish. She was *not* going to cry. "You were nearly naked."

"I just woke up," he bit out tightly. A muscle at his jaw ticked and he pulled in a deep breath. "I sleep naked. You *know* that."

Madison quivered in anger as she scoffed at his statement. "And the kissing part?"

"Maddie, *she* kissed *me*. Not the other way around."

She turned away, rubbing a hand over her heart, trying to stem the tide of pain that was threatening to consume her. "And even though you outweigh her by over a hundred pounds, you just couldn't stop her, right?" She squeezed her eyes shut. "Just stop it, Gavin. I don't want to hear any more of your lies."

"What do I have to do to make you believe me?" he growled in frustration. He stood right behind her, so close that she could feel the heat emanating from his body. "I have *no* reason to stray from your bed."

Madison whirled around and confronted him. "*I know,*
Gavin. I know because I did everything you wanted me to do
in that bedroom. *Everything.*" She blinked back the tears. "I gave
you my heart."

"Then why would I turn to another woman, Maddie?"

"I don't know." Her voice broke. "You tell me."

Gavin looked at her earnestly, taking her hands in his. "This
is all just a misunderstanding. Come home, babe. We can work
this out."

She pulled away. "You hurt me."

"You think I'm not hurting right now?" he countered gruffly.
"You don't think it hurts to come home and find you gone?
That you trust me so little you won't believe me when I tell you
I'm not lying?"

Madison was too steeped in her pain to listen. "I told you
that infidelity was the one thing guaranteed to drive me away,
Gavin."

"Damn it, Maddie—"

"I want a divorce." The words hung in the thick atmosphere.

Gavin paled. "*What?*"

"I want a divorce," she repeated dully.

"No!"

"I-I can't trust you anymore. I should have listened when
people told me we didn't know each other well enough to get
married."

"Who said that? Your mother? She never liked me, Maddie."

"But she turned out to be right." Madison tried to keep the
bitterness from her voice, but she couldn't. "Look at what happened to us."

Gavin held her tight. "I'm your husband. You should believe
me."

Misery engulfed her. "It was a mistake to get married."

"Not for me. I knew I wanted to marry you the moment I saw you." His voice rang with conviction.

"You wanted to sleep with me, you mean."

"You felt the same way." He pulled her close, ignoring her resistance, wrapping his arms tight around her. "There's more than just lust between us, Maddie. We both know that."

She wiggled out of his arms. It hurt too much to let him hold her, knowing that he'd gone to another woman. "It's too late. I want a divorce, Gavin."

A muscle in his jaw ticked. "No fucking way."

"You don't have a choice."

His eyes flashed angrily. "I didn't cheat on you."

Madison trembled, close to the breaking point. "Please, stop. Just . . . stop."

"I'm not lying," he growled. "Don't you care enough about us to want to know the truth?"

Madison turned away. When she'd met Gavin, she had a small inkling of the kind of life he led. Successful and handsome, his social life had been featured in multiple magazines. What had made her think she could keep him satisfied when there were a number of women ready and willing to please him? She was just a simple coffee shop owner, not a glamorous social butterfly who would willingly look the other way while her husband played around. Marrying Gavin had been a dream, a temporary one. The words her mother said on her wedding day echoed in Madison's mind. *Don't be a fool. I knew from the moment I met him that Gavin is not the type who'd be satisfied with just one woman. Men like him never are.*

"Goddammit, Maddie. Don't do this."

Madison clutched at a nearby chair and forced herself to

confront him. "We were never meant to be together, Gavin. Let's just accept that."

Anger emanated from every inch of his six-foot-four frame. "Bullshit. We have something, Maddie. Don't just throw it all away."

She couldn't hold back the tears anymore. "Don't you see? We don't have anything in common. We . . . we don't even know each other that well. It was too soon. We shouldn't have gotten married."

"Is that what you really think? That getting a divorce is the best thing to do?"

"Yes," she choked out. In the next moment, she gasped as he pulled her into his arms. Gavin clamped his lips over hers, thrusting his tongue inside her mouth. Madison resisted, feebly struggling against his hold, desperately holding back the response that he could arouse with little effort. The kiss turned persuasive, carnal. *No fair.* Her thoughts scattered, her mind became fuzzy. A tidal wave of hunger swept over her, wiping away all thoughts of resistance.

He ground his hips against hers. "Only you can make me feel this way, Maddie. I ache for you. I can't sleep at night." Her tank top was no obstacle to the questing fingers that pushed it out of the way. Like a starving man, Gavin suckled her nipple, pulling on her deeply.

Madison felt the jolt directly to her sex. She rubbed against him, as much a slave to the need as he was. Gavin slipped a hand under the elastic waistband of her shorts, wasting no time, plunging into the wetness of her pussy. She gasped, knowing she should stop him before it got any further. But her body refused to follow her mind's instructions. When Gavin laid her on the couch and disposed of her shorts, she remained pliant.

His eyes gleamed hotly. "You're mine, Maddie. You'll *always* be mine." Like a fine-tuned instrument, he played her body with consummate skill, arousing a need only he could assuage.

Tingles of electricity raced up and down her skin. "Th-this is wrong," she moaned. Her words were at odds with the way her thighs splayed open for his touch, primed and waiting.

He squeezed her nipples. "Come home with me."

Her eyes fluttered at the sharp pleasure and pain that reverberated in her flesh. "N-no," she managed to gasp.

"I didn't cheat on you." He licked her from the top of her slit to her ass, lingering wickedly to rim the small ring of muscles there. Madison gasped. "I didn't lie." He buried his face in her soaked folds and ate her hungrily. Within moments, she was panting, racing toward that one little place that could offer her oblivion, even if only for a short while.

"Gavin . . . " Her plea turned into shock as he abruptly stopped.

"Do you believe me, Maddie?"

Her body quivered with need. "Why are you doing this?"

"I want you to trust me. I want you to let me explain what really happened that day, and most of all, I want you to come home, Maddie. But you have to learn to trust me."

A fat tear rolled down her cheek. "What's the point, Gavin? I saw you. I was there."

"You *thought* you saw me cheating, but it's not true," he insisted, frustration ringing in his voice. "I've given you the space I thought you needed. But enough is enough. I want you to come home." His hot gaze swept over her. "We can make this marriage work."

"You broke my trust. I-I can't live with that. Can't you see?"

His face hardened into an angry mask. "So what are you

telling me? It's over? Just like that? Tell me, Maddie. Tell me to my face that we're over."

Her heart splintered into a million tiny pieces. "It's over."

"What about this?" His hand swept over her. "You fell into my arms like you always do. You were as hungry for me as I was for you. Can you turn your back on that?"

"Yes." Forcing that lie from her lips was the hardest thing she'd ever done.

Gavin was silent for so long that Madison finally raised her eyes to look at him. His dark eyes were dull and lifeless. "I'm not going to beg, Maddie. I'm not going to plead that you give us another chance, that you believe me when I tell you I didn't cheat on you." The distant, icy tone underscored the cold fury etched in his handsome features. "I can't force you to do what I want. Just remember what you're throwing away here." He left, closing the door softly behind him with a decisive click.

He was gone. Alone, Madison was consumed by a gnawing emptiness inside. She rocked on the couch, wrapping her arms around her middle. Hot, unfulfilled need washed over her. She longed for his touch, ached for the release that he could give her. But at what price?

Oh Gavin. She began to weep for what could have been, for the love she still felt for him, for their life together that had been abruptly cut short. If only he hadn't cheated. *If only.*

"JESUS, WHAT THE HELL happened?"

Gavin opened his eyes and blinked, trying to focus. "Wes?"

Wesley Halverson swept empty liquor bottles out of the way

before hefting him into a sitting position on the couch. "You're drunk out of your mind."

Gavin groaned and cradled his head in his hands. "*Was* drunk. Last night. What time is it?"

"It's Monday morning, nine o'clock," Wes drawled, taking the chair across from him. "What's going on, man?"

"Monday?" Gavin repeated, incredulous. "Christ."

"Judging from the number of bottles scattered around here, either you had one hell of a party and I wasn't invited or there's something going on here that you need to tell me about."

Gavin rubbed his face. His eyes felt gritty and his mouth felt like it was full of cotton. "What are you doing here?"

"I've been calling you since yesterday. When you didn't answer, I got concerned." Wesley frowned. "What the hell is going on?"

"I got drunk."

Wesley snorted. "That much is obvious."

Gavin slumped against the couch. "Maddie left me."

"Say that again?"

"She left me." Without glossing over any details, Gavin told him the whole story. "I didn't expect her to show up like that. And *damn* Kimberly for getting me into this mess in the first place."

"That woman was trouble from day one," Wesley grumbled. "All she saw were dollar signs on you."

Gavin shut his eyes tightly. He didn't give a fuck about Kimberly. "Maddie wants a divorce."

"Shit. Did you try to explain?"

"Maddie has . . . trust issues. I tried but she won't listen. She's convinced I cheated on her." Anger and frustration knotted inside his chest. "I *didn't* cheat on her, Wes. Why won't she believe me?" He clenched his fists. "I love her. I had no reason to even look at another woman. Why can't she see that?"

Wesley sighed. "I believe you. In all the years I've known you, I've never seen you act this way over a woman."

Gavin raked his fingers through his hair. Maddie was different from all the other women he'd known. From the moment they met, she'd made him feel things he'd never felt before. "This whole thing has got me so wired. I'm her husband. She *should* trust me."

"Yeah, but if she has trust issues like you said . . . well . . . it's just not easy."

"Fuck easy," Gavin bit out, furious. "She told me she wants a divorce. Just like that." He snapped his fingers. "She'll throw everything away and not even try to work things out."

"Gavin, man, anger isn't going to help you right now."

Gavin pushed off the couch and stalked to the window. "But I am angry, Wes. I married *her.* I promised to love, cherish and honor *her* for the rest of our lives. Doesn't that count for anything?" He gritted his teeth. "If Maddie thinks I'm going to beg her to come back, she's dead wrong. I'm done with this whole fucking mess."

Anger and resentment flowed through him, hardening his resolve. Gavin was sick of defending himself. He closed his eyes, the stinging pain of heartache slamming into him for the first time in his life. Madison had been the only woman who'd cut a path straight to his soul. Every fiber of his being was against letting her go. If she truly loved him, she wouldn't be so quick to resort to divorce. If it was so easy for her to throw away their marriage, then their relationship truly was over.

2

Wesley stared at Gavin across the length of his desk. "You look like shit." Gavin shifted on the plush, oversize leather chair. "Gee, thanks. Nice to see you too, Wes."

"What the hell have you been doing?"

"Working," he answered curtly. Too restless to sit, Gavin stalked to the window. The view from Wesley's downtown law office was impressive, the beautiful skyline bathed in bright Southern California sunshine. But he hardly noticed it. Instead, he gazed at his reflection in the tinted glass. Wes was right. He did look like shit. In the month since Maddie had left him, he'd been plagued by insomnia and his appetite was shot. Worse, his latest manuscript was due in a month and he hadn't written anything worth a damn.

"I think you need help."

Gavin scoffed at that. He ran a hand through his hair and looked over his shoulder at the man who was his best friend as well as his lawyer. "I assume there's a reason why you wanted me to come here today? Because I assure you, I'm not in the mood for a sermon right now."

Wesley frowned. "Have you had lunch? I can have Marie get you something from the deli downstairs."

His stomach roiled at the thought of food. "No thanks."

"Are you trying to kill yourself?"

If he was, it wasn't working. "That would probably be a good idea," he muttered. "But no, as it happens, I'm not."

"This self-pity bullshit has got to stop."

Gavin narrowed his eyes. "Fuck you. I don't need this. I'm outta here." He strode to the door.

"She filed for divorce."

He froze, his mind going blank. He turned around slowly. *"What did you say?"*

Wesley exhaled loudly and stood up, jamming his hands in his pants pockets. "Maddie filed for divorce. I got the papers yesterday from her lawyer."

Cold fury welled up in Gavin's chest. *She actually went through with it. She actually filed for divorce.* Madison was really done with him, done with their marriage. He pulled in a deep breath, desperately trying to come to terms with it. He swallowed the lump in his throat and forced the word past his lips. "Fine."

"What?" Wesley asked, clearly shocked. "Just like that?"

"What do you want me to say? That I'll fight it? That I'll never give her a divorce?" Gavin shook his head. "If she wants to get out of this marriage, fine. I'll give her a fucking divorce."

"You're going to let Maddie go?"

Pain sliced into his heart. "I don't have a choice, do I?"

"Keep telling yourself that, maybe you'll believe it," Wesley muttered.

"What do you want me to do, Wes? Force myself on her?

Hell no. I've never loved another woman the way I love her. If she wants to end our marriage, then so be it. I can't be with a woman who's incapable of trusting me."

"Gavin—"

He raised a hand. "I won't fight it. Give her whatever she wants."

"Alimony?"

"Yeah." God, he needed a stiff drink, even though alcohol didn't really solve anything. He could drink himself to oblivion, much like he'd been doing lately, but it only masked the pain. It never took it away. What he needed was to move on. Get on with his life.

"*Whatever* she wants?" Wesley persisted.

"Whatever she wants. Give her the fucking divorce, give her half my money. Hell, she can have all of it. I really don't care anymore."

"Is this what you really want?"

"What I want doesn't seem to matter."

"You don't want to try to talk to her again? One more time?"

He pulled in a shaky breath. "It's over."

For a moment, Wesley looked as if he would argue some more but finally he nodded. "All right. I'll arrange a meeting to iron out the details. You'll have to be present, of course."

At the thought of seeing Madison once more, his pulse jumped. It had been thirty-six days, five hours and—he glanced at his watch—twenty-eight minutes since he'd last seen Maddie, naked and splayed on the couch, trembling beneath his hands. It had taken all of his strength to walk out the door. Gavin shook his head. "No."

"No?" Wesley echoed in disbelief.

"I don't want to see her." Coming face-to-face with Maddie

while they finalized the dissolution of their marriage would be the last straw. To see her and know that she wasn't his anymore would surely be the blow that finally killed him. No. It was better that they didn't see each other. Wipe the slate clean and move on. "I don't want to see her again."

WHEN THE SUN PEEKED THROUGH the early morning clouds and began to cast a warm glow over the still-quiet city, Madison gave up trying to sleep and got out of bed. Today was *the* day. At ten o'clock sharp, she, accompanied by her lawyer, was scheduled to meet with Gavin and his lawyer to discuss their divorce.

Divorce. Her heart tripped over the word. It was hard to accept that her marriage was coming to an end. Had it really been over a month since she'd left Gavin? It seemed longer.

After taking a shower and drying her hair, she applied her makeup carefully. *I'll be fine. I'll recover.* After all, she was only twenty-eight, plenty of time left to find a trustworthy man to fall in love with and have a family. It was unfortunate that Gavin wasn't that man.

Walking to her closet, Madison tried to decide what to wear. This was the first time she'd see him again after he'd left her apartment. One part of her wanted to blow him away and remind him of what he'd lost. The other part mocked her for caring. *Damn him.* He was still tying her in knots.

Deciding on an ultraconservative black suit, she pulled it out and laid it on the bed. The jacket buttoned down the front and the skirt reached exactly to her knees. It had the right tone of unapproachable formality she wanted to convey. Madison sat down in front of her dresser and ignored the quick twinge of pain in her heart. Too late for regrets.

Gathering her thick hair into a twist at her nape, she secured it with a clip and smoothed down the sides. She slipped her feet into black, chunky-heeled pumps before looking at her reflection in the mirror. The effect was severe, and not in the least sexy. Good. That's what she wanted.

The coffee shop was full but not crowded when she came down from her apartment. Madison nodded to Kelly, one of her part-time employees, and headed to a table in the back where her lawyer sat waiting for her.

"Good morning, Dana."

Dana Hightower looked up from the notes she'd spread out on the table and gave her a smile. "How are you feeling today? Ready for the meeting?"

"Ready as I'll ever be. I want to get this over with."

Dana gathered all the papers together before stuffing them into her briefcase. "I'll try to make this as painless as possible. Shall we?" Madison followed her out to the car, thinking that the woman's petite frame and pretty features were totally at odds with her reputation as a shark in the courtroom, with a long list of divorce cases she'd successfully represented.

"We have to discuss a settlement for you." Dana pulled out smoothly into traffic. "Your husband has considerable assets."

"I don't want his money," Madison enunciated carefully. "I'm not asking for anything."

"You shouldn't be so quick in making these decisions," her lawyer chided gently. "Gavin Cahill is worth a lot of money."

"I don't want anything."

"Not even the house? A nice financial settlement?"

Madison shook her head firmly. "Nothing."

"You never know when you might need it," Dana reminded her in a mild voice.

She breathed deeply. "I'm doing fine. My coffee shop is all I need."

"Then what is it you *do* want?"

"I just want a divorce so I can get on with my life." Saying the words out loud always resulted in a familiar twinge in her heart. Would the pain ever go away? With time, maybe. And she had nothing but time at this point. For her to be able to start another chapter of her life, she had to close the book on her disastrous marriage. She needed to put Gavin completely out of her life . . . forever.

Dana pulled into the underground parking garage of the high-rise building that housed Gavin's lawyer's office. They rode in silence as the elevator swiftly rose to the fortieth floor. Madison wiped her damp palms down the sides of her skirt. Her heart was starting to beat erratically.

"Remember," Dana reminded her in a low voice, "let me do the talking, okay?"

"Not a problem." Just being here tied her stomach in knots.

The law offices of Halverson & Auburn occupied the entire floor of the building. The receptionist was a stylish blonde who wore fashionable eyeglasses and a headset.

Dana approached her. "Hello. We're here to see Mr. Halverson."

The young woman pressed a button on the console, talking in low tones before she addressed them once more. "Somebody will be out to see you in a moment."

While they waited, Madison glanced around the plush

reception area. She'd met Wesley on numerous occasions, but had never been to his office. She fought the urge to fidget. She tried to relax, half anticipating, half dreading seeing Gavin once more.

A woman dressed in a cream-colored suit ushered them into a large conference room furnished with a long, polished table and cushioned chairs.

Taking the seat next to Dana, Madison tried to quiet the butterflies flitting around her stomach. She pulled in a couple of deep breaths. The door opened and a man came in dressed in an impeccable gray suit with a neat tie, a thick file folder in hand. Madison schooled her face into a polite mask. Wesley Halverson was a handsome man with sun-lightened hair and a charming smile.

"Ladies," Wesley greeted them warmly. He extended a hand out to Dana. "Wesley Halverson." Then he turned to Madison. "Hello, Maddie."

Madison nodded, unable to muster a smile. "Wesley."

He put the files down on the table and sat. Dana frowned. "Where is your client, Mr. Halverson?"

"Mr. Cahill won't be able to make it today."

Madison clamped her lips together. *He couldn't even be bothered to show up.* He probably didn't want to see her. Now, why should that thought hurt? She should be relieved that she didn't have to face him today instead of being disappointed.

Her attorney was none too pleased. "I thought we agreed that all parties would be here today to discuss the dissolution of this marriage. How are we supposed to do that if your client is not here, Mr. Halverson?"

"Call me Wesley, please." His eyes sought out Madison's. "Gavin is under a very tight deadline, Maddie. There was just no way he could be here today." His eyes slid to Dana. "As to the matter of this divorce, my client is prepared to cooperate and does not intend to fight it."

He does not intend to fight it. The words swam in Madison's head. She pulled in a deep breath in an attempt to ease the tightness in her chest. That was good, right? So why did she have the sudden urge to weep?

"All right. Let's proceed." Dana opened the file in front of her and perused the papers.

Wesley spoke first. "My client is willing to pay alimony, whatever amount your client wishes."

That took Madison by surprise. Why would Gavin do that? To soothe his guilty conscience? "I don't want—"

"Madison," Dana warned softly. She nodded to Wesley. "Go on."

"Gavin is also willing to sign over the deed to the house in Pacific Palisades." As Madison sputtered in denial, Wesley looked at her directly. "He wants you taken care of."

Dana smiled. "All right, then." She picked up a pen and began to write.

"No. I won't *accept* anything from him," Madison declared firmly. "I just want a divorce." Dana looked at her in disbelief but Madison stood her ground. "Nothing else. And I won't change my mind about that."

Wesley frowned. "But Gavin wants to—"

"What he wants no longer matters here," she interrupted firmly.

"Madison, I'd like to remind you that under the laws of the state, you're entitled to half of your husband's assets." Dana's voice was mild but the message was clear. She'd be a fool not to take what Gavin was giving her.

"No, Dana. That's final."

Her lawyer pursed her lips before she relented. "Whatever you say."

As Dana and Wesley discussed the other legalities of the divorce, Madison tuned them out. Money, or the fact that Gavin had a lot of it, had never mattered to her. She'd have given everything she owned to be able to go back to the early days of their brief marriage. Their honeymoon had been beautiful and unforgettable, full of love and laughter. They'd talked about having children in the near future, maybe four, even five. Gavin had wanted a big family and she'd agreed, weaving daydreams of little children running and playing around the house.

Madison swallowed, blinking back sudden tears. It was foolish to long for those times. Soon her marriage would be dissolved forever. The anger that she'd initially felt at Gavin's betrayal was gone. In its place was pain and regret.

When the two lawyers wrapped up their discussion, Madison breathed a sigh of relief. Dana extended her hand to Wesley. "I'll send you the final papers for your client to sign."

As they shook hands, Madison made her way to the door. She needed to get out of there before she completely broke down and made a fool of herself.

"Maddie?"

"Yes?"

Wes pulled her into a hug. "Good luck."

"Thanks," she whispered, closing her eyes for a moment. Fearing she might burst into tears, she opened the door and hurried outside, past the receptionist, heading directly to the elevator. She was barely aware of Dana getting into the car with her.

"Are you all right?" Dana asked, her voice tinged with concern.

No. "Yeah, I'm okay." But even to her ears, the words rang hollow. She didn't have Gavin anymore. She was never going to be fine. Ever.

GAVIN WATCHED MADISON THROUGH the two-way mirror in Wesley's office, hungrily tracing the features of her face, lingering on the full, pouty lips that never failed to stir him. He'd tried to stay away but he couldn't. When he had shown up earlier today, Wesley had been surprised. But Gavin didn't trust himself enough to come face-to-face with Maddie. He was starving, famished for her. Up close, he might have been tempted to touch. This was safer. He just wanted to see his wife again.

Except she wouldn't be his wife for much longer.

He took in her appearance, examining the beautiful, thick hair she'd twisted into a knot at her nape. She knew damn well he didn't like it when she put up her hair like that. And that suit. He was sure she'd come here dressed in that severe schoolmarm look expressly to tick him off. It'd had the opposite effect.

The suit jacket couldn't contain those magnificent breasts of hers. Though she'd buttoned the thing up to her neck, her breasts thrust tightly against the soft material. His imagination ran riot, bringing to mind visions of her generous flesh cupped softly in a lace bra. His cock stirred to life, lengthening under the denim, making his jeans damn uncomfortable.

When she stood up, his eyes caressed her rounded hips, wishing she would turn around so he could see her ass pushing softly against her skirt. The modest skirt couldn't even begin to disguise her shapely legs. And what was up with those ugly shoes? He knew she had a preference for strappy, high-heeled, drive-a-man-crazy stilettos. Did she think if she dressed down she would be undesirable to him? She could be dressed in a burlap bag and she'd still give him a hard-on.

Madison may have broken his heart but she still could make him want her like he wanted no other woman.

Gavin clenched his fists. God, it had been too damn long since he'd held her in his arms. It was all he could do not to burst into that conference room, push her against the wall and fuck her—to hell with the spectators. His mouth watered as he followed her progress to the door until he couldn't see her anymore.

Wesley walked in. "You should have joined us."

He slipped his hands inside his pockets. "She's as beautiful as ever."

Wesley shook his head. "Man, you're still lovesick. Why the hell are you divorcing her?"

He'd asked himself that question many times. He was no closer to an answer now. "It's for the best."

"I never thought I'd see the day when you just gave up without a fight. That's not the best friend I grew up with." Wesley threw him a challenging stare. "The Gavin I knew would march over to Maddie's apartment, fuck her brains out and then tell her hell would freeze over before he'd give her a divorce."

I'd still love to fuck her brains out. At that thought, heat swirled in his belly. His wife was the hottest woman he'd ever had in his bed. "Can't beat a dead horse, Wes."

"I still think you gave up too easily." When Gavin didn't answer, Wesley shrugged. "Look, if there's truly no hope left for you and Maddie, then maybe we should go out tonight. Grab a drink or something. We could go to a bar, pick up a woman and get you laid. Maybe that's just what you need."

"Been there, done that," he muttered. He'd gone out, fully

intending to bring a woman home to sink into and forget his wife, even for a little while. When that had failed, he'd called up an ex who'd always made it clear she was available to him, whenever he wanted. He'd gotten as far as kissing her, then . . . nothing. He didn't get hard. And after the same thing happened again with a different woman, he'd given up. He just couldn't muster any enthusiasm.

But one look at Maddie and his cock had snapped to attention, ready to play, eager for her pussy. Pathetic, that's what he was. *Fucking pathetic*.

Gavin straightened his shoulders, suddenly needing to get far away from everything. "I'm going up to the cabin. Just send me the papers to sign when you get them."

"How long are you gonna be there?"

"I don't know." He shrugged carelessly. "As long I need to be there, I suppose." The cabin in the mountains had always been the one place where he could go to think, where he could find peace of mind. It was also where he and Maddie had shared some of their happiest moments.

It was time to exorcise her ghost from his life.

He'd start there and work his way up, until all traces of Madison were gone and he could finally move on.

AMANDA WALKED THROUGH THE DOOR and pointedly eyed the wide array of pots and bowls littering the kitchen counter in Madison's apartment. "All right. What's the emergency, Maddie?"

Kylie, who sat on a bar stool, snickered behind the can of soda she held to her lips.

Madison glared at Kylie and kept on stirring cake batter. "What makes you think there's an emergency?"

"Because you cook and bake in massive quantities when something is bothering you," Amanda supplied dryly, running her fingertip over the rim of the bowl, swiping some of the delicious mixture.

Maddie gave a snort and swatted Amanda's hand away. "I invite you two over for a home-cooked meal and this is the thanks I get?"

Kylie grinned. "I'm glad you don't have too many of these crisis episodes, Maddie. My hips can't take it."

"I just felt like cooking, that's all."

"Uh-huh," Amanda mocked over another mouthful of batter. "Kylie, remember that time she broke up with Randy Nielsen right after the prom?"

"Yup. That was the first time she cooked us a four-course meal. There was so much food left over that I took some home and told my mom I made it to impress her."

Amanda laughed. "And remember when she didn't know how to break up with Bill? You know, the one with the tragically short tongue?"

Kylie burst out laughing. "Who could forget that? He couldn't . . . ah . . . perform certain things well because of that particular handicap." She gave a dramatic sigh. "Too bad. If not for that, he was an okay guy."

Madison rolled her eyes and checked the pot roast.

"Exactly," Amanda quipped. "Maddie baked soft and chewy chocolate-chip cookies that were to die for. Those cookies alone were responsible for the five pounds I gained that summer." She swiped some more batter and licked her finger. "And remember when Maddie left Gavin and stayed at my apartment for a couple of weeks?"

"Oh, yeah," came Kylie's reply while she sniffed the soup simmering on the stove. "That was the big one. She baked us six different kinds of cake in one day." She groaned. "I still haven't gotten over that white chocolate cake, Maddie. *Unbelievable.*"

"I know." A blissful sigh came from Amanda at the memory. "I'll never forget that one."

"All right, all right," Madison interrupted, exasperated. They knew her too well. "There *is* something."

Two pairs of interested eyes, gleaming with anticipation, swung around to look at her. Kylie narrowed her eyes. "Let me guess. You decided to stop pining for Gavin and got laid last night?"

Amanda jumped at that. "Ooh, ooh, you finally went out with John?"

"No, nothing like that." Just the thought of sleeping with someone else was . . . well, unpalatable right now. Madison sighed. "I filed for divorce."

The two women were shocked, momentarily speechless. Amanda recovered first and reached for Madison's hand. "Oh, sweetie, why didn't you tell us?"

"I don't know," she confessed. "I guess I just didn't want to talk about it. I'd planned on telling you the news after we ironed out all the details."

"Did everything go okay?" Kylie asked.

"Gavin didn't even show up." Madison couldn't keep the frustration out of her voice. "He let his lawyer take the meeting. Wesley said that he had a deadline he couldn't miss."

"Wesley, huh?" Kylie lit up with sudden interest. "I

remember him. He was Gavin's best man at your wedding, right? He's cute."

Amanda frowned. "Focus, Kylie. We're talking about Maddie now." She put an arm around Madison. "Tell us what happened."

"Gavin agreed to the divorce."

"That's a good thing, right?" Kylie was puzzled. "Why do you look so sad?"

Madison's shoulders slumped. "It's just so difficult. I'd prepared for this meeting, telling myself I could see him again without feeling angry." She bit her lip. "I guess I was a little disappointed that he couldn't even be bothered to show up to discuss our divorce."

Amanda and Kylie exchanged knowing glances.

"What?" Madison asked.

"You sound disappointed that you didn't see him, Maddie," Amanda observed gently.

"I do?" she hedged. "Well, maybe I was. I just thought that . . . you know . . . I'd see him one last time."

"You miss him," Amanda commented. "That's perfectly normal. We know how hard you fell for Gavin. Something like that doesn't go away quickly. It's not easy to just completely erase somebody you love from your life."

"What you need is some form of catharsis," Kylie declared, nodding her head wisely.

"Catharsis?" Madison echoed.

"You need to purge all the hurt you feel and focus on the good times. Let go of the bitterness and the anger. That's the only way you can move on."

Amanda nodded. "Kylie's right. Bitterness warps the mind and all that."

"How do I do that?"

Kylie shrugged. "Any way you can. Find some emotional release, something that will drain the heaviness, the lingering pain from your heart."

Later that night, Madison poured herself a glass of wine. The kitchen was once again immaculate, no trace left of the cooking and baking frenzy she'd indulged in. Amanda and Kylie had long since left, sent off with carefully packed boxes of cake and cookies. She turned off the light and made her way to the darkened bedroom and sat on the bed. Her muscles felt stiff. She rolled her shoulders and neck, hoping to ease the painful tightness. The tension began to gradually seep from her body. She'd been on an emotional roller coaster from the moment she'd gotten up and dressed to go to the meeting. Thank God the day was almost over.

Madison relaxed against the pillows and sipped her wine. Her life had been doing just fine . . . until she met Gavin. What was that movie where the heroine confesses to the hero, "You had me at hello"?

Once, she'd grimaced at the clichéd dialogue. Nobody said or did those things anymore. Little did she know that was going to happen to her. Gavin had swept her off her feet, making her disregard all the precautionary measures a woman living in this day and age swore by.

Don't sleep with a man on the first date. Madison blushed at the memory. She'd slept with Gavin the night they'd met.

Don't let lust rule your head. She'd *certainly* done that. After Gavin kissed her for the first time, she'd been hopelessly lost.

And last, the rule that she learned from her very own mother. *Don't trust a man with your heart, because sooner or later, he'll break it.* It had been her mother's mantra, something she'd drilled into her daughter early on.

Madison had plunged headlong into a hot, torrid affair with Gavin Cahill, culminating a couple of months later in a small, elegant wedding. She supposed it was inevitable that they would get married. They'd been inseparable since the night they met. And the sex . . . *wow.*

She squirmed restlessly on the bed at that thought. Sex with Gavin had been incredible. In the bedroom, he had been her lover and her master. He'd taught her exactly how to please him. In return, he'd done things to her she had never even imagined. He'd known just how to use his cock—long, thick and mouth-watering—to drive her crazy. Their sex life had been rich and varied, never boring. Gavin had been perfect for her in every way.

Her nipples tightened under her shirt, rubbing against the cotton material, suddenly sensitive and painful. With shaky fingers, she pulled it over her head. The tips of her breasts were hard and tingly, made even more so by the rings she still wore. *Gavin's nipple rings.* Even after everything that had happened, she couldn't bring herself to remove them.

With the tip of a finger, she rubbed the stiff nub caught in the delicate gold circle. Heat washed over her. Her pussy clenched with need, moisture pooling between her legs. It had been so long since she'd felt his touch. She pulled at her nipple, elongating the tip, imagining it was Gavin's talented fingers working it. The slight pain only aroused her more.

Madison slipped her hand under the waistband of her shorts and through the edge of her panties, parting her legs wider. She sought and found her aching clitoris, shuddering with need. She swirled around it, tugging gently at the clit ring—another token from Gavin that she couldn't bear to remove.

Hungry for his touch, she did the next best thing. Madison undressed and lay down on the bed. She slipped her fingers inside her sheath, drenching the digits in her warm wetness and began to pleasure herself. In her mind, it was *his* strong fingers plunging in and out of her sopping vagina, gently pulling at her ring, the overwhelming pleasure drowning out the slight sting of pain. She brought her other hand up and fondled her breast, working the aching tip until she was moaning and writhing feverishly on the bed. Madison whimpered, driven by intense need. It had been so long and she needed it so bad . . .

She came, her inner muscles contracting hungrily around her fingers. "*Gavin!*" His name exploded from her lips as she crested, revealing the stark need she harbored deep in her soul.

Afterward Madison burst into tears, overcome once more by a horrible feeling of emptiness. What had just happened was a temporary solution to the hunger gnawing at the very center of her being. She hugged a pillow tightly, pressing her tear-streaked face into the soft folds. Touching herself was a feeble, ineffective replacement for what she really needed. She needed the real thing. She needed Gavin.

3

Six months after signing the divorce papers, Madison had to admit she was a fraud. Her life was a never-ending cycle of dreaming about Gavin when she was asleep and longing for him when she was awake. In the company of others, she presented a happy front, but alone, her mask crumbled and she gave in to tears. It was a lonely existence. Too many times she'd thought of Gavin. Where was he? What was he doing? More important, who was he doing it with?

When his latest novel had come out, she'd immediately gone to the bookstore and bought a copy. How many times had she stared at his picture on the inside of the book jacket? And when he'd hit the bestseller list once again, she'd been tempted to pick up the phone and congratulate him. She'd scoured countless magazines and newspapers for any news of him. When he'd been snapped at a lavish gala with a stunning woman clinging to his arm, a hot stab of jealousy had lanced her heart. It tortured her to think that he was dating again. Over and over, she looked at the picture of him with the beautiful woman in the red dress. She couldn't stop herself.

Madison threw the magazine in the trash can. This had to stop. Kylie was right. What she needed was to start over completely. Gavin was getting on with his life, so should she. But how was she supposed to do that? She had absolutely no desire to date at all. The sudden ringing of the phone interrupted her pity party. It was Wesley.

"Gavin is selling the cabin in the mountains."

Madison was stunned. "B-but he loves that place."

"Believe me, I'm just as surprised as you are."

The cabin was where they'd spent their honeymoon. Why would he possibly want to do that? Unless . . . Madison drew up short. The answer was pretty obvious. *He's cutting all ties with me.* He was getting rid of everything that reminded him of their marriage.

"My instructions are to let you know in order to give you a chance to get whatever you want from the cabin," Wesley continued.

Madison swallowed. She'd left numerous pictures back at the cabin, most of which she'd taken herself. Their wedding album was also there, as well as other mementos of their time spent together.

"I'm sorry for the short notice, but Gavin would like this taken care of as soon as possible." When she didn't say anything, Wesley uttered a sigh, clearly uncomfortable. "I know this must come as a shock to you, Maddie."

"A-a little," she admitted.

"If you're not interested, he'll hire somebody to take care of it and get rid of everything."

"No!" she blurted out in a rush. "D-don't do that. I want

them back." This was her chance for a much-needed catharsis, to let go of the bitterness and hurt. Going back to the place where she and Gavin had been the happiest would be an enormous release. To go there for the last time would be the cathartic event Kylie said she needed. She made a sudden decision and said, "I'll fly up there. This weekend."

"You will?" Wesley asked doubtfully.

"Yes. If that's okay with Gavin."

"Of course it is. He specifically told me to let you know so you could have the chance to get them yourself."

"I'll book a flight for Friday."

"Okay. Sounds great." Wesley paused. "I'll inform Gavin. You know, just to make sure he won't be anywhere nearby."

"Thanks," Madison managed to say before she hung up. She dropped onto the couch, her legs shaky. This was further proof that Gavin was indeed moving on. If he could do it, why couldn't she? She needed to do this, desperately. For the last time, she'd like to see the place that bore witness to the love that she and Gavin once had. Then she could finally put Gavin and their failed marriage behind her and move on. Picking up the phone, she booked a flight to Colorado.

THE ROCKIES LOOMED IN THE BACKGROUND as Madison filled up the tank of her rental car, shivering under her thick parka. There was a distinct chill in the air, and the temperature seemed to have dropped drastically. She ran inside the local convenience store, where it was blessedly warm, and bought a bottle of water. The man behind the counter recognized her. "Mrs. Cahill, right?"

She smiled, not bothering to tell him she was the ex–Mrs. Cahill. "Yes."

"You headin' up to the cabin?"

Madison nodded. "Yes, I am."

He indicated the clouds gathering in the sky. "Looks like a nasty storm brewing. Be careful."

She looked over her shoulder at the thick clouds that covered the sky. "I should make it there in good time. Thanks." But as the car ate up the miles leading away from the town of Cripple Creek, Colorado, the clouds suddenly appeared more ominous than she'd first thought. She began to feel nervous as the first snowflakes started to fall. Gripping the steering wheel tightly, she pushed on, saying a quick prayer that she'd make it to the cabin before this turned into a full-fledged storm. Her prayers went unanswered. The snow started falling harder. It was still a couple of hours until sunset, but visibility was almost zero as the snow fell thicker and faster.

Not for the first time, Madison thought about turning around. She could barely see in front of her. But she was close, she knew it. To turn around now would mean that she would spend even more time driving in this horrible weather. Apprehension filled her as she looked in vain for a mile marker or something to tell her where to turn. There was nothing but blinding white powder blanketing the countryside. *Damn it.* If she hadn't been delayed at the car rental counter at the airport, maybe she would have been safely to her destination already. A savage winter storm was suddenly raging and she was in the middle of it.

Madison adjusted the thermostat of the car heater. Along with the cold, she began to feel very real fear as she inched forward on the deserted road. The windshield wipers couldn't move fast enough to clear the view and she could barely see in front of her. Why hadn't she turned back earlier when it had been safe to do so? *Stupid, stupid, stupid.* She could only hope that she reached the turnoff soon and got to the cabin in one piece.

Her hopes quickly dimmed even further. She was essentially driving blind, following a road that she couldn't even see anymore. Her heart pounded. Beneath her gloves, her palms were damp. *God, please just let me get there in one piece.* She was trying to verbally bolster her courage by chanting "I'll get there, I'll get there" when she hit a big rut in the road and jolted to a stop. Madison shrieked in terror. The car was tilted sideways, the right front fender dipping low, hanging over something she couldn't even see.

Her heart pounded. *Okay. Calm down. Panicking will not help in this kind of situation.* Gingerly, Madison put the car in reverse, stepped on the gas and tried to turn the wheel. The tires spun uselessly. The engine groaned as she revved it, but the car didn't budge. She did it again. Nothing happened. She stayed right where she was.

A choked sob escaped her throat. *What am I going to do?* The car was stuck. Taking a deep, calming breath, she tried to peer through the windows. Where the hell was she? She couldn't see anything at all, no clue as to where exactly she was. Flipping her cell phone open, she dialed 911.

No response. Madison glanced at the screen. There was no signal. Refusing to give in to the panic threatening to suffocate her, she tried again, punching the three numbers that would send help to find her.

Again, nothing.

Don't panic. Trying again, she carefully punched the

emergency number once more. When she got the same result, she pounded the steering wheel in frustration. She took a deep, steadying breath. *Think, Maddie.* Her options were limited. Going out in the storm would be sheer stupidity, since she didn't have the faintest idea where she was. Staying in the car seemed like the wise thing to do. Pulling her parka closer around her, Madison zipped it up and peered outside her window. *Please, God, let somebody come along to find me.*

She picked up her purse and checked the contents for food. All she found was a half-eaten candy bar she'd bought at the airport this morning plus the water she'd bought at the store in town. She'd have to save the candy bar for when she got really hungry. God only knows how long she was going to be stuck here.

Time slowed to a crawl. Madison huddled deeper in her thick parka, thankful she'd at least done one thing right and put on sensible clothes. Every few minutes, she'd try her cell phone again, only to get the same results. Frustration mounted along with fear, but she forced herself to stay calm. She was stuck in the middle of nowhere. It wouldn't help at all to become hysterical.

But as the snow continued to fall unabated and with ever-increasing ferocity, it was getting harder and harder not to panic. She shivered. Every few minutes, she let the engine run so she could turn on the heater. But as soon as she turned it off, the cold came back with a vengeance.

The wind howled incessantly, rocking the small car, jolting her nerves further. Darkness fell and with it, Madison's hopes of being rescued. In the inky blackness outside, she'd given up even trying to see anything. She rubbed her gloved hands together, just needing to move. In the time she'd been in the car, she'd gone from anger to self-pity to blaming herself for even wanting to come out here. Now she just felt hopeless. Tears pricked at the corners of her eyes as she reclined the seat all the way back. If she was going to die, she might as well be comfortable.

Madison eyed the empty candy wrapper on the passenger seat. No food. No more water either. At least the heater was still working, giving her some warm air. But luck wasn't on her side. At that exact moment, the engine sputtered and shook before it fell silent. She eyed the gas gauge in dismay. Empty. She shivered. Would she die of hypothermia out here? How long would it be before she was found? A few hours? Worst-case scenario, a day maybe? Several people knew where she was headed. Surely they'd send out a search party for her once they realized she'd been caught in the blizzard.

A bright light shone into the car, jolting her upright. The sudden pounding on the window elicited a small cry of terror from her lips. A gloved hand cleared the snow from the windshield, the beam from the flashlight briefly illuminating a masculine face. Madison blinked. Gavin? After fumbling with the lock, she opened the car door and all but fell into his arms.

"Of all the stupid, brainless fucking things to do," he roared, "this takes the cake, Maddie. Didn't you check the weather report?"

Fear, panic and terror were instantly wiped away, replaced by giddy euphoria at being found. She shivered in the freezing temperature, raising her voice to be heard over the howling wind. "Oh, thank God you found me." She hugged him on impulse. "It-it's so cold."

Gavin's jaw tightened dangerously as he threw another, bigger, parka over her, zipping it up quickly and tightening the hood over her head. "How do you feel?" he asked gruffly, once again shining the flashlight in her face.

She brought a hand up to shield her eyes. "I-I'm cold but okay. The heater was working until I used up the last of the gas just a few minutes ago."

"Get on the snowmobile."

"M-my stuff."

"I'll get it," he told her curtly. He reached inside the car for her purse and small case and stowed them on the trailer attached to the back of the snowmobile. "Let's go. We need to get you out of this cold."

Madison climbed behind him, sliding her arms around his waist. It felt good to hold him. She blinked back the tears of relief that threatened to fall. Gavin had found her. She wasn't going to freeze to death in the car.

He started the engine. "Hold on."

Madison hung on for dear life. Even through the thick parka he wore, she felt his shifting muscles as he maneuvered the vehicle. Snowflakes pelted her cheeks as they sped through the darkened night. Madison buried her face in his back, immediately assaulted by the smell that was uniquely Gavin. *Damn.* His body heat seeped through the layers of clothing that separated them. Even as cold as she was, her body stirred. *Don't go there.* She didn't feel that way about Gavin anymore. It was just a natural human reaction after being rescued from a potentially fatal situation.

With a sigh of relief, Madison spied faint lights flickering through the dark. Gavin covered the last hundred yards in record time before pulling to a halt right at the front steps of the cabin. Disengaging her arms, he quickly stood up and gathered her things.

Madison hurried up the steps. The lights of the cabin were blazing like a welcoming beacon in the middle of the sea. A plume of smoke rose from the chimney. *Oh, to be warm again,* she thought longingly as she followed Gavin through the front door. The delicious heat emanating from the large fireplace enveloped her instantly. She closed the door, relieved to be out of the freezing weather.

"How are you feeling?"

Madison shook the snow from her jeans and parka. "I'm fine, thanks." She winced at the breathlessness in her voice. "Damp and cold, but okay. How did you know I was caught in the storm?"

"Frank, the owner of the local store, radioed me. He said you got some gas a couple of hours back and wanted to check if you'd made it here okay. It shouldn't have taken you long to get here. I knew right away that you were lost somewhere out there. I drove up and down the road searching for any sign of your car." Gavin frowned. "You made a wrong turn and ended up on Gold Camp Road instead of Highway 67."

Madison flushed. "It was snowing so hard I really couldn't see in front of me. I would've frozen to death out there if you hadn't come along."

His dark gaze was unreadable. "What are you doing here, Maddie?"

Butterflies danced in her stomach at being this close to him again. "I-I . . . " She pulled in a deep breath. "Wesley told me you were selling the cabin. I wanted to get some things from here and . . . " she trailed off. *Get a grip, Maddie.* "You're not supposed to be here," she finished lamely.

Gavin ran a hand through his hair. "I was scheduled to leave a couple of days ago but decided to stay."

"You didn't know I was coming?"

"There's no telephone here, remember? Wesley probably left a message for me at home."

Madison flushed. "I'm sorry for showing up here unannounced." He was clearly uncomfortable with her presence. "If I'd known you'd be here . . . "

Their eyes met and held. Slow, insidious heat invaded her veins. Madison tried to ignore it, but it was impossible. There was a curious tingling in the pit of her stomach, and the significance of their situation hit her. They were alone in a secluded cabin, miles from anywhere, trapped inside by a powerful blizzard. Just her and Gavin.

"Strip."

"Excuse me?"

His lips quirked with faint amusement. "Get out of those damp clothes before you catch pneumonia. I suggest you jump in the shower and get warm. I'll toss your clothes in the washer."

Her cheeks felt hot. What did she think he was asking her to strip for? To have sex with him? How embarrassing. *Get your mind out of the gutter, Madison.* "Give me a minute." Lifting her chin, she marched to the lone bedroom.

The bedroom was just as nice and comfortable, courtesy of the small fire that burned in the antique woodstove. Gavin had lovingly refinished it himself. The great stone fireplace in the living room was nice and functional, but he'd fallen for the charm and ageless grace of the old wood-burning stove.

Madison glanced around. The king-size bed was still here, as well as the pine dresser and matching nightstand. Nostalgia hit her hard at that moment. This was where she spent some of the happiest days of her life with Gavin.

Hearing a sound behind her, she whirled around. Gavin motioned to her jeans and sweater. "Clothes?" At her hesitation, he gave her an amused smile. "I've seen it all before."

Madison ignored that and went into the bathroom, slamming the door shut. Shivering, she hurriedly peeled off the parka, her sweater and undershirt. Next came her damp jeans. She bit her lip. Should she take off her underwear and give him that too?

"All of it, Maddie," his voice boomed from the other side of the door.

Did he read minds now too? Irritated, she pulled off her underwear, thinking now was not the time for modesty. Opening the door, she cracked it just enough to extend her arm outside and drop her clothes. Shutting herself in once more, she walked into the shower stall and turned on the water. In no time at all, the room was immersed in rising steam. Madison stepped gratefully under the hot spray.

Soon, she felt close to normal and wasn't freezing anymore. Grabbing a plush towel from the rack, she wrapped it around her securely before pulling the door open. Her small case sat on top of the bed. Madison grabbed her clothes and quickly donned them. She hadn't really counted on being snowbound, and she only had one day's change of clothes with her. The rest of what she had packed were toiletries plus an extra pair of underwear and socks. With any luck, the storm wouldn't last more than a couple of days at the most.

She ran a brush through her damp hair, took a couple of deep breaths and left the sanctuary of the bedroom.

Gavin was placing steaming bowls of chicken soup on the table, along with a couple of thick sandwiches. "Hungry?"

"Yes. Thank you." While she'd been in the shower, he'd

changed into a fresh pair of jeans and a flannel shirt. The casual clothes enhanced his sexy masculinity. *Stop! Don't even start thinking of him that way again.* But she was fooling herself, because she couldn't keep her eyes off the tight backside encased in soft, well-worn jeans when he stood up to get their drinks. When he slipped into the chair across from her, she quickly averted her gaze, pretending a serious interest in the hot soup.

Madison tried to follow Gavin's lead and act nonchalant, but failed miserably. Thick, uncomfortable silence descended between them. The cabin seemed to have shrunk in size, dominated by his presence, further fraying her sagging defenses. She dragged much-needed oxygen into her lungs, only to realize it was permeated with his scent. Again and again, her eyes were drawn to him. As surreptitiously as she could, she examined his face. He looked the same, in fact, even better than the last time she'd seen him months ago. His hair was a little longer, but it suited him somehow. Lips that she'd loved to nibble on seemed to taunt her with their tempting presence. He could make her weak with just one kiss. One stroke of his damp tongue would trigger an avalanche of reaction from every single one of her nerve endings.

Her pussy clenched.

Madison groaned silently. Even now, after months of separation, she was reacting to his presence like she was in heat. What had happened to all her avowals of putting Gavin completely out of her life? It was a joke. Just like it was fate's cruel trick that she'd ended up stuck in this cabin with him while a blizzard raged outside. Once again, her eyes strayed to his lips. Her nipples tightened under her shirt, reminding her she still wore the rings he gave her. Slow, syrupy wetness pooled between her legs. This was a man who could turn her on with just one scorching look. Desperate to stop her runaway thoughts, she blurted out the first thing that came to her mind. "Thanks for dinner."

Gavin shrugged. "It's no big deal."

What now? Madison didn't know what to say after that, so she kept her mouth shut and just ate. After she was done, she brought the dishes to the sink. Gavin followed suit. "I'll wash up," she offered. There weren't many dishes, and she was done in no time at all. Madison wiped her hands with a dish towel, lingering by the sink, desperately wishing she could hide in the bedroom. She couldn't sneak away, no more than she could stop her eyes from being drawn to Gavin as he stared out the window, his hands on his hips. For a moment, she looked her fill. She'd been on intimate terms with that body, spending endless hours exploring every mouthwatering inch of it. Again, her senses responded to just being this close to him. Her gaze strayed lower, irresistibly drawn to his taut buttocks. *Stop looking at his ass.* When she looked up, Madison was shocked to see his reflection looking right back at her, the glass giving him a clear view of her face. *Oh, great.* He'd caught her checking him out!

Madison flushed. "Ah, um, maybe I can start to sort through some of the personal items I left here and decide which ones I'd like to take with me."

When he faced her, he looked faintly amused. "All the stuff's in there." He pointed to the antique trunk that doubled as the coffee table before positioning his big body in the chair next to the window.

Determined to divert her wayward thoughts, she sat on the throw rug and pushed open the heavy lid. The first thing she saw was their wedding album. Right after they were married, she and Gavin had spent a month here at the cabin. Foolish romantic that she'd been, she'd asked the photographer to ship the photos up to her. She hadn't wanted to wait until they got back to Los Angeles to see them. She traced their embossed names on the cover. Against her better judgment, she flipped it open.

Madison was assailed by memories as she looked through picture after picture of her and Gavin. Smiling. Kissing. Laughing. Gazing into each other's eyes. Oh God, this was killing her. With more force than was necessary, she closed the album and put it aside. She reached inside the trunk once more and pulled out more photos. This time they were the ones she'd taken of Gavin chopping firewood. She'd caught him in the act of swinging the ax, a soft sheen of sweat glistening damply on his tanned skin. She'd taken several pictures of him, even one where he'd jokingly flexed his muscles for her.

The next one was of her, asleep, with only a thin sheet slung across her body. She remembered that one too. Gavin had ended up slipping into bed with her and gently waking her up with hot, deep kisses that inevitably led to other, more pleasurable, things.

Releasing a shaky breath, Madison dropped the entire stack of photos on top of the wedding album. This was harder than she'd thought.

"Had enough?" His dark, compelling eyes were locked on her.

Madison's pulse jumped. "I didn't think it was going to be this difficult."

"We had some happy times here, Maddie."

"Yeah, we did." It was hard to speak past the lump in her throat. A burning question hovered on the tip of her tongue. She'd been silently debating the wisdom of asking it, but how could she not? She needed to know. "Why are you selling the cabin?"

"It's outlived its usefulness. I don't intend to come here like I used to."

She was the reason. Madison was certain of it. The thought didn't sit well with her at all, triggering confusing feelings of remorse. "But you *love* this place. This was where you could get away to think and write. You restored this place, picked every piece of furniture that's in it and once told me this is where you found peace. How can you let it go?"

Gavin gave her a long, enigmatic look. "Don't ask questions, Maddie. You might not like the answers."

Her heart thumped anxiously. "I want to know why."

"This cabin is filled with memories of our life together and I don't want to remember that anymore. Is that honest enough for you?"

She flinched. "I'd hate for you to lose one of the things you love the most just because of what happened to us."

"I don't need it anymore. I find that I don't need a lot of things since our divorce became final."

"I'd really rather not talk about the past. This cabin—"

Gavin's dark eyes narrowed. "Why not talk about it? I've got nothing to hide. I didn't cheat on you."

Madison turned away, unwilling to venture into their turbulent past. That only seemed to incense him further.

"You refused to listen to my explanation, refused to believe me." His tone was dangerously cold. "*You* left *me*."

Madison trembled as she grappled with painful memories. She felt on edge, unsettled, her emotions seesawing dangerously. "We can't undo what's been done."

"You're *so* goddamn positive that I cheated on you."

"I *saw* you," she snapped, goaded beyond endurance.

"You gave up on us. You didn't want to try to work things out." The cold anger in his voice lashed at her. "You threw away what we had without even giving us another chance. Instead, you let the poison your mother planted in your head dictate your actions. Don't even pretend I'm to blame for everything," he finished tautly.

Madison uncoiled her legs and stood. She blinked back the tears, trying to regain her composure, staring at the greedy flames that licked at the split logs in the hearth. Fighting was not going to get them anywhere, and rehashing the reason for their divorce was a moot point.

The silence was tense and uncomfortable. How were they supposed to coexist while trapped in the storm? There was nothing to be achieved by being at each other's throats. She'd come here to let go of the past, for God's sake, not dredge it up again.

Armed with this conviction, she faced Gavin. "I don't want to fight. Whatever happened in the past is over. None of that matters anymore. I know you've . . . moved on." Under his unrelenting stare, she flushed and tried to smile. "I mean, I've seen your picture in magazines. The woman you're with, she's very beautiful."

Gavin crossed his arms over his chest. "If I didn't know better, I'd think you were asking me if I'm dating her." His eyebrow rose in faint challenge. "You lost that right when you divorced me, Maddie."

Her smile died a quick death. "Forget it. I don't know why I even mentioned it."

"Are you jealous?"

Her face felt hot, all the way to the tips of her ears. "Of course not," she replied quickly. Too quickly. "I, ah, I'm dating someone too." As soon as the words were out of her mouth, Madison wanted to smack her forehead. What on Earth had possessed her to say that? Was it her way of salvaging some pride after finding out her ex-husband was dating again? "I just think it's time we put the past behind us and try to become friends," she finished lamely.

Gavin's face was carved from stone. Had she not been reeling from the big fib she'd just told, Madison would have recognized that as a sign of impending doom. "You're *dating* someone," he repeated, his voice low and throbbing with intensity.

A cold knot formed in her belly when he pushed from the chair and came toward her. She took a step back. "Th-that's a good thing, right? I-I mean, we . . . we shouldn't let what happened to us get in the way of living normal lives again. You know, bitterness warps the mind and all that," she said breathlessly.

He didn't stop until he was only inches away from her. Awareness hit her squarely in the chest, gathering in the already sensitive tips of her breasts. She had the strongest urge to rub them against him, to find relief from the need pulsing in her pussy. "What are you—" Madison jumped when he grabbed her hand and placed it on the front of his jeans.

Oh God. His cock was thick and hard beneath her palm. "This is what you do to me, Maddie." His breath washed over her, as hot and urgent as his words. "I look at you and I get a fucking hard-on. I imagine you naked, laid out on my bed for me to feast on." His hand tightened over hers, forcing her to clamp around the long shaft under the soft, worn denim. "I want to see your nipples adorned with the rings I gave you. I want to lick and suck them until you beg me to bite you."

Madison shuddered, her knees almost buckling from under her.

"I want to spread your legs and lick you all over. Most of all, I want to suck you through your little clit ring." He pulled her tighter against him, thrusting against her hand. Of their own volition, her fingers curved around him, molding his shape eagerly. "Are you still wearing it?"

Madison swallowed. She felt feverish, her blood turning molten as it raced through her veins. "Gavin, I—"

"I want to fuck you, Maddie, so bad I can almost taste it. I jack off at night thinking of you tied up in my bed, remembering your pussy wrapped around my cock like a wet glove while you begged me for more."

A whimper escaped her lips. Hunger exploded inside her, drowning out the persistent voice that warned her not to let him do this. She'd been too long without him, too long denied his touch. She was starving for him.

"Most of all, I remember how your ass clamps so sweetly around me as I fuck you there. That's what I think about when I come, Maddie. That gets me through the night. But in the end, it's not enough. It's never enough." With his other hand, he cupped her nape and tipped her face back. "You still think we can be friends?" he snarled, jerking her hand away and thrusting her from him. He went inside the bedroom and slammed the door shut behind him.

The silence in the cabin was deafening.

Madison trembled, panting hard, falling back on the couch. Need vibrated through her body, concentrating in the soaked folds of her sex. She squeezed her thighs together, moaning softly. How was she supposed to stay here with Gavin and not go insane from wanting him? She looked at the bedroom door, hunger eating away at her common sense. For months, she'd fooled herself into thinking she didn't want him anymore, that she was over him, that she could move on with her life. Yet tonight, as soon as he'd touched her, every cell in her body came to stinging, pulsing life. The pain of betrayal, the months of separation and the bitterness of divorce melted away. She was right back where she'd started, with Gavin holding her body and her heart in the palm of his hand.

The inevitable was about to happen. She'd lost the war when he'd rescued her from the storm. From the first moment she'd seen him again, the chemistry that had always simmered between them had begun to work its magic on her susceptible senses. It was undeniable. Unstoppable. Irresistible.

She moved toward the closed bedroom door and opened it. Gavin stood by the window, stiffness lining every muscle, his fists clenched as he looked out at the dark night. When he eventually faced her, Maddie was singed by the intensity of his gaze.

"You have five seconds to get out of here. I'm *this* close to throwing you on the bed and saying to hell with the consequences."

Madison trembled, awash with need. She couldn't get beyond wanting to be with Gavin again, beyond having him inside her once more. Let tomorrow take care of itself.

"I'm warning you. I'm hungry, Maddie. I won't be easily satisfied." His eyes pierced her with heat. "Get out now while you can."

With shaking fingers, she gripped the hem of her sweater and pulled it over her head, tossing it off to the side. Holding his gaze, she unbuttoned her jeans and shimmied out of them. The air was so thick she could have cut it with a knife, but she didn't waver. In moments, she was completely naked, her body bared to his gaze.

Gavin sucked in a harsh breath.

Madison knew she was playing a dangerous game, but she could no more stop this than she could stop breathing. Tonight was about Gavin.

"You had your chance," he growled. In no time at all, he covered the distance between them, grabbed both her hands in his and pulled them over her head. "No regrets."

"No regrets," she confirmed huskily.

He pushed her against the wall, at the same time clamping his mouth on hers, wasting no time in preliminaries as he thrust his tongue inside in a blatantly erotic kiss that devoured her. It was unrepentant, carnal and hot.

Her mind turned hazy with wanting. "Let me touch you."

"Hell no. If you do that, this will be over before we even start." With his knees, he nudged her legs wider apart, forcing her to ride him. The denim rasped against her aching clit.

It felt *so* good. "Oh, yes. Right there."

With one hand, Gavin fumbled with the button of his jeans. Madison moaned, consumed with urgency. "Hurry."

"Damn it," he muttered in frustration before he finally got the button through the hole. He pushed his zipper down, his massive erection spilling against her belly.

The feel of the soft skin encasing his hard flesh drove her insane. "Gavin," she cried out. "I need to touch you."

With a curse, he finally let her go so he could push his jeans down his thighs. Madison instantly wrapped her hands around his cock, fisting it, sliding up and down, fascinated by the broad, bulbous head where a drop of liquid already quivered on the slit. She bent to lick it.

"Oh no, you don't." Gavin cupped her ass and lifted her against the wall. "You'll get that later."

"I want it now," she moaned, automatically wrapping her legs around his hips.

"I've got to fuck you now, Maddie," he gritted out. "I've got to feel your pussy clenching around me or I'll go insane."

He'll go insane? She was teetering on the edge of madness as the ridged head rubbed against the slick opening. With one mighty thrust, Gavin impaled her to the hilt. She uttered a shaky sigh, lost in the bliss, her eyes closing as she absorbed the delicious feeling of having him inside her once again.

"I've come home," he rasped against her skin.

Madison opened her eyes and met his. An incredible feeling of tenderness overcame her at his words. She wrapped her arms around his neck and pressed her lips to his, unable to come up with a response. The kiss soon turned urgent, rapacious. Gavin slapped a hand on the wall and braced his legs on the floor. His hips thrust inside her with ever-increasing speed, catapulting them swiftly into that place where only the two of them existed.

"Yes. Yes. Yes," she chanted, her breath hissing at every slide and push. The rhythmic friction created the most delicious feeling.

"I'm sorry, babe," Gavin panted, his warm breath mingling with hers. "It's been too long."

"Don't be." Madison tightened her inner muscles around his cock. Biting her lip, she felt the first tingling gathering in her lower belly. The first splash of his seed against her inner walls triggered her climax. Delirious, she cried out as she came.

"Fuck. *Maddie*."

She savored the sharp pleasure of their orgasms. Gavin had always loved coming with her, loved the feeling of her inner muscles contracting tightly around his shaft as she milked him. Tears gathered in the corners of her eyes at the all-consuming pleasure. After months of separation, this first joining had been quick and intense. She'd only now realized just how much she missed this physical closeness with Gavin. She'd been starved for it.

Long after she stopped trembling, Maddie couldn't bear to let him go. Her mind was still buzzing with satisfaction when he moved them over to the bed, gently laying her down. She sighed, burrowing into the soft mattress, basking in the soft aftershocks that still pulsed through her. Her eyes drifted shut. She'd rest, just for a moment. It felt so good to be in his arms again.

4

GAVIN EXAMINED THE FAINT signs of satiation that edged Madison's serene profile as she slept. Unlike her, he couldn't sleep at all. He'd been jolted by the shock of what had just happened. The whole feverish encounter left him reeling, both from the pleasure and the unexpectedness of it, and he had yet to recover. He couldn't believe that Madison—his ex-wife—was in his bed once more.

When she'd divorced him, he'd resolved never to see her again, never to speak to her again, and most of all, never to touch her again. She'd broken his heart and put him through hell. Despite all that, when he'd realized she'd gotten lost in the blizzard, he'd driven like a madman through winding, desolate and icy roads trying desperately to find her, praying that he wasn't too late. When he'd opened the car door and seen Madison again for the first time in months, he'd known right away the battle was lost. His anger and resentment melted away like snow under a hot desert sun. He snorted. It'd been appallingly easy to forget all his resolutions about this woman, who still had a stranglehold on his heart *and* his cock.

In the dim light of the bedroom, her skin glowed with a soft, luminous sheen. She moaned and rubbed her foot against his before shifting to lie on her back, presenting him with a full view of her body. His gaze strayed lower, devouring the picture she made. God, she was so fucking hot he couldn't get over it. Full breasts, small waist and rounded hips. The very first time he'd seen her, he'd fallen like the proverbial ton of bricks. He'd foolishly thought that once he'd had her in his bed, the intensity would lessen. He'd been wrong. He only wanted her more.

There wasn't anything he'd asked that she hadn't done. He'd loved her lack of inhibition, her eagerness to play. Maddie had enjoyed being tied up, blindfolded, handcuffed and restrained. Their bedroom had become a playground, a place for adventure that added spice to their new marriage. But in the end, all that had paled in comparison to how right he felt with her. In the short time they'd been married she made him happy, brought laughter into his life and soothed his frustration on days he couldn't write anything that made one iota of sense. She'd never complained when he immersed himself in his writing for hours on end, always there for him when he finally emerged. Their life had been perfect until the day she'd caught him with Kimberly outside his hotel room.

His jaw tightened. Kimberly was a pain in the ass who couldn't quite accept that their one-night stand was just that. The thing with Kimberly had been over before he'd even met Maddie, but he'd been a fool to get involved with her in the first place. The woman had ambushed him outside his hotel room that fateful day. He'd fired her on the spot, but the damage had already been done. He'd already lost his wife.

Madison uttered a soft sound. Gavin stared at her face, peaceful in sleep. The feelings he'd tried to suppress for so long clawed their way to the surface, wrapping around his heart until he couldn't breathe. What had made him think he was over her? The desire, the *need* to claim her physically, had never gone away. It was a constant, gnawing ache that had been his sole companion during the long, lonely nights after their divorce.

Madison was here, within reach once more. They were alone in a remote cabin, stuck in a blizzard. This was his chance to win her back, to rekindle the love that had always existed between them and to prove to her that they belonged together. She still wanted him. He'd have to build on that to win her heart back, because tonight he'd realized one thing. He could *never* let Madison go.

She's mine. She'll always be mine.

Touching one nipple, Gavin rubbed it until it stiffened. Her breasts had always been ultrasensitive, made even more so by the gold rings she'd willingly worn for him. He leaned down and lapped at it, alternating between sucking and gently biting, insistently drawing her from sleep. He knew the exact moment she woke up by the way she arched into his mouth.

"Hi." He skimmed his lips across the fragrant valley between her breasts, sniffing the delicate, feminine scent of her skin as he traveled across to the other one. With his tongue, he traced the full swell in ever smaller circles, teasing but never quite touching the waiting tip. "You still wear my rings."

The deep breath Madison took brought her flesh closer to his mouth. "I-I just never had the time to . . . to get another set," she moaned.

As excuses went, that one was lame. Gavin didn't argue, instead pulling her into a sitting position. He quickly reached into the bedside drawer and pulled out leather ties. "Arms over your head, Maddie."

Excitement glowed in her eyes. Madison raised her arms, crossing one wrist over the other with unabashed eagerness. He bound her to the headboard, piling pillows behind her to cushion her back and leaving enough room that she could shift to her side if necessary. She licked her lips, her breath coming faster. Gavin pushed her legs apart, positioning himself in between before sitting back and just gazing at her. His cock rose long and stiff between his legs. It seemed all the blood in his body pooled between his legs. Madison's gaze fell on his shaft, hunger written plainly on her features.

Instead of giving in to her silent plea, he cupped her breasts in his hands, kneading them exactly how she liked it, alternating between gentle squeezes and firm pinches, worrying the tips with his fingers. "I used to suck your nipples for hours, Maddie, remember? It drove you crazy when I clamped these."

Madison trembled, her hips subtly rising on the bed.

"Tell me what you want," he invited, his own senses rioting at her responsiveness.

"You know what I want," she replied in a helpless, breathless voice. "Please."

"This?" He used his teeth to pull at the stiff crest before biting down on the pliant flesh.

She shuddered, her breath catching sharply. Her eyes were glazed with lust. *"More."*

He sucked her briefly, enjoying the little sound of distress she made when he pulled back. Again and again, he manipulated the tips through the sexy gold rings, driving her arousal higher. He used his mouth, his teeth, his lips and his hands to stimulate her further, loving the soft, breathy moans she uttered.

Gavin slid his fingers down the flat plane of her belly, coasting over smooth, silky skin. Madison had gone still the instant he did that. Hot anticipation shone in her beautiful face. He cupped the backs of her knees and pulled them up. In this position, she was completely open to him.

He parted the puffy, soaked lips of her pussy. Savage satisfaction filled him to see the hood ring piercing her clit and the fragile little "G" pendant that hung from it. He thumbed the swollen nubbin, gathering her juices and swirling them around the pulsing spot. Driven by a compulsion he couldn't resist, he asked, "Have you slept with anyone?"

"Have you?" she countered huskily.

He didn't even hesitate. "No."

"B-but that picture in the magazine—"

The little catch in her voice told him it was a difficult statement for her. Gavin looked into her eyes, wanting her to see the truth of what he was about to say. "Had they printed the entire picture, you would have seen Wesley standing on the other side of the woman in the red dress, who happens to be his sister, Susan. She works for the museum that had the gala that night." Madison remained silent. It rankled that she didn't believe him instantly, but he was determined to work through that. "At this point," he continued quietly, "I don't need to lie to you, Maddie. We're divorced. It doesn't matter if I've slept with anyone or not."

She flinched at the truth of his words. "You're right, of course. It's none of my business."

"But I *am* telling you that there's been no one since you left me." He placed his palm over her mound. "You said you were moving on. What exactly does that mean?"

A shadow of unhappiness flickered in her eyes. "Maybe we

shouldn't talk about this at all. It's only going to lead to trouble."

He grimaced. "True. Talking never did us any favors." He pulled back, cutting off any physical contact. Did her refusal to answer mean she'd already slept with somebody? Possessiveness rose to his throat, threatening to choke him. To even think of another man's hands on her body, touching her, kissing her, was like a jagged blade cutting through him.

Madison went still. Gavin's handsome face flashed with something that looked suspiciously like pain. The unexpectedness of it surprised her. Was it the natural reaction of a man to the thought of his ex-wife sleeping with somebody else? Or was that hurt unique to him because he still cared? Was it even possible?

This was dangerous territory they were entering, one that could potentially bring more heartache to her later on. Yet when Gavin had declared in that utterly serious tone that he hadn't slept with anyone and had no reason to lie to her, she believed him. Their divorce was over and done with. Any confession he made about being with somebody else was of no consequence. Even so, she was relieved and strangely happy to know that he hadn't. "I haven't slept with anyone either."

His breath hissed in at her admission. "I'm glad."

"Me too."

"I think it's time to reacquaint your body to my touch."

Heat swept over Madison. There was no need for any reacquainting. Her body had never forgotten its master. Her nerve endings were already singing, eagerly waiting for the gentle bite of his teeth, the merciless pounding of his cock—even the sting of his hand on her ass.

"Maddie?" he prompted as he gently pulled once more at the delicate gold nipple rings.

Madison drew in a sharp breath, dazed by the familiar plea-sure-pain that radiated from the aching tip. God, it had been so very long. Hunger tormented her, licking at every inch of her skin. She couldn't stem the needy whimper that escaped her lips as he continued to play with her, stoking the fire inside her with stunning ease. They were creating their own tempest that could rival the snowstorm that raged outside.

Swallowing, Madison dropped her gaze to Gavin's straining cock. It was swollen, thick and heavily veined. It was hungry for *her*. Stinging heat rushed to her vagina, soaking it with even more moisture. Her clit throbbed with sharp anticipation.

"Look at me."

Something stirred within her at the quiet command in his voice. She knew what it was. It had always been inside her. It was the very basic need to submit to his every wish.

"I want to play, Maddie." Gavin delivered a light, stinging slap on her bare mound. Pleasure reverberated through every cell in her body. Intense, hot lust curled from her inner muscles and spread inexorably from the tips of her toes to the ends of her fingers, coming together to merge in her sensitized nipples. "I'm greedy." He slipped his fingers inside her once more, delv-ing deep, bringing a gasp to her lips. "I want to do everything at once."

Her senses were battered by the prospect of once again expe-riencing all that they'd shared together. *"Oh yes."* She was barely able to say the words.

Gavin captured her lips. Madison responded with everything she had, running her tongue along his lower lip before delving deep inside to absorb his unique flavor.

His fingers worried her nipple through the ring, pulling, pinching, squeezing. Every touch intensified the heavy ache in her lower belly, just enough to keep her teetering on the edge, hungry for more.

Gripping her hips, he shifted her lower body slightly to one side, exposing her ass. The ties holding her wrists had enough play that she was able to move comfortably. Even canted to her side with her wrists bound over her head, she was still able to lock her eyes on him, wanting not just to feel everything but to see it. Sliding his hand caressingly over one buttock, he rubbed her skin lazily. She held her breath, knowing what he was about to do. Gavin had an obsession with her ass.

He was not one to disappoint. Slipping his right hand in the warm crevice, he trailed his fingers down to her anus and teased the puckered orifice. Swirling lower, he delved into the crease, gathering up moisture. When he finally came back up and rubbed against the tight ring of muscles, gently slipping past it, Madison released the breath she'd been holding, her lips slightly parted.

"It's been a long time, Maddie," he murmured gruffly. "I'm dying to be here." He worked in another digit, easing past the tightness, getting her used to being penetrated *there* once more.

It felt so good. She moaned when he slipped his thumb inside her, working it in until his palm was flat against her mound. She began to undulate against him.

The feeling of being deliciously helpless swelled as he continued to work her with his magical fingers. Through the fog of pleasure clouding her mind, she knew she was getting close, so close . . . When he pulled back, she moaned in protest.

"Shh," he murmured. "I'm not going to rush this." His face was a mask of hunger, calling forth a deep, answering need inside her.

Gavin settled once more between her splayed legs. His gaze

was dark and hot. "This will always be with us, Maddie. You can't deny it, and neither can I."

It was the truth. She'd realized it as soon as she'd stepped inside the cabin. No matter what had happened between them in the past, no matter what would happen to them when they left the cabin, *this* would always be there, between them.

Gavin shifted to his knees. Madison swallowed at the sight of him, naked and aroused. Beautifully sculpted from his wide, muscled shoulders to his flat, trim waist and the long, thick cock that jutted proudly from a nest of dark curls, Gavin took her breath away. "I want you in my mouth," she whispered.

He stood on the bed, bracing his long legs on either side of her, positioning the wide, bulbous tip right at her lips.

"Suck it," he instructed hoarsely.

Opening obediently, Maddie trembled as he slowly drove the head between her parted lips. He was huge, wide. She rubbed her tongue just under the ridge of the head, exactly as he'd taught her, and earned a soft grunt in response.

Gavin went in carefully, feeding her one delicious inch at a time. She breathed through her nose as she took more and more. Her cheeks hollowed as she sucked his flesh, moistening him on the long, slow slide back up before pulling him in deep once more.

"Come on, babe," he whispered roughly, his free hand threading through her hair. "You can take some more."

Even as she took a couple more inches, there was still plenty left. Madison relaxed her throat and sought to take him deeper, loving the way he tightened his hand on her hair, reminding her he was in control.

"God, yes. Just a little bit more. I want you to take the whole thing."

She took him until she could take no more, until he was touching the back of her throat. He had both his hands in her hair now, guiding her movements during the long, slow suck she gave him.

"You always knew just how to suck my cock," he groaned. "Like that, babe."

He was almost more than she could handle, her lips stretched impossibly wide. Her nipples tightened and wetness dripped down to her upper thighs. She'd always enjoyed taking him between her lips, loved giving him this pleasure.

Gavin was fucking her mouth, alternating short strokes with longer, deeper ones. "God, yes. Get it nice and wet, Maddie. It'll be inside you soon, babe," he whispered, urging her on.

Moaning, Madison caressed with her tongue the thick vein that ran under his shaft before rimming the head and then sucking him deep. He let her go on for another minute, his hands clenching and unclenching in her hair before he finally pulled out of her mouth altogether. At the soft sound of protest she made, Gavin grimaced. "No more, or this'll be over before we even start."

As he stepped off the bed, Maddie admired the lean, muscled strength etched in the graceful line of his spine. Gavin might be a bestselling author, but he wasn't a sedentary one. He regularly worked out in the gym and ran up to five miles a day. Even his feet were as beautiful as the rest of him, long, narrow, perfectly shaped. A sharp thrill went through her. For tonight, at least, he would be hers again.

When he turned to face her, Madison caught her breath. He held a large butt plug in one hand and a tube of lubricant in the other. Anticipation kicked her sharply in the stomach. His progress back to her side was slow and deliberate. Her eyes were wide as she watched him squirt a thick line of lube on the plug, spreading it with his hand. She shivered. It had been so long . . .

Gavin didn't have to tell her what to do; she already knew. She raised her hips when he slipped a pillow underneath her, and opened her legs obediently. He worked his finger in first, gently stretching her, lubricating the little puckered opening. Old habits die hard, so she knew to look at him while he rubbed the tip of the plug against her, never breaking eye contact, letting him see everything she felt. Deliberately relaxing, she was none-theless unable to control the sudden jump of her pulse when he worked the tip of the plug inside her ass. Holding the toy in one hand, Gavin put the other to good use, manipulating her aching clit until she arched off the bed. Moments later, he finally eased the plug past the tight ring of muscle.

Madison let out a long, low whimper as it slid in all the way, until the cold, flat base rested against her bottom. She pulled deep, shuddering breaths into her lungs, feeling stretched to the limit. Gavin ran his palms up and down her inner thighs, patiently letting her get reacquainted with one of their favorite toys.

"Tell me it feels good," he commanded gruffly.

She couldn't deny it. "Y-yes."

"You're so sexy, Maddie," he muttered, bending to lick a dis-tended nipple. "Lying there with a plug up your ass, begging me with your eyes for more." He kissed her, his tongue delving into her mouth. "I need to taste you."

She writhed on the bed, as much as she could in her posi-tion. At the first touch of his mouth on her pussy, she trembled violently. Gavin was a master at everything he did. Every lick and lap, every foray inside her slit was measured to drive her insane. When he pushed the plug in and out her ass while he ate her, she toppled over the edge. With a cry, she bucked against him and came.

He rode it out to the last tremor before he got to his knees. He slid his hands behind her knees, pulling her legs up before positioning the plumlike head of his cock at her entrance. His progress was slow, the tight fit made even more snug due to the plug still lodged in her backside.

"Jesus." He breathed roughly. He held her steady when she would have moved. "Easy, baby. It's a tight fit."

Madison whimpered, her breath hitching sharply as he slowly worked his way inside her. "Gavin," she moaned, tortured and pleasured. He merely grunted in response, gritting his teeth as he slowly slid in to the hilt. She couldn't breathe, couldn't think, filled to the brim. Tossing her damp hair away from her face, she pleaded, "Fuck me now."

Gavin pushed in and out, his pace agonizingly slow. Eyes glittering darkly, he rubbed a thumb over her lips, slipping it into her mouth. Madison bit the fleshy part of his finger.

"Harder. I want it harder," she begged shamelessly. It had been too long since she was with him like this.

"Damn it." Gavin moved incrementally faster, driving her against the headboard. Pleasure exploded inside her, an insistent throbbing that battered her senses. In a low voice, he told her how much he wanted her, what she was doing to him, what he was feeling. His erotic words washed over her, his words of praise—sometimes gentle, sometimes frankly sexual—heightening her pleasure. When he gently pinched her nipples, she moaned and asked for more, craving the pain and the pleasure that went along with it. Her breath came in heavy pants as he stroked in and out of her slick channel with long, mind-blowing thrusts that jammed the plug even deeper in her ass.

It was too much. With a scream she had no hope of holding back, Madison gave in to the exquisite release. She shuddered convulsively, gasping, whimpering as he plowed on without mercy, giving her no quarter. A second later, Gavin groaned and she felt his hot seed jet inside her. The bedroom was filled with a cacophony of soft moans and whispers.

Gavin slumped over her. He released her wrists from their restraints, pulled them down and rubbed her arms gently. Madison lay limp and boneless against him, drained and satiated. He arranged her so she was lying on her side before gently pulling out the plug. He got up and went to the bathroom, returning with a warm washcloth and tenderly cleaning her. Madison didn't utter one word of protest when he came back to bed with her after he was done.

Drowsy with satisfaction, she snuggled against him. "Gavin," she murmured softly before she gave in to sleep.

5

⁂

THE WIND WAS STILL howling when Madison woke up. Rubbing her eyes, she glanced at the small clock radio on the bedside table, surprised to see it was almost nine o'clock in the morning. Gingerly shifting under the heavy arm that lay across her waist, she took in Gavin's sleeping face. A thick lock of dark hair fell across his forehead, his lashes formed half-moons on his cheeks. His nose was far from perfect. It had a slight bump in the middle, something he'd acquired in a fight when he was a teenager. His lips were beautifully shaped and had the power to turn women into weak-kneed, lust-crazed creatures. Including her. Resisting the temptation to look under the thick blanket, she tiptoed out of bed. Gavin must have gotten up sometime in the middle of the night and added more logs to the woodstove, for the fire was still going. She stood by the window watching the snow flurries that fell endlessly on the already white ground. The storm hadn't abated.

Madison moved into the bathroom and turned on the

shower, shivering slightly in the cool air. Steam rose as she stepped into the tiled cubicle, raising her face to the delicious heat of the water. Now that it was morning, what was she going to do?

She picked up the shampoo, squirted some on her hand and worked her hair into a lather. Last night proved that she was still susceptible to Gavin. Nothing had changed. It had been like that from the moment they first met. Their eyes had locked across the room and she had known with the first sting of hot awareness that she would end up with him . . .

"HELLO," HE GREETED HER with a sexy smile. "I'm Gavin Cahill."

His dark brown eyes were like velvet. "Madison," she replied, her voice husky. He was standing close—so close that the expensive wool of his suit brushed against her dress. He was much taller than she, even in her heels she had to look up at him.

When his gaze dropped to her lips, she'd licked at them nervously. He was staring at her hungrily, making no effort to mask it. The music, the buzz of conversation, the clinking of wineglasses faded into the background until she was aware only of him.

"Let's find a quiet place."

There was no asking, no hesitation, just a direct invitation to leave with him. "Uh, th-the party," she stammered. "Wouldn't it be rude to just leave?"

"Do you want to stay?"

She could smell the mint on his breath. Their lips were mere inches apart. "Not really," she admitted huskily.

He trailed his hand down her bare arm before capturing hers. "Let's go, then."

Without a thought of the friend who she had come to the party with, Madison willingly let him pull her through the throng and out the ballroom door. Silence enveloped them as he took her farther down the carpeted hallway of the large estate, seeming to know exactly where he was headed.

"Where are we going?" she asked breathlessly.

"Right here." He pulled her inside a darkened room, a small lamp illuminating the desk in the far corner. In the dimness of her surroundings, she could only make out the stacks of books on built-in shelves and plump leather couches in the middle of the room.

"What are we—"

He backed her against the wall and swooped down to take her lips. Her mind scattered into a million pieces and she responded instinctively, opening her mouth to let him in. He swept inside her mouth like he owned it, thoroughly kissing her senseless. By the time she became aware of her surroundings once more, the halter top of her dress was down to her waist.

"Beautiful," he muttered, palming her breasts. When he squeezed her nipples, she moaned. When he inserted a thigh between hers, she obligingly parted her legs. And when he growled as her dress got in the way, she didn't stop him when he pulled it up her legs and bunched it around her waist. She rode his thigh, slightly off balance, forced to hang on to him. He sucked on her neck and kneaded her ass, sliding his hands inside the silk of her panties. She was whimpering, fevered, wanting more. She'd never done anything like this, had never let a perfect stranger take such liberties. Her knees almost buckled when he took her hand and placed it on the erection that strained against the front of his trousers.

She didn't even think of stopping. It was all so urgent, so demanding, that her head reeled. There was a desperate hunger to the way they touched each other, sweeping aside all common sense and caution.

"I need to be inside you," he murmured harshly.

"I know," she replied urgently. She felt his fingers as he made quick work of his pants. "Hurry." In the next second, he freed himself. She looked down and swallowed, marveling at the beauty of his flesh. He ripped her underwear and she gasped, not in shock, but at the heat of his hand as he cupped her mound.

"So hot." He shifted slightly away and fumbled impatiently with his wallet. He handed her a foil packet. "Put it on me."

She bit her lip, tearing open the square. His groan reached her ears as she rolled the condom down the length of his shaft. He lifted her off the ground, wrapped her legs around his waist and smoothly slid into her pussy. Their simultaneous groans of pleasure broke the silence.

To Madison, it was unlike anything she'd ever felt before. She caught her breath, only to release it slowly as he began to thrust in and out. It wasn't slow, it wasn't tender. It was a mad coupling combined with the sheer desperation of needing to have each other. Her orgasm hit her hard. She shuddered, holding tightly on to him. She was dimly aware of Gavin following her, feeling the delicious swell of his cock as he came.

When he gently put her back on her feet, she straightened her clothing, at a loss for words. Picking up her torn panties, Gavin slipped them into his pocket. "Let's go." He took her hand once more and led her out into the hallway where a few people were chatting. She blushed and averted her eyes as they emerged into the warm evening air. He took her to his house and she spent the night. She didn't want to let him out of her sight. She got ready to go home the next day, already thinking of when she could see him again, when he suggested she just pack up some clothes and spend another night with him.

One night turned into two. Two turned into three and so on. More and more of her things ended up at his place until she finally stopped going home altogether. By the end of the first month, they were living together.

A month after that, they were sitting out on the terrace, enjoying the balmy night air and looking at the twinkling city lights. Madison leaned against Gavin and listened as he talked about his latest book and the publicity tour that was sure to follow. She loved listening to the sound of his voice, deep and low, intimate, as if she was the only person in the world he wanted to talk to.

Gavin chuckled. "Maddie, are you listening to me?"

Rubbing her cheek against his chest, she closed her eyes in pleasure. "Uh-huh." She could sit there forever and just listen to him talk, enclosed in his arms, feeling loved.

He fished something out of his pocket and held it in front of her. It was a diamond ring, square cut, set in a simple platinum setting. She twisted around and faced him, her heart beating as fast as a jackhammer.

"I think it's about time you made an honest man of me, don't you agree?"

"Oh Gavin."

"Marry me, Maddie," he said gruffly. "Let's make this permanent."

She must have said yes, because the next thing she knew, he

was slipping the ring on her finger. Gavin insisted they marry soon. Two weeks later, they were married in a simple ceremony with only close friends and family in attendance.

After the wedding, her mother had pulled her aside. "I certainly hope you know what you're doing, Madison."

She blinked. "What do you mean, Mom?"

Janice inclined her head over to where Gavin stood, surrounded by his friends. "A man like that, you think he's going to stay faithful to you?"

"Mom," she chided, shocked that her mother could say such a thing.

"I only want you to go into this with your eyes wide open. Men like Gavin Cahill will never be satisfied with just one woman. Look at your father. Believe me when I say that you need to protect yourself and get ready for any eventuality."

Madison fought to keep her voice light but she failed. "Gavin loves me and I love him. He's not like Dad."

Janice scoffed at that. "We all start out with the best intentions, honey. But mark my words, even the strongest of men succumb to temptation."

Unable to listen any longer, Madison murmured an excuse and left, weighed down by sadness. Her mother's bitterness over her husband's repeated betrayals had warped her view of men and marriage. Over and over again, she'd hammered into Madison that men were not to be trusted, planting in her young mind a real fear of infidelity. Why today, on her wedding day, would her mother choose to spread her bitter poison?

Madison's head began to throb and she headed swiftly to the ladies' room, needing a moment alone. Gavin suddenly appeared, a look of concern on his face.

"Maddie?"

The tightness in her chest eased as she looked into his eyes. His very presence comforted her. Gavin would never cheat on her. Her mother was wrong about him.

He smoothed the wisps of hair away from her face, his touch tender. "What's wrong?"

The worry in his voice lessened her anxiety. She mustered a smile. "You made me the happiest woman alive by making me your wife." She would have preferred that nothing marred this day, but she had to get it off her chest, had to hear him reassure her. "I just want you to know that I love you."

His dark eyes softened. "I love you too."

She rubbed her cheek against his palm. "You know that . . . that if there's anything that would drive me away, it's infidelity." She rushed on. "I've seen what it can do to a marriage. I don't want that to happen to us."

Gavin pulled her close, tipping her face up to press a gentle kiss on her lips. "I would *never* be unfaithful to you."

His voice rang with sincerity. Just like that, all Madison's doubts melted away. She hugged him tightly, closing her eyes. "I know. I just needed to hear you say it."

WITH A SIGH, MADISON pulled herself back to the present and rinsed her hair. She'd been naïve and trusted him completely. Closing her eyes, she reached for the soap and jumped when it was placed in her palm.

She opened her eyes to see a very naked Gavin standing in the shower stall with her.

He grinned. "Good morning. Did you leave me any hot water?"

She tried not to let her gaze stray lower. Just having him this close was enough to raise her temperature. "I'm sure there's a lot left."

Stepping close to her, he adjusted the nozzle so the water would hit them both. "Still, it might be better to shower together. All in the name of conservation, of course."

Not knowing what to say, feeling off-kilter, she didn't demur when he started soaping her. His touch was as hot as the water when he rubbed the soap against her skin, lingering on her breasts. Madison reveled at the sheer sensuality of his touch. He was determined to get her clean, soaping and rubbing every crevice, every curve. When he wandered between her legs, she stopped him with her hand.

Gavin grinned. "I'm making sure you're clean everywhere. Come on, Maddie, open up."

She obediently opened her legs, willing to play the game. Maybe because in the back of her mind, she knew this was temporary. A fantasy she was living while the storm raged outside and they were isolated in this cabin in the woods. For a short time, nothing else existed except her and Gavin. Not their divorce, not his infidelity, and certainly not all the anger and pain she'd bottled up.

Just for a little while, she reassured herself, she'd play along and live out this surreal dream of being with him again. She'd enjoy it while she could.

Gavin was thorough. By the time he was done, she'd been soaped from head to toe, and her breathing had turned heavy. He handed her the soap, clearly expecting her to return the favor. Madison eagerly ran her hands over corded muscles that flexed under her touch. Wanting him to be as affected as she was, she soaped him thoroughly, taking special care with the hard flesh that rose high and proud between them.

When he finally rinsed, his lips were pulled into a tight line and the teasing grin was gone. He kissed her, their wet bodies sliding against each other. Her eyes fluttered shut. There was something about long, deep, intimate kisses that spoke more than words could say. She lost awareness of time, their lips melded to one another. By the time he let go, she was clinging to him, grateful for his arms supporting her.

Madison lowered her face, trying to hide how a simple, poignant act like kissing could affect her so deeply. Only in the past twenty-four hours had she realized exactly how much she'd lost when their marriage fell apart. It hit her hard, pressing like a heavy weight on her chest.

Trying to stop her churning thoughts, she dried off and combed her wet hair while Gavin brushed his teeth. The scene was reminiscent of old times, when they would share a shower at the start of every day. The simple intimacy of the situation struck her hard, adding to the already deepening feeling of loss. She missed sharing her life with him.

The lights flickered for a moment before coming back on.

Gavin grabbed a towel from the rack and wiped his face. "The power's probably gonna go out soon. I'm surprised it didn't go out last night." He wrapped the towel around his hips and opened the door. "Don't take too long. I'll make us some breakfast."

Another burst of nostalgia hit her. Even though she'd loved cooking for him, Gavin oftentimes insisted on making their meals. It was his way of unwinding after a long day of writing. She would arrive home from the coffee shop to find him in the kitchen whistling softly as he cooked.

Though it was difficult to ignore the flood of painful memories, it did her no good to dwell on the past. Madison twisted her damp hair into a coil on top of her head and dressed. She emerged from the bedroom just in time to see Gavin put eggs and bacon on a plate. The scent of fresh coffee wafted on the air, and slices of bread popped up from the toaster.

Going on autopilot, Madison poured Gavin a cup of black coffee. She hadn't forgotten that part. After fixing her own, she handed him the mug and sat down at the table.

At that moment, a particularly strong gust of wind rattled the windows. Startled, she whipped around to stare outside. The weather hadn't let up. How long was this storm going to last?

"It'll keep up for probably another day or so," Gavin stated, answering her unspoken question. "Don't worry. I've got all the supplies we'll need in the shed out back."

She chewed on her toast. "You're going to miss this place when it's sold."

"This was the one place where I could write with no inter-ruptions. The isolation worked well for me."

Her heartbeat tripped. "What about your writing?"

"I'm looking at a house somewhere else."

Madison stilled. "Far away?"

"I'm thinking somewhere in Europe. Maybe a nice place outside of London."

Dismay filled her at the thought of him a whole continent away. "Th-that sounds great." She tried to smile but failed. "What's important is you'll be able to do your work. I know you'll miss this place though."

"It's time to move on. I've been here since July."

Her eyes flew to his. He'd been here since . . .

"I've been here since the divorce became final. The only time I went back was for that museum gala I'd promised Wesley's sis-ter I'd attend." His expression was intense as he leaned forward.

"Why are you surprised? You didn't expect me to seek solitude and lick my wounds? Did you think I'd go out and party the very same day?" He frowned. "You expected me to just shrug off the fact that you filed for divorce and go on my merry way?"

She couldn't deny that she'd thought exactly that. "I thought you'd be happy that you were free."

"I was devastated, Maddie." His dark eyes flickered with anger. "Then I was pissed. Pissed that you could trust me so little and leave me so easily."

That left her speechless.

Gavin pushed his plate away, his jaw tight. "I'm going to the shed to get some more firewood and get the generator ready." Walking to the door, he shrugged on his parka and pulled on thick gloves before stepping outside.

Madison couldn't move, shocked and dumbfounded. All this time, Gavin had hidden away in this little cabin licking his wounds. Unable to sit there a minute longer, she quickly washed the dishes and put them away. But still he hadn't come back. Peering out the window, she couldn't make anything out. Getting worried, she pulled on her parka and followed him outside. Heading to the side of the cabin, she found Gavin loading up a cart with various items. It was snowing so hard she could barely see in front of her, but she went to him anyway.

"What can I do to help?" she asked, raising her voice to be heard over the wind.

If he was surprised to find her there, he didn't show it. Instead, he handed her a bag of canned goods to add to the ones in the pantry. She quickly walked back in the warmth of the cabin and put them away. Gavin followed not far behind and closed the door. The cart was full of firewood and bottled water and other things she couldn't see.

"The generator is ready to go anytime the power goes off. So don't worry, we're not going to die in this storm."

"I'm not worried," she replied cautiously, trying to gauge his mood.

The sudden crackling of a radio broke the thick silence between them. Gavin strode to the corner where his computer was and pressed a button on the ham radio she hadn't noticed was there. He talked to a man who identified himself as the sheriff. From the sound of it, Gavin had a pretty good rapport going with the man, who was checking to make sure he was okay.

Madison wandered over to the window and sat looking out. He'd stayed here alone for months after their divorce became final. He'd sought solitude. He'd wanted to get away.

But that little voice in her head was quick to remind her that all this had happened because she'd caught him with another woman.

Frustration hit her. God, she wished she could just clear her thoughts. She was confused. Her emotions were jumbled. She couldn't shake off memories of her life with Gavin, even though she knew it was no use rehashing the past. Feeling Gavin's gaze on her, she reluctantly turned.

Just then, the power suddenly went out. Although it was not yet noon, it was dark outside. The fire in the hearth cast dancing shadows on the wall. When Gavin started to turn on a gas lamp, she stopped him. "It's nice like this. Maybe we could just save the lamp for tonight when we'll really need it?"

He shrugged and sat across from her.

"How's your mother?"

"Fine," he replied curtly. "Thanks for asking."

She bit back a sigh, refusing to be deflated by his demeanor. "I liked your mother, Gavin. She was always nice to me."

"At the moment, she's enjoying herself on a Caribbean cruise." He paused. "She liked you too. Always has." The close relationship he had with his mother was something she'd never had for herself. Marilyn Cahill had been warm and caring, eager to get to know her daughter-in-law.

Once again, Madison's gaze strayed to Gavin. She resisted the urge to fidget, something she always did when she was nervous. His mood was difficult to read, and she didn't know what else to say. This uncomfortable silence was hard on her nerves.

"How's the coffee shop?"

"Thriving," she replied with a small smile, grateful that he'd initiated conversation. "The store next door to me is closing. I'm thinking of taking that space and expanding."

"Things are going that well, then?"

At least they were talking. "Oh yes. Right now, I have four part-time employees, college students who need extra money. I like interacting with people, meeting customers, getting to know regulars." She drew her knees up under her chin. "When I was growing up, I helped out at my aunt's coffee shop every summer. It was then I realized I had a knack with people."

"You've made a success of it. You should be proud of yourself."

Madison flushed. "It's something I can truly call my own. When we were together, it helped keep me busy too. I mean, as soon as we came back from our honeymoon, you went back to writing."

"I was under a deadline at the time, Maddie."

"I know that," she rushed on. "I wasn't implying anything. It's just that, the times we were together, most of them were spent in—"

"Bed," he finished for her. "You don't have to remind me."

"It's the truth. Talking was the last thing we did. And then you were busy with your book tour and, well, you know the rest."

A thoughtful look came over his face. "You think we rushed into getting married without really knowing one another?"

"We really *didn't* know one another, did we?" Her smile was rueful. "There are still so many things you don't know about me."

"You told me a little about your father."

Squirming uncomfortably in her chair, she shot him a chiding look. "Yes and let's not go there right now."

Gavin stared at her broodingly. "I've been a selfish bastard, haven't I? I married you then buried my head in my work, only coming out long enough for mind-blowing sex." He ran a hand through his hair. "Was I a lousy husband?"

A wave of sadness hit her. "No. Not lousy. Just . . . busy."

"Is that why you decided to surprise me that day at the hotel?" he suddenly asked. "Because we hadn't been spending enough time together?"

"Well . . . " she hesitated, realizing they were venturing into extremely sensitive territory. "I just thought it would be nice to surprise you."

"I'm sorry for putting my work before you."

"It's in the past, Gavin." Her voice was heavy with the regret that weighed her down. "There's nothing we can do to bring it back now, is there?"

Gavin abruptly pushed himself out of the chair and opened the door, pulling his parka from the coatrack.

"Where are you going?"

"For a walk."

"In this weather?" He didn't answer and stepped outside. "Gavin—"

The door slammed. He was gone.

Madison debated whether to follow him outside, but decided to just stay put. He knew the area well, even though a thick blanket of snow was currently coating it. That thought did little to ease her apprehension. Anything could happen out there. "Damn it, Gavin. What a stupid thing to do."

She sat by the window, anxiously waiting for him to return. The snow fell rapidly, and the intensity of the storm hadn't lessened. Peering outside, she could see nothing but white. Where was he? It was freezing outside, and visibility was near zero. Her glance strayed to her watch again and again as she counted the minutes. When he failed to return after fifteen minutes, her anxiety deepened. She chewed on her lip. Gripping the windowsill, she searched for any sign of him, even a glimpse of his dark parka. Nothing. Time crawled by. Madison paced in front of the window, hoping to sight him right away. She sat down. She got up again. After half an hour, she was wringing her hands. Her nerves were stretched thin. *I'm going to kill him. What if something happens to him out there?*

Cursing her stupidity for not following him, she agonized and worried about him. *Please let him be okay. Bring him back to me.* She teetered between anger and tears, biting her nails nervously. Talking about the past never did them any good. When would they learn not to dredge up what had happened during their brief marriage? It was over. Finished. They should've left well enough alone. Now Gavin was out there somewhere and she was terrified he was hurt or trapped in this awful weather. She eyed the radio he'd used earlier. How hard could it be to figure out how to use it? It looked simple enough. She'd just made up her mind to try calling the sheriff when she heard the heavy thud of boots on the porch. Before he could even open the door, she'd beaten him to it.

"Where the hell have you been?" she demanded, her anger born out of fear. "I was so worried!" She shut the door behind him and glared at his back.

Gavin shook the snow from his head and carefully put his parka back on the coatrack. When he faced her, his features were grim. "Were you worried I was going to die and leave you here all alone?"

Fury swelled to her throat so fast it almost choked her. "Of all the stupid things to say." Tears welled up in her eyes. "I thought you got lost, hurt or worse, buried under all this stupid snow! You're such an ass, Gavin." Madison pushed him aside, stalked into the bedroom and slammed the door. She sat at the far end of the bed, quickly swiping away her tears. What an insensitive boor. How could he think that her safety was the reason she was worried? *This is what I get for caring what happened to him at all.* It seemed like one way or another, they always ended up hurting each other.

She stiffened as the door opened. The bed dipped as Gavin sat behind her. Refusing to look at him, she tipped her face away, still simmering with anger.

"I'm sorry." His voice was low, quiet. "I didn't mean to worry you. I was actually in the shed freezing my nuts off. I needed to think." Madison closed her eyes when Gavin laid his hands on her shoulders and began to knead softly. He ran his thumbs over her nape, burrowing under the tendrils of hair that had escaped from her twist. He worked his way down her back, his fingers pressing with just enough pressure to get rid of the tension that tightened her muscles. "Okay?" he murmured against her ear.

Under his soothing touch, her anger melted away. Madison knew he was trying to make amends. "Yeah." It felt so good to be in his arms, knowing he was here safe with her. She didn't stop him when his fingers drifted to her front and pulled off her sweater off and unclasped her bra.

In the glow of the embers in the woodstove, her rings glinted softly. Gavin rolled his palms over her nipples. She moaned softly. He pushed her to stand up and turned her around to face him, working on her jeans. Shadows danced on the angles of his face, highlighting the slash of his cheekbones and the dark intensity of his eyes. Placing her hands on his shoulders, she obediently raised her legs one after the other and kicked free of her jeans and underwear. The atmosphere was hushed, hazy. Neither of them said a word, as if by unspoken agreement. Words would have ruined the moment.

He tugged her back down onto the bed before quickly shedding his clothes. Naked and aroused, he knelt between her parted legs, his hooded gaze sweeping over her.

Gavin ran his palms up and down her body, heating her with his touch, spreading fire everywhere. When he came to her breasts, he pinched the tips. She moaned at the sharp, piercing pleasure-pain. He drew his hand over the slight bump of her belly before coasting down to the roundness of her hips. With a fingertip, he traced her hip bone and swirled over her bare mound glistening with moisture. Without any warning, he delivered a light slap to the bare mons.

Madison shuddered.

He did it again, this time aiming his hand so that he hit her swollen clit dead-on. She moaned but didn't move. She knew this game well, had played it many times with him.

In quick succession, Gavin delivered four more taps to her pussy, all in varying degrees of intensity but always hitting the little nub that swelled impudently from between the wet labia. Madison bit her lip, her breath coming in quick pants, loving the delicious sting of the blows on the sensitive mass of nerves. *More.*

His eyes were locked on her mound. "So pretty. Plump and pink." A finger swiped moisture from the cleft, spreading it around lazily. Her pulse jumped crazily as he delivered another tap. She rose off the bed, arching closer to him. But the warning tap he delivered on one buttock made her sink back down on the soft mattress. "Don't move."

Pushing her legs apart, he flicked at the ring with his finger. The brief movement jarred the stiff button, and she moaned. He played with her, working the sensitive point until she felt like bursting. Helpless against the need ripping through her, she undulated her hips, trying to get his finger to slip inside the sopping slit that so needed him. "Gavin—"

"Not yet." Positioning his big body between her legs, he pulled open the puffy lips and blew on her, sending the delicate pendant bumping against the swollen nub. Madison trembled, in tune with every little thing that happened to her down there. With his tongue, he licked the swollen nub, tracing and shaping, lifting and gently tapping.

She clenched the sheets until her fingers hurt. She couldn't stand it. Gavin alternated between deep and firm licks to light, barely there touches. She panted, moaning softly, pleading incoherently. Anything, *anything* to let him know how much she needed him to fuck her now.

"Patience, Maddie," he instructed her in a voice that throbbed with heat. "You can't come yet." He buried his face between her legs, working his tongue in the soaked crevices, sinking deep inside her.

She reared off the bed, a cry breaking from her lips. "Oh God." The need for release frayed her control. Sweat broke out on her body as she desperately tried to hold back. Even the deep, measured breaths she took only provided temporary relief. "Gavin, I don't think I can wait," she cried out in desperation.

He ignored her plea, eating her with an intensity that shredded her restraint. Madison shuddered violently. When he gently bit down, she cried out. "I'm coming," she gasped. "I can't hold it . . . "

Sharp pleasure slammed into her, her pussy clenching tightly as she came. His name was a litany on her lips as she rode out the sensations. Gavin was merciless, pushing her up and over after the first intense wave. Madison was delirious from the sensual assault, racked with powerful aftershocks of pleasure.

He held her in the circle of his arms until the tremors gradually ebbed, soothing her with gentle touches, murmuring sweet words in her ears. The bed dipped as he got up. When she was finally able to open her languorous eyes, the sight before her made her go weak at the knees.

Gavin knelt on the edge of the mattress, spreading a thick line of lubricant on his palm. His eyes were locked on her as he coated his erection liberally, from the broad head to the root. His intent was plain, and she wasn't about to stop him. She didn't *want* to stop him.

"Get up."

Madison stood gingerly, her thighs heavy with renewed lust.

She greedily eyed his beautiful body as he sat on the bed and leaned against the propped-up pillows and headboard. Excitement raced up her spine as she waited for what was going to happen. Gavin spread his legs, his shaft rising from its nest of dark curls like a thick sword. He let her look her fill for a moment, taking his well-oiled cock in his fisted hand and caressing it with slow, deliberate motions. Maddie trembled, knowing what was to come, helpless against the tide of lust that swept over her.

He indicated the thick tube lying on top of the sheet. "Prepare yourself."

Her knees almost buckled under as she picked up the tube of lubricant. His eyes were hooded, half closed, but she knew he was watching her closely. Jagged anticipation streaked through her. She was already looking forward to the forbidden. It was the most basic and primal act of possession, one that she wouldn't deny him. Her hands trembled as she applied the thick lube between her buttocks, dipping inside the tightly puckered muscle again and again, knowing it would ease his entry. When she was done, she licked her lips and waited.

"Come here."

Madison was under his spell, bound by his will, unable to do anything else but obey. Getting on her knees, she moved to his side of the bed.

"Straddle me."

Her heart was trying to beat its way out of her chest as she swung one leg over him. Shaking, she shifted until her knees were on either side of his waist.

"Open yourself for me, Maddie." Gavin's voice was low and hypnotic.

She did as he asked, holding her buttocks open, biting her lower lip. It was difficult to maintain her position when she was quivering so much, but somehow she did it.

Gavin rubbed the lip she'd bitten, soothing it with a soft touch. "Take me inside you."

Madison descended in slow increments, pausing when she felt the head of his cock against her puckered entrance. Taking a deep breath, she pushed down gently, slowly, forcing herself to relax, feeling the broad tip ease inside the tight muscles. The lubricant aided his entry, but it was still a very tight fit.

He grunted but remained perfectly still, letting her set the pace, letting her take him in.

Madison took in a couple more inches, savoring the exquisite combination of pain and pleasure in taking him this way. Tossing her head back, she desperately held onto what little control she had left. Gavin played with her clit, gently tugging at the ring, swirling around it, adding to her arousal. She paused, reacquainting herself with the hard flesh impaling her ass. With a slight shudder, she took more inside her, never letting up until he was seated to the hilt. She was on sensory overload, her breathing uneven and raspy. This was the ultimate mastery of her body.

He slid his hands up to her breasts. Gavin worked the tight buds into aching tips, every tug and pull calculated to drive her insane. "I've waited so long for this to happen again. Move, babe."

Gripping the headboard with white-knuckled intensity, Madison obeyed. She slid all the way up until he almost slipped out, before gliding back all the way down. The dark curls tickled her wet pussy as she undulated above him. Her ears buzzed with the pleasure as she took him deep again and again.

Gavin took her breast and suckled hard. Madison moaned, her lust-glazed eyes locked on him as he pulled at the nipple caught in the ring. The slight pain intensified all the other sensations swimming through her as she bounced on his lap.

Gavin slipped his fingers inside her slit, crooking the digits and starting a mind-blowing pumping motion. She whimpered a plea—for what, she didn't know—when he thumbed the aching bud, rubbing sensuously without interrupting the in-and-out movement of his fingers.

"Tell me how you feel, Maddie."

"I feel . . . I feel . . . " she trailed off, unable to form an answer.

"Good?"

"Y-yes," she breathed, moving faster. "It feels so . . . I can't . . . Oh Gavin—"

"Fuck me faster," he growled.

Under the shadow of the flickering firelight, she did as he bade her, taking him deep with ever-increasing speed. Her skin glistened with perspiration, their damp breath mingled. Gavin wrapped his other arm around her waist, holding her tight, all the while plunging his fingers in her pussy and sucking the nipple closest to his mouth. Stars exploded behind her closed eyelids. Madison gritted her teeth, skating on the edge of insanity, knowing she wouldn't last for long.

"I want to feel your ass clenching sweetly, tightly, on me. Come, Maddie," he rasped.

The floodgates opened. She cried out as her orgasm exploded through her body. Intense, almost painful pleasure rolled through in a giant wave, robbing her of all thought. She clamped down on his fingers; she clamped down on his shaft. "Gavin. Gavin," she chanted mindlessly as she absorbed the pain and pleasure of their joining. He cupped her nape and drew her lips down to his. Madison poured everything she felt into the kiss. She never wanted it to end.

"Maddie," Gavin groaned, thrusting, his cock swelling impossibly bigger a moment before he blasted his seed inside her. Madison sought his lips, her tongue delving within to tangle with his in a heated duel. She couldn't get enough of him, clenching around him as he rode out his own pleasure. Her heart pounded in her chest, gradually slowing back to normal until the very last shudder was wrung from her body.

"Whatever else that may have happened between us, Maddie, we have *this*. We'll always have this."

Madison buried her face in his neck, silent tears coursing down her cheeks. She wept for what was and what could have been. Her heart ached, and for a moment, just for a moment, she wished she could wipe away everything that had happened between them and start over. He was right. They did have this. But would it be enough to carry them through the pain and uncertainty they would have to endure?

It wasn't. Trust was something that was earned, not freely given. They could never go back. Their time together in this cabin was just a dream, a fantasy they were living out while the storm raged outside.

Madison didn't say a word as Gavin cleaned her up, her heart twisting at the gentle way he cleansed her with a warm, damp cloth. Afterward he cleaned himself before sliding under the sheets with her and gathering her in his arms. Neither of them said a word. There was nothing left to say.

The storm lasted for a couple of hours more, then miraculously in the late afternoon, it stopped. The dark clouds parted and the sun peeked through, a feeble beacon of brightness that instead of making her happy, only intensified her sadness. The storm was gone and soon—as soon as the roads were cleared—she was going home, leaving Gavin for good.

6

THE ROAD CREWS WORKED all night to make the roads passable. While Maddie showered and got ready, Gavin remained in constant contact with the sheriff, making arrangements for the local garage to pull her car from the ditch she'd driven into and return it to the local rental agency she'd gotten it from. "Put the charges on my tab," he instructed the person on the other end before turning off the radio.

"I'll pay you," Maddie assured him quietly, emerging from the bathroom. "Just send me the bill and I'll take care of it."

"It's no big deal. Are you packed and ready to go?" At her nod, he strode to the door. "I'll meet you outside."

Madison took one last look around before slinging her purse over her shoulder and picking up her overnight bag. The personal items she'd chosen to take were all carefully packed in a box, ready to be shipped. It wasn't much, just some early pictures of her and Gavin, plus the wedding photos and a few personal items. She looked around once more. This was probably the last time she'd be in this cabin, which held so many memories of her life with Gavin. Soon, this chapter would be forever closed. Once he moved out of the country, she'd probably never see him again.

An engine started outside and revved. Madison pushed aside the sadness closing in on her. *Stop being silly,* she scolded herself. This time with Gavin had been nothing but a dream. Now it was time to go back to the real world, back to the lonely reality of her life.

Gavin met her at the bottom of the steps, standing next to a gleaming black SUV. He helped her inside before stowing her bag in the trunk. Silence reigned in the car as they drove through town. She shot him a puzzled look. "Aren't I supposed to get off here?"

"I'm taking you to the airport." His reply was curt, and he didn't even glance at her. As a final blow, he turned on the radio, filling the truck with soft jazzy music, discouraging any conversation. Madison stared out the window, taking in the blinding white of the snow-covered countryside. She didn't know why he was taking her to the airport. Things had been strained since they'd woken up that morning. Gavin was in a strange mood, brooding and quiet. At this point, plagued by her own depressing thoughts, she didn't even want to risk conversation.

Madison breathed a sigh of relief as he pulled into the airport terminal parking lot much later. The tense atmosphere had been nearly unbearable, the air thick and uncomfortable. She got out of the car, mentally readying herself to say good-bye. When Gavin pulled out an expensive-looking suitcase along with her bag, she frowned. "What are you—"

He merely turned away and headed into the building. Clamping her mouth shut, Madison hurried to keep up with his longer stride. When he didn't go to the airline counters, she finally pulled his arm to stop him.

"I need to check in."

"Not over there, you don't" was his calm reply. "I'm going back to L.A., you can ride with me." He continued walking, emerging in a hangar for private planes and charter jets.

"I can take a regular plane," Madison protested, having to almost run to keep up with him. "Gavin, will you *stop*?"

He finally did and gave her an impatient frown. "Our flight is scheduled to take off in twenty minutes. We have to board now."

"I didn't know you had your own plane," she blurted out like an idiot.

He shrugged. "It's chartered. I don't like flying. I like to be as comfortable as possible and commuter airlines are certainly not that." He glanced at his watch impatiently. "We're on a schedule here, Maddie. And don't give me any nonsense about not wanting to fly back with me. I'm going to L.A. too, so why not go together? Any more questions?"

She shook her head.

He headed for a jet that was idling on the runway. Madison followed his instructions like an automaton, choosing a seat in the plush cabin and buckling up. Gavin spoke to the pilot before closing the door to the cockpit and taking the seat across from her. Soon afterward, the plane taxied down the runway and took off. Gavin looked out the small window, appearing deep in thought.

In a way, she was glad he was ignoring her. This whole day had exhausted her, emotionally and spiritually. She felt like she'd been through the wringer, and it wasn't over yet. To say that her feelings were conflicted was putting it mildly, but she chalked it up to just being with him again. Whenever he was around, she just couldn't think straight. Once she was back on solid ground, on her home turf, she'd see things clearer and realize that she and Gavin were never meant to be together. This was only temporary. The time they'd spent together at the cabin would have to last her a lifetime.

Madison gasped in surprise when Gavin unceremoniously unbuckled her seat belt and yanked her out of her seat and pulled her into his lap. "What are you doing?" she asked, her heart beginning to thud heavily in her chest.

He didn't answer. Instead, he kissed her. Madison moaned under the onslaught. It was fraught with frantic hunger, mixed with an element of desperation. The misery that plagued her at the thought of never seeing him again was buried under the avalanche of need that welled up in her. She wanted this, needed it, just as much as he did.

Slipping his hand under her sweater, Gavin pushed it up and over her head in one quick movement. He disposed of her bra easily, exposing her breasts to his gaze. Her nipple rings glinted in the dull cabin lights as he bent and laved the stiff tip with his tongue.

Her mind went fuzzy. She whimpered when he sucked her deep into his mouth. Balanced precariously on his lap, she arched and offered him the other, bringing it close to his mouth, quivering in need as he lavished it with the same attention. Liquid heat traveled like electricity along her veins, raising her temperature, bringing instant flooding to her pussy. Needing to touch him, she fumbled with the buttons of his shirt, whimpering a faint protest when he didn't make a move to help her at all. Gavin was too busy laving her breasts, licking every inch of skin within his reach. Knowing he found so much pleasure in her body was more potent than any aphrodisiac. This time, pleasing him, taking him higher than he'd ever gone before, was very important.

Madison climbed off his lap and pulled him up. With a greed born of desperation, she pushed his shirt off his shoulders and fastened her lips to his skin. He tasted so good. She knelt, working on the fastening of his jeans, moaning in triumph as she pushed them down his muscular legs to the floor. On the way back up, she skimmed her lips up his thigh, bypassing his cock, and slowly slid up his chest to end at his neck, suckling the skin softly before she stepped away from him.

She shook her head when Gavin made to reach for her, motioning him to sit back down. In the isolation of the cabin, their eyes made contact and for a brief moment, Madison allowed the love she still felt for him to shine through. In that instant, they shared what was probably the most honest moment between them. Love and regret shone in her eyes, the same two emotions mirrored in his gaze.

She shimmied out of her jeans, slowly pushing them down her legs, taking her underwear along with them. Naked, she stood before him, feeling not one iota of shame or embarrassment, or reluctance or second thoughts. This time was for him.

Propping a leg next to his thigh, she moistened a finger with her tongue before trailing it down to one stiff nipple, slipping inside the gold ring and tugging gently. His eyes flashed with heat, glued to her finger as she swirled it around and around the distended crest.

Sliding her finger down over her belly, Madison reached between her legs and was instantly engulfed in warm, sticky moisture. Widening her stance, she slipped her fingers inside, tracing her labia, dipping in and out, circling from side to side. With her other hand, she drew back the lips, exposing her swollen button and the ring, along with the gold pendant. Madison never took her eyes away from him, noting his heightened color, the flared nostrils and the muscle in his jaw that ticked. Gavin was aroused, highly so. He wrapped his hand around his engorged flesh.

Giddy with desire and nearly out of her mind from the need tearing at her, Madison caressed herself in front of him, uncaring that just beyond the cabin door were the pilots, and that one could walk in at any moment. Gavin was as indifferent to the threat of discovery as she was, never taking his eyes away from her glistening labia.

She massaged her clit, going around and around, under and over. At his impatient growl, Madison rubbed her fingers against his lips, coating them with her moisture. Gently slipping inside the warm cavern of his mouth, she shivered as his tongue lapped hungrily at her, cleaning her fingers meticulously, sliding between each digit and savoring her taste.

"No more games." Gavin curved his hands around her buttocks and pulled her close, burying his face between her legs. Her knees buckled under her and Madison clutched the seat for support. He ate her voraciously, slurping his enjoyment, greedily inhaling her scent before plunging his tongue inside her slit.

Madison cried out, closing her eyes at the sharp pleasure that pulsed through her. She let him do what he wanted, offering her body to him without any words. Holding her tighter, Gavin explored every single inch of her dripping pussy, lashing at the bundle of nerves nestled between the folds before taking it between his lips and sucking hard.

She shuddered and bucked in his arms. He groaned, the

rough sound humming over her skin. She bit her lip and tried to hold still, but found that she couldn't, grinding against his face. "Oh God, Gavin."

He thumbed the hot bud, devastating her with the slow and deliberate way he rotated the fleshy part of his finger against it. Nearly insane, she ground her hips against his hand, needing firmer, harder contact. But he denied her even that, and continued to thumb her lightly, almost casually.

"Please," she cried softly. "I need more."

He finger-fucked her in measured beats, adopting a slow, lazy rhythm that didn't even begin to satisfy her. A strong tremor rocked her. "Gavin, hurry."

He stroked her faster. Madison opened her legs as wide as she could, inviting more of his touch, consumed by the need thundering through her veins like molten lava. He pulled away and stood, turning her as he positioned her in front of him. He pushed her legs wide apart and bent her slightly at the waist. Without hesitation, he plunged inside her, taking her from behind.

Madison moaned in bliss. She didn't want gentleness at this time—she wanted it rough and primal. "Yes . . . yes." She shivered as he pulled out entirely before plunging back in again. His hands latched onto her breasts, squeezing and pinching her nipples, driving her insane.

"Fuck me harder," she begged with mindless abandon.

His hips slammed against hers, making quick slapping sounds as he fucked her deep, again and again. Her senses whirled. Her heart pounded. Madison cried out again and again, uncaring if anybody else heard her pleas.

Gavin released his hold on her breasts, wrapped a hand in her thick hair and tugged her head back. He placed his lips in her ear and swirled his tongue around the soft shell before whispering, "Come for me."

As if his words triggered her release, a huge wave of pleasure slammed into her, robbing her of breath, wringing a harsh cry from her throat. Gavin didn't stop pounding into her through the shudders that racked her body, stroking in and out until he let out a mighty groan and went over the edge. She couldn't move, satiation rendering her boneless. Limp, she barely stirred when he reached for her clothes and dressed her. He pulled on his shirt and jeans before he sat back down and pulled her back onto his lap.

"We belong together, Maddie. Can't you see that?"

Her heart tore in two at his words. She placed a finger on his lips. "Gavin, no."

"Yes," he countered in a low, intense voice. "I love you, Maddie. Until the day I die, you will be the only woman for me. These last two days proved that we can be together. I want to try, Maddie. I want you to give us another chance."

Madison swallowed the lump in her throat. "We'll just end up hurting each other again."

Gavin took her hand and placed it over his heart. "I don't know what else I can do or say to make you believe me that I didn't cheat on you. I can only swear that what you think you saw that day was not what happened."

She closed her eyes, feeling the strong rhythm of his heart under her palm. His voice rang with sincerity.

"I didn't lie to you then and I'm not lying to you now." He closed his eyes and held her tight. "If you truly think there's no hope for us, that you can never trust me, then tell me now, Maddie. Tell me you don't love me anymore and I'll leave you alone forever."

Madison hid her face in her hands and let the tears flow. Did she really want to go back to long nights of dreaming about Gavin when she could have the real thing? Life without him was an empty existence, one day blurring into the next. Before long, life would pass her by and she would lose this chance to be with him again. No other man could ever make her feel the way Gavin could. But the fear was still there, squeezing her heart. But the love she felt for Gavin fought for equal space, reminding her of its existence, stronger and longer lasting than the fear she harbored. The love never really went away.

She buried her face in his neck, soothed by the warmth of his skin. "My father was the local football hero," she began in a soft voice. "The small town he grew up in worshipped him. He could do no wrong. My mother was the high school girlfriend he got pregnant. They had to get married before they had me."

"Maddie, you don't have to tell me this."

"I want to tell you the whole story. I want to explain, somehow, why I'm the way I am."

Gavin kissed her forehead. "All right."

"It wasn't long before he got tired of being tied down to one woman." Madison breathed deeply. "He made it known that he wasn't satisfied with my mom, that he wanted to play around. She couldn't stop him, enduring the humiliation over and over again as he went from one woman to another. People looked the other way. What's worse, they blamed my mom. It was somehow her fault that her husband strayed."

"Jesus."

"She became very bitter. Finally, when I was about nine, we left him. All my life, she'd warned me about not trusting men. Men are incapable of being faithful, she said. Men can never be satisfied with one woman. On the day of our wedding, she told me I was a fool to marry you. That we would never last, that you weren't the type to stay faithful to me." She sniffled. "I tried, Gavin. I really tried to put her words out of my mind."

"Then you saw me with Kimberly."

"I was crushed. Most of all, I was devastated that my mother had been right. All I could think about was getting away from you as soon as I could, before I got hurt even more." She stared into his eyes, wanting him to understand. "I told myself I should have seen the signs. Kimberly used to call at home when you weren't there and drop little hints about your 'relationship.'"

"She *what?*"

Madison nodded. "She was your publicist. I couldn't complain about her presence around you. She told me you'd been lovers, that you and she had an arrangement. She didn't care that we were married. She still wanted you. Don't you see, Gavin?" she asked. "What was I supposed to think after all that? I tried to ignore her, tell myself that you couldn't possibly be sleeping with her. That she was lying. Then you left for your book tour." Her voice broke. "You know what happened next."

"I slept with her once, long before I met you. *Once,*" he emphasized. "And the woman never got over it. She kept thinking there was more to it than just a one-night stand." Gavin sighed, stroking her hair. "Maddie, I'm really sorry she subjected you to all that bullshit. Had I known, I would've put a stop to it immediately and fired her right away."

"I thought I could handle it," she murmured, still hurting from the memories.

"It's my fault too," he admitted in a low voice. "I should have tried harder to get you back. But I was angry and proud. I wasn't going to make a fool of myself and beg you to come back when you didn't want me anymore. I damn near killed myself drinking, just to forget about you."

"I'm sorry I didn't believe you." She'd been foolish and blind, wallowing in the pain, not realizing what she'd lost. "Can you forgive me for not trusting you?"

"Our past makes us the people we are. You can't help yours." He gently drew her hair back from her face. "I'm not letting you go again."

Madison swallowed, tears flooding her eyes. She didn't deserve this strong, caring man who still loved her despite what she'd put them both through. She cupped his face. "I love you."

He pulled in a sharp breath. "Do you really think you can trust me, Maddie?" he asked, utterly serious. "I need you to do that before we can move forward."

"Yes." Her words rang firm and sure.

Gavin held her close. "I will never willingly hurt you."

She rubbed her cheek against him. "I know. It's not easy to erase the painful memories of my childhood, but I'll work through it. You mean more to me than anything else."

"We'll do whatever we can to make it work. Anything, Maddie. As long as we're together. Any doubts, any questions, we'll handle it together."

Madison buried her face in his neck. "All right."

His arms wrapped around her. "I thought of all sorts of things that I could do to persuade you to stay with me when we got back to L.A.—I even thought about keeping you locked up at home until you'd listen to me."

"Locked up, huh?" She licked his ear. "I think I like that idea."

"Yeah?" He slipped his hand under her sweater. "I even have handcuffs and whips. Plus all the toys we need."

Madison laughed happily. "Sold. You can have me."

"But you have to be good, otherwise, I'll have to spank you."

She licked her lips. "Sounds exciting."

"You're mine forever, Maddie."

She skimmed his cheek with her lips, smiling. "Forever. That sounds nice. Is that a promise?"

"It's a goddamned guarantee." He kissed her deeply. "Marry me again."

Happiness chased away the last remaining doubt in her heart. "Yes. Yes." She rained kisses on his lips. "I'll marry you whenever, wherever you want. And this time, we'll make sure its forever."

Epilogue

GAVIN STEERED HIS WIFE into a quiet corner of the art gallery and palmed her ass. "This party sucks. Let's go home, babe."

Madison giggled. "Will you stop it? This is Kylie's boyfriend's first show. She'll be crushed if we leave so soon."

"You call this art?" he drawled in her ear. "A three-year-old can draw better."

"Shh. Don't say that out loud. Kylie really likes him."

His finger brushed against her nipple, lingering for a longer touch. "What happened to that Dave something-or-other?"

She leaned closer, pushing her breast against his hand. "He's *so* last week." When he gently pinched her nipple, she bit back a moan. "No fair. You can touch me but I can't touch you."

He chuckled. "You're welcome to touch me anytime."

"Hello, Gavin."

At the sugary-sweet voice, Gavin stiffened and turned around. "Kimberly."

Madison's blood began to simmer as she faced the stunning woman dressed in a revealing black gown.

"Darling, it's been a long time. You're looking well." She devoured Gavin with her eyes.

Madison stepped forward. "There's nothing you have to say that we're interested in hearing," she snapped, deliberately being rude. She barely restrained herself when Kimberly released a dramatic sigh, casting a disparaging look at her strapless red gown. *At least I don't look like an overly made-up doll. I bet she looks horrible without all that war paint.*

Kimberly's perfectly shaped eyebrows rose. "Your wife's scary, Gavin. No wonder you preferred me, darling."

His jaw tightened. "I never preferred you, Kimberly. You just couldn't take no for an answer."

Kimberly's laugh grated on Madison's nerves. "Did I get you in trouble that day at the hotel? That was just a small payback for how you treated me like shit, like I was some groupie." Her eyes glinted with malicious triumph. "Even though we didn't have sex, what's important is *your wife* thought so. That was enough for me." She tossed her head and turned toward Maddie. "Although what he sees in *you* is beyond me."

Madison clenched her fists. It would be so easy to give in to her anger and hit Kimberly. She wanted to wipe that smirk off her face, but in the end, the other woman wasn't worth it. "It's simple, really. He loves me." She cocked her head, stepping close to her. "Do you know that there are *several* places on the body where I could hit you and not leave a mark? Now why don't you leave us alone before I do that?"

Kimberly paled beneath her makeup but lifted her chin. "I've got somebody else now. Way better than Gavin. You can have him." She disappeared into the crowd.

Gavin burst out laughing. "Bravo, babe. That was good."

Madison grinned, wrapping her arms around him. "Can you ever forgive me for believing you would be attracted to that . . . that *bitch?* I was so stupid."

Gavin smoothed a hand down her back. "Nothing to forgive. That's all in the past, Maddie. We've started a new life together. Consider what happened tonight closure."

"I'm sorry for not trusting you. To think of all the time we wasted and the pain I could have spared both of us."

"Forget it. What matters to me is that we're together again and that you trust me."

"I *do* trust you."

"That's enough for me. I'll happily spend the rest of my life proving that I love you and no one else."

"I don't deserve you," she murmured.

He gave her a wicked grin. "You can make it up to me as soon as we get out of here."

"I'd love to." Her eyes swept over the crowd. "Although I really would've loved to have kicked that woman's ass."

Gavin laughed. "Sheathe your claws, woman. She's not worth it. Now kiss me."

"With pleasure." She leaned up and gave him a hot, tongue-tangling kiss.

He held her tight against him. "Come on, let's go home."